Crime
of
Passion

JOHN BOORMAN

When Agamemnon arrived home from Troy his treacherous wife said, 'Step down from your chariot, my lord, but let not your foot touch the earth. Walk upon this crimson carpet set before you.'

Agamemnon knew that only gods walk on such richness. 'I am mortal man,' he said. 'I cannot trample on these tinted splendours without enraging the gods.'

Aeschylus

ONE

Shadow of a Smile was the 8 PM film in competition at the Cannes Film Festival and its director, Daniel Shaw, stepped on to the red carpet alongside his star, Alison Mulhoney. Her full-length frock cascaded in frothy layers to the carpet, and when Daniel offered her his arm he inadvertently trod on one of the dress's trailing effusions. Alison shot him a withering look before summoning the radiance she needed to present to the three hundred photographers banked up on both sides of the red carpet.

Daniel looked back and beckoned his wife, Hope, to join him. She shook her head and clung to the comfortable arm of the film's producer, Jack Diamond, whose other arm supported his wife, Bella. They watched Alison swirling and posing for the frantic snappers.

'She's a goddess,' said Jack, reverently.

'Of what?' said Hope. 'They all had jobs, didn't they, the Gods?'

'How about the Goddess of Eastman Kodak?' said Bella.

'Eastman Kodak is on the skids,' said Jack Diamond. 'Film is finished. Those cameras are all digital.'

The projection of *Shadow of a Smile* was drawing to a close. On the screen in tight close-up, the luminous Alison Mulhoney shed a single teardrop, which the forty-foot screen magnified to the size of a ping-pong ball as it made its slow-motion journey down her high cheekbone. Daniel recalled that after thirty takes he had given up on getting Alison to cry. The tear was CGI, a computer-generated image. That globe of saline water had taken two operators eighteen hours on their terminals to get right and had cost $30,000 – and to Daniel it still looked fake. It looked like a tear all right, but not hers. It came out of her eye as though escaping incarceration.

'Now?' Alison asks her ailing lover, who, a wider shot, reveals is cradled in her arms in a composition nudgingly like the *Pieta* of Michelangelo.

'Yes,' he replies, 'now.'

She pushes the needle into his arm with a gasp that Daniel hoped would metaphorically suggest sexual penetration. As the lethal dose of morphine floods his bloodstream, her lover sighs in post-orgasmic content.

As the end credits crawled up the screen, applause erupted. Daniel had had other pictures in competition at the festival, and he knew that almost every film was applauded. He squeezed Alison's hand. Both their hands were moist with the cold sweat of anxiety. They slipped and slid together like miniature sumo wrestlers. In a spirit of equity, he groped for his wife's hand on his other side, but it was not on offer. The event was being televised close-circuit in every bar and festival office, every hotel room, and somewhere amongst the forty thousand press, forty-five thousand producers, distributors, actors and directors, she knew that her jealous lover would be keeping an eye on her.

At this moment, more than anything else in the world – even the Palme d'Or or his wife Hope's estranged affections – Daniel wanted to urinate. This would become a dilemma in the next few minutes because the applause, sitting or standing, its intensity and duration, would be carefully measured and noted, and affect the fate of the film. He would urge it to go on, but for the sake of his bladder, he needed it to be over. He regretted his lack of restraint at the champagne reception before the screening, where all those whose fortunes rested on *Shadow of a Smile* had gathered to fortify themselves for the ordeal.

The applause faltered, then a spotlight illuminated Shaw and his star. Pierre Dachenet, the gloomy French press attaché, sitting behind Daniel, leaned forward to hiss in his ear, 'Stand up.' Daniel stood; so did Alison. The applause surged. He turned and bowed to the crowd and flapped his hands in an upward motion, urging his producer, Jack Diamond, and writer, Brad Tullio, to rise too. They both stood and bowed. The applause flagged again. The credits on the screen were celebrating the contributions of the Honey Wagon driver and Alison's masseur. Pierre hissed to Daniel, 'Kiss Alison, kiss her.' Daniel obeyed and Alison hugged him, wallowing in the rising applause. She had the ecstatic radiance of Bernadette communing with the Holy Virgin. Daniel noted that at last she was truly beautiful. After all those weeks of cajoling, bullying, pleading, flattering, tricking her into a performance, wanting to love her but never achieving even affection, she was now incandescent. His heart opened to her. He looked into her eyes, eyes that shot past him to the blur of faces offering her adulation. He did not exist.

Now, having watched the film with the eyes of an audience, he knew that it did not quite work. The history of the project unspooled in his mind as the aural flattery of applause rattled around his ears; the thrill of the first idea, the excitement of writing the script with Brad Tullio; they had both felt that this was the one, the Ur-movie they had been put on this earth to make. He had wanted Kristin Scott-Thomas, but the financiers had demanded a bigger star. Alison was wrong for the part but he had compromised, since it had been the only way to get it made. In the happy expectation of shooting in Manhattan, he had rented an apartment and put the children in school there, but it had proved too expensive to shoot in New York, so they ended up faking Manhattan in Bulgaria, with post-production in Stuttgart in order to get German tax-shelter money. Hope, his wife, was stuck in New York, and he hardly saw her or the children for eight months. Feeling abandoned, she took up with an old boyfriend, Paul, whom she had known when she was single and working as a dancer. What had started out as an escapade to spite her husband had developed into an exquisitely painful love affair.

'Film is war,' as Sam Fuller defined it. 'You shoot and are shot at, battles are won and lost.' You hope that the film is not fatally wounded by compromise.

The three thousand black-tied, ball-gowned members of the audience dutifully kept the applause alive but, despite Pierre's protestations, Daniel led his team from their seats up the long aisle towards the exit. Cannes protocol demanded that no one leave until the director and stars had left. There are further rituals back on the long red carpet, where the insatiable photographers await the disgorging stars, and behind the snappers, the fans, the autograph-hounds and the mildly curious.

But Daniel had to pee. Following him blindly, his entourage found themselves piled up at the entrance of the men's toilet.

Two hundred people in evening dress sat down to dinner. The cost was shared between the festival and the sales company. After a great deal of haggling, the festival put up 40 percent, and Phyllis Silverstein, whose task it was to sell the film, put up the other 60 percent – making a dent in the $300,000 from the film's budget allocated for sales expenses. Gilles Jacob, no longer programming the festival, as he had for twenty years, was still president, and behind the scenes, the most *grise* of *eminences*. He floated among the tables greeting the guests he had invited – present, and hopefully future, contributors to the finances of the festival. The jurors were invited to all these events but mostly stayed away for the sake of their *amour-*

propre, so Daniel was surprised to see John Boorman, President of the Jury, talking with Gilles. Daniel tried to interpret his presence at the dinner. The jury would have seen the film at the 8 AM press screening that morning, when two thousand critics and hacks from forty-eight countries staggered in with their hangovers, clutching their press kits, and many snatching an hour's sleep during the film. All eyes panned with Boorman as he approached the top table. Would he speak to Daniel; would his body language reveal his feelings about the film? Boorman passed Daniel, tossing him a friendly wave and a nondescript smile which all present tried to decipher. He headed to the other end of the table towards Daniel's wife Hope. She had choreographed a dance sequence in Boorman's last film. There was something at once too intimate and awkwardly formal in their greeting. Daniel watched them kiss, and Boorman whisper in her ear. They laughed, sharing a confidence. Had they had an affair? Surely not. He was much too old. Daniel had always trusted her, been sure of her, but perhaps this thing in New York was not the first betrayal. Shamefully, his first thought was, would it help or hinder his cause, would Boorman's fondness for Hope make him sympathetic to the film, or less so. Daniel had sometimes been called 'the new Boorman'. Did he resent that, or was it flattering?

Brad Tullio, the suave Italian screenwriter, was watching Daniel's reaction closely through his dark smiling eyes, amused and relaxed as always. His task was to explore and translate Daniel's intuitions and intentions. When Billy Wilder was asked how he and his writing partner I.A.L. Diamond shared the work, he replied, 'He writes down the words and I go into the cage.' The writer is not at risk. Brad had no desire to tame lions. Lee Marvin once advised a young director on how to deal with actors, 'All you need is a whip and a chair.'

'It's not you, Daniel,' said Brad, 'it's Cannes. Infectious paranoia.'

Daniel winced and tried to control the twitch in his left eye.

'Every time I promise myself I'm going to be aloof and detached, but I always get sucked in,' said Daniel. 'I'm disgusted by the person I become in this place. All I want to hear is people trashing the other films in competition.'

'You know what they say,' said Brad. 'To be really fulfilled, it's not enough to have a hit. It's necessary that your best friend has a turkey.'

Quentin Tarantino loomed over Daniel's shoulder, his big moon-faced smile embracing the whole table. Jack Diamond, the producer, and Fred Schneider, Daniel's agent, fawned over him.

'Hi, Quentin,' 'You look great, Quentin,' 'Terrific tux, Quentin.' How they loved his name passing their lips. The men beamed and the women metaphorically curtsied.

Alison, still in the afterglow of the applause, stood and fell into his arms. He was, Daniel thought, what I will never be: Hollywood royalty. He was anointed.

'I was blown away. It was so wacky, I bought it,' Quentin gushed. 'That opening, the anamorphic compositions, and those landscapes, it was, like, straight out of *Deserto Rosso*. And the party scene in the gay bathhouse: boy, that was Fellini on speed. And the last act was pure Bergman, devastating, and her face when he died, that tear rolling down her face was like her life ebbing away. Jesus.' He leaned down to Daniel's ear, 'I heard a rumour the tear was CGI.' Daniel managed a convincingly scoffing laugh, 'No, no, what bullshit, Quentin, she's a great actress. She can do anything.'

'Except cry, is what I heard.'

'Well, now you know different.'

Quentin patted and squeezed Daniel's shoulder, 'Great movie.' His attention had drifted to the next table. 'Hey, there's Sean Penn,' he cried.

Quentin gathered up his goodwill and took it to the next table. Virtue was sucked from Daniel's table as the Tarantino effect shifted onto Sean Penn, hotly tipped for the Best Actor prize.

'He plays a hunchback. A shoo-in,' said Jack Diamond ruefully.

'But a hunchback *and* a club foot. That's too much for Cannes,' said Daniel. 'That's an Oscar performance, not a Cannes performance.'

Daniel's agent, Fred Schneider, had sat silently polishing his enigmatic yet knowing smile. When he pronounced, the table fell silent, attending to the oracle. 'Not Sean – Sebastian,' he decreed, and the name flowed like warm oil across the table; they all fluttered with pleasure and excitement. Sebastian was the lead actor in *Shadow of a Smile*, and also Fred's client. Fred had put Sebastian and Daniel together and packaged the picture, taking an extra fee. They all waited for further enlightenment, but none was forthcoming. Sebastian was now in New Zealand, shooting Peter Jackson's new film, and Fred was negotiating to have him be the next Bond: a $20 million gig. Fred felt an inner glow as he contemplated the deal and mentally credited his $2 million commission. Brad was the one person at the table who did not revere Fred, possibly because he had offered himself as a client and been gently rejected. 'Conflict of interest,' Fred had claimed. 'You and Daniel are buddies but you surely will come to blows one day, and I would find myself in the middle of a divorce, caught in the crossfire.'

Consequently, Brad loved puncturing Fred's pomposity.

'You think hunchback is too much for Cannes, Freddie? Our AIDS is sexier? It's more "today"?'

Jack Diamond flicked his eyes around in alarm.

'Keep it down, Brad. We never say Sebastian has AIDS in the picture. He's dying, but we don't say what of. Let the gays think it's AIDS, if they want. But we have that line, like it was something he caught from the water in the Nile. Let's keep it that way,' he chided, wearing his responsible-producer face.

Daniel noted that Hope was drunk, and that her blonde hair was escaping its severe bondage. She was literally letting her hair down, letting herself down, and her voice was louder than she intended it to be.

'Oh, come on, Fred, don't be so mysterious. Spill the fucking beans,' she said.

Fred's career had been built on strategic pauses. While everyone around him, though exponents of a visual medium, frantically filled every gap with words, Fred had abrogated to himself what Hitchcock called 'dog's feet' – the pause. And he took one now, let it run, and finally pronounced, 'The jury.' They waited, puzzled, but Fred offered no further explanation.

Jack guessed: 'They have something against Sean Penn?'

Brad: 'Lot of gays on the jury?'

Fred's latest wife, a very young, confused blonde who had been fitfully studying for conversion to Judaism, was defiantly swilling champagne, despite Fred's stern, reprimanding eyes, and now felt emboldened enough to speak. 'Ask him how many of the jurors are clients of the agency.'

'Wow,' said Jack, genuinely moved by the insidious penetration of Hollywood power.

Daniel was fretting because Fred had avoided pronouncing on the film, despite having been offered several openings. Unable to endure it any longer, Daniel blurted out, 'So what did you think of the movie, Fred?'

Fred looked up with a querying eyebrow, a pause.

'Our movie,' added Daniel weakly.

The table hung on Fred's heavy, drooping lips. Fred raised his eyes to the distant wall as though re-projecting the film from memory. His large bulk shifted in its seat, reproducing, Daniel feared, restlessness while watching the movie. Fred allowed himself another lavish pause, then, 'You did it, Daniel. It was all up there on the screen.'

A further pause, then confirmation, 'Every single frame.'

The table seemed pleased and relieved by that, but Daniel knew that although Fred never publicly lied, he also rarely told the truth.

'It's everything you wanted it to be,' was another of his pieties. So, his reputation grew because he was never proved wrong, just as the most enduring studio executives are the ones who never green-light a project, and therefore never father a failure.

A tap on Daniel's shoulder. He looked up at the kind, lined face of a man in his late sixties who was disappointed that Daniel did not recognise him.

'Nigel Bateman, Daniel.'

Daniel jumped up and gave him a hug. Nigel was unused to such effusion, and his body stiffened.

'Nigel, I didn't recognise you in a tuxedo, I've only ever seen you in a white overall.' 'Were you happy with the print, Daniel?'

Nigel had timed and graded Daniel's last three movies at Technicolor. His excessively deferential manner invited bullying. Directors confronted by the shortcomings of their movies often blamed the labs, and berated Nigel. Daniel had done so himself, frustrated by the deficiencies of Eastman Kodak film stock, which had been devised to flatter the skin-tones of white movie stars. The emulsion was far too saturated, and there was little Nigel, or anyone else, could do about it. 'A little more Cayenne, Daniel?' He counted it a privilege to be on first-name terms with his directors and liked to confirm it constantly.

'Touch less Magenta, Daniel?' 'Two points denser, Daniel?' Mole-like from thirty years of night-work in the lab, developing negative and making rush prints, he had emerged into the light of day eight years ago, promoted to a grader, and day-work. He had remarkable sensitivity, and a religious devotion to his work. Filmmakers abused him but always asked to have him back, and hated the younger, cocky graders who watched the films with condescension at best, and more often with ill-concealed contempt. The graders were the first people to see the finished film – when directors were at their most vulnerable. A print of *Shadow of a Smile* had been made brighter and with more contrast especially for Cannes, to contend with the long throw and huge screen. Technicolor would send the grader to keep an eye on the print, as a perk.

'It was a fine print, Nigel.'

'Thank you, Daniel.'

He hovered at Daniel's shoulder. Daniel turned back to his guests, but Nigel patiently persisted.

'This is my last job, Daniel. Retiring.'

'Oh no. What are we going to do without you?'

'It's all going digital, the grading, Daniel. I'm too old to work a computer.'

Daniel offered muttered sympathy but was privately elated at the prospect of digitally grading his films. It allowed de-saturation, revising the lighting, and absolute control.

Bella, Jack Diamond's wife, walked towards the table. Her severe dress, chosen to conceal her figure, had the contrary effect, her shapes and curves offering the faintest of erotic hints. Men penetrated her camouflage with darting looks. Her long auburn hair was an ungovernable riot of curls leaping out of her head, half concealing her face, and suggesting incipient passion. She sat down, alert, tense, critical. She had been conducting an interview with the distinguished French director Bertrand Tavernier. The interview was the beginning of her forensic process, which would involve watching his films and speaking with his actors and collaborators. She sought Jack's welcoming eyes. She needed him to anchor her, handle her, indulge her. He was immensely proud of her, and pleased with the effect she had on men.

'Good interview?'

She nodded.

'In English or French?'

'French.'

Bella spoke several languages. She had studied semantics at Harvard. She'd done her thesis on Wittgenstein.

'I asked him one question, and he spoke brilliantly for an hour.'

'What was the question?'

'Were you in love when you made this movie.'

Alison perked up. 'Was he?'

'In love with the film. In love with the actress. In love with the process.'

She sat down next to Jack, and they squeezed hands beneath the table. Although Jack chuckled at Daniel's jokes, encouraged him, indulged him, backed him – and was the last man in Hollywood to smoke a pipe – he nevertheless often left Daniel feeling gloomy. In contrast, Bella's pessimism and (often unnecessary) honesty cheered him up no end. She had never interviewed Daniel, his close association with her husband put him off limits, and she seemed neutral, to negative, about his work.

Jack had wounds from her honesty, so it was with some trepidation that he asked her, 'Get any sense of the press reaction?'

'To what?'

'To our movie.'

'The French loved it. The Americans thought it was soft, and the English, as ever, faint praise. And there was something about a CGI teardrop they kept on about.' Daniel winced. To prevent the plastic tear from shedding its lachrymose gloom over the table once more, Jack tapped his knife on a glass and stood up. He folded away the smile from his kind face and put on a deeply serious air that was on the verge of comical.

'I just want to say this. Whatever happens here, Daniel, you made one hell of a movie. Alison, I'm proud to have my name on a movie that is illuminated by your performance.'

Alison managed a regal smile of modesty.

'Sorry Sebastian couldn't be with us. He was damn good – better than good. We talk about chemistry; well, this was it. You and Sebastian. Sparks coming off the screen.'

Jack was defining exactly what the film lacked, Daniel realised. It was Hollywood inversion, making a taboo negative into a wishful positive.

'And I want to thank Fred and the agency for their help in putting the picture together,' Jack continued. 'He bullied the studio into submission. I know all we got was a prints-and-ads deal, but he found us soft money too. Fred, I owe you one.'

Fred acknowledged this with a slight, sage nod, as befits an oracle.

An agitated Pierre Dachenet hovered at the table. He whispered to Daniel and then to Alison, putting Jack off his stride.

'And Hope,' Jack went on, 'sorry. So sorry. It was going to be just great. Making a movie in Manhattan. You and the kids moving there and all. My fault. Had to do it in Bulgaria to save the picture. You were so brave about it. Thanks for your . . . '

The speech petered out as Daniel and Alison crept quietly from the table, guided away by Pierre for a live interview on Arte TV.

' . . . your understanding.'

Hope, now fuelled by Moët, flared up at Jack.

'Understanding? I was dumped! And there he is, slinking away again. Everything has to be sacrificed for the movie. And for what? For this . . . this . . . '

Jack took the blow on the chin and fell back into his chair.

Hope got to her feet, knocking a wine-glass over. She wanted to storm off, but was too shortsighted to locate the exit. She stood, swaying and peering across the blur of tables. She fumbled in her purse for her glasses, then checked herself. She was not going to put them on in front of all these people. Her fingers located her lipstick. She felt a desperate craving to feel the scarlet slash of Chanel Rouge Noir across her mouth. While she was thinking it, she became aware that she was doing it, and her brain, functioning in jerks and jumps, informed her that this action meant that she was very drunk. Jack sent urgent signals to Bella – hands, eyes, twitching eyebrows – the Morse Code of marriage. She sent irritable but compliant messages back, and finally stood up and took Hope by the arm.

'Let's go fix our faces.'

'I just fixed mine.'

'Well, try it with a mirror.'

At the door of the ladies confessional, they brushed against Meryl Streep. Hope, in her louche manner, fell upon her.

'Oh. My. God. You, you were so beyond everything in . . . in . . . '

She failed to recall the name of the movie starring Meryl, which she had seen the previous night. Meryl kindly supplied the title.

'*Polite Hysteria.*'

'Yes, *Polite Hysteria.* Wonderful.'

Meryl extricated herself with effortless aplomb.

'How can you be so perfect,' Hope asked. 'You act like an angel. You hung on to your husband. Lovely grown-up kids, men still desire you, how do you do it?'

'Read what your friend wrote about me in *Vanity Fair,*' said Meryl. 'She told me more about myself than I wished to know. I said "ouch" five times when I read it.'

Hope turned to Bella accusingly.

'How could you?'

Bella herded her through the door with an apologetic smile for Meryl.

Hope sat on the toilet seat with her mobile phone to her ear.

'I know they're asleep; I still want to talk to them.'

Bella, leaning against a washbasin, watched Hope coolly through the open door of the stall.

'No, don't wake them. I'm sorry, I'm silly, I'll talk to them in the morning before they leave for school . . . . Yes, of course. No school tomorrow. Sunday. Oh Sophie, I'm so pissed.'

Hitching up her hair, Hope peered at Bella through the mirror.

'Thanks for the rescue,' said Hope. 'Dragging you away from the table.'

Bella managed a wan, forgiving smile that irritated Hope.

'Don't you ever let go, Bella? You're so fucking poised. Just the way you stand makes me feel like a slob. And I was a dancer. A dancer with stretch-marks.'

'I wish I could be as loose as you, as spontaneous,' said Bella – and meant it.

Hope lifted her breasts up in her bra, straightened her back, pulling all her bits together.

'I can't imagine you making love, Bella. I just can't see you out of control. Is Jack a good lover? He looks too comfortable.'

In all the time their husbands had worked together, they had never talked intimately. Bella was amused and touched by Hope's openness. She chose her words carefully.

'He's sensitive and considerate.'

'I wonder if anyone ever said that about a movie producer before.'

They both got a fit of giggles.

'Don't you ever feel like taking a lover?' said Hope.

'It's all very delicately balanced in my marriage. We're both surprised at how well it works, so we try not to disturb anything.'

'I've taken a lover. An old lover – I mean a previous lover, before Daniel. Well, he is old too, as it happens, older than Dan – which seems to upset him more than anything. I would have thought a young lover would have bothered him more. Anyway, it's fucked me up; I'm all fucked up.'

'So Daniel knows about it?'

'Yes, I told him. I was so angry at being dumped. I wanted to hurt him and I hated hurting him. I love him so.'

She stared at the stranger looking blearily back at her from the mirror.

'Daniel disappears into his movies, and when he surfaces he expects me to be exactly the same. Turn me off, turn me on,' she said.

Back at the table, Alison's young lover, Lance – an out-of-work American actor – had sat silently through the meal, but now found himself alone with a Hollywood producer and a top agent, Brad having gone off table-hopping. Lance seized his moment.

'I mean, like, is it better to be with a smaller agency, as I am, where you mean something, or be a nobody in a big agency like yours, Mr Schneider, that, like, has more leverage with the studios? Like I say, Stan Cohen is not just my agent, he's my best friend. He breaks his balls for me.'

'But you'd fire him in an instant if I'd take you on,' said Fred.

'No, I'd sure have to wrestle with a decision like that,' said Lance, with a show of Actors Studio torment. Fred fixed him with an eye practised at reading the wiles of young actors.

'You want my advice?'

'Yes, sir.'

'You have a skill. Use it.'

'I know I am a good actor, sir.'

'Not acting, fucking. Alison is a star. She has the muscle to oblige her agency to take you on. Keep your pants zipped until she does.'

Jack felt sorry for the boy, who looked crushed.

'I saw you in *Beastly Bikers*, Lance.'

'Really?' said Lance in alarm. He had scratched it from his CV, it was so awful.

'You were good and open and honest,' said Jack softly. 'Don't lose that. The problem for actors is that they often need to be ruthlessly ambitious to cut it, but that can kill off the very thing that made them appealing in the first place,' said Jack, thinking of Alison.

The boy expressed his gratitude with a show of modesty and humility, and called them both 'sir' in every breath, but could not altogether conceal his resentment. Why don't these old farts move over and give youth its due, he thought.

It was 2AM when Daniel arrived back at the Carlton Hotel with his bow-tie in his pocket and his shirt open. There were a couple of diehard autograph-hounds in the lobby. He knew them and gave them a nod. He walked past but they overtook him and blocked his path, shuffling backwards.

'Great movie, Daniel.'

'How would you know? You haven't seen it.'

'Daniel, do me a big favour. Would you sign these five cards?'

'You got me this morning.'

'I know, but with five Daniel Shaws I can get one Steven Spielberg.'

Amused, he signed them. There were a few stragglers in the lobby. He glanced in at the bar on his way to the elevator. Nigel had been waiting for him. He jumped up from his stool and ran after Daniel.

'Sorry to bother you, Daniel.'

'It's all right, Nigel. What is it?'

'I've been trying to get my nerve up, Daniel.'

'What for?'

Holding it reverently in both hands, he presented a script to Daniel. In forty-eight hours, Daniel had had scripts from two waiters and three festival volunteers.

'Took me five years, Daniel, this opus. You're the first to see it.'

Nigel winced as Daniel rolled it up, disappointed that Daniel did not show it proper respect.

'It may take me a while, Nigel.'

'No problem. I'll wait down here until you finish it.'

'Nigel, it's 2 AM in the morning. I'm dead beat; I'm talking weeks, maybe months.'

Nigel stood his ground. Having found his courage, he was not going to back down.

'It's good, Daniel. I see films all the time, and this is better than all of them.'

Daniel felt a surge of anger and was too tired to conceal it.

'Better than mine?'

Nigel was belligerent: 'Yes, Daniel, 'fraid so.'

'Do you know how many scripts get made,' said Daniel, exasperated. 'Every Hollywood studio makes maybe two in fifty of the ones they develop themselves, that they finance and spend big money on. Then there are another two thousand a year submitted by experienced writers and agencies, and on top of that there are thousands of unsolicited scripts that don't even get read.'

Nigel had his chin thrust out, and his eyes were blazing.

'Even so, Daniel. Even so.'

Daniel turned away and stepped wearily into the elevator.

He reached the door of his room and hesitated, for two reasons. Firstly, could he face another episode of recriminations in the continuous but endlessly inconclusive discussion of their tottering marriage, particularly if she was still drunk? Secondly, he felt bad about Nigel. He went back to the lobby, but Nigel had gone. The day had started with a difficult press conference, where even those who admired the film felt there was something intangible missing. Then a succession of interviews right through the day. Like most directors, when he was finally finished with a film after two years' work, his interest in it was at its lowest ebb, but it was at this point that he was required to extol its virtues to critics and journalists. He felt like a whore. Fellini had once suggested that all the directors should get together and agree to make the films for free, but be paid for the interviews.

He felt empty, hollowed out. Back in the room, he was relieved to see that Hope was asleep, her clothes strewn across the floor, lights blazing. He took a shower, dimmed the lights and levered his long, lean frame into the bed. Hope shifted in her sleep and rolled towards him, her face only a foot from his. He felt insubstantial, with no sense of self. He recalled how Hope's zest and earthy humour had always anchored him, and how he missed it, how he needed it. An overwhelming love for her engulfed him, and he forgave her in his heart, and acknowledged his own sins of omission, and commission, for driving her into the arms of another man. He kissed her lightly and tenderly. Her mouth opened and she kissed back passionately. He responded, and took her in his arms. Her eyes opened as she surfaced from sleep. She cried out. He was the wrong man. She turned away angrily.

In the bedroom of the coveted seventh-floor corner suite of the Carlton, Jack and Bella lay in the huge *bateau* bed with their three-year-old son Orson – named after Welles, of course – lying asleep between them. Outside, rich young men in open-top sports cars were still cruising the Croisette lusting after starlets; beyond, the feeble waves of the Mediterranean flapped prissily against the manicured beaches of the hotels. Indigent, aspiring filmmakers in sleeping bags were scattered across the sand. Further out twinkled the armada of yachts lying at anchor, hired by producers and distributors who were out to impress.

It was the invariable custom of Bella Diamond to give an account of her day to her husband in a dreamy, numinous stream of consciousness. Her sharp, critical mind was put to rest, and she allowed her subconscious to float up and wander at will. She mused on her encounter with Hope, and speculated on the dynamics at the dinner table, and how the screening had been received.

'You know, Jack, only the films seem real at Cannes. The people are all fake . . . fictional. I see them all losing their grip on themselves – even you, darling Jack, the most rooted of men . . . . I watch you emotionally levitating . . . drifting away from me . . . becoming strange . . . a stranger . . . and Fred, with that calm absolute control . . . even in him, I see cracks appearing . . . I can smell the sulphur, the molten magna about to erupt in his mind . . . that's what gives him his power, the threat of the inert volcano . . . he scares me . . . and Daniel, at the screening, sandwiched between his wife and his star, both floating off out of his control . . . he's become a wraith. I could see his substance leaking away . . . sucked into all those cameras . . . and Hope, drinking to hide her radiance . . . . She tries to dull it down in front of Daniel. Love is so treacherous, so selfish, so . . . '

She was drifting from dreamy to dreaming. Jack stretched his arm over Orson and took her hand. The tentative, opening move in their ritual. Her hand fluttered, which signalled that he could take the first turning in the maze. He slid out of the covers and walked around to her side of the bed. Her eyes were closed and her breathing had shallowed. He knelt on the floor and brushed her hair and neck with his mouth, and waited for a response. She stirred and sighed. He slipped his hand under the sheet and ran it delicately and slowly down her body until he reached her Venus mound. He threaded his fingers through her silky pubic hair, so unlike the tumultuous tangle that framed her face, another country. He ran his middle figure delicately down the groove of her vulva, up and down, waiting for permission to enter. He had been in a dead marriage, with children

25

who were strangers to him. As he had gradually abandoned the religion of his fathers for a vague humanism, his wife had become a fanatical Zionist and had influenced the two boys to take the same course. They despised him for his secularism. He had been forty-eight when he'd met Bella, five years ago. She had interviewed him – and mesmerised him. He had never understood what she saw in him. He was running to fat, balding, with poor eyesight, but he was kind and gentle, selfless and generous. When he asked her why, she said, in one of her numinous humours, 'We fall in love at the dictate of a child wanting to be born' – and thus he discovered the vein of romanticism beneath her sardonic and rational mind. He had married 'out', and so was a dead man to his sons. He wrote to them every week, but they never responded. He was awash with guilt. On those occasions when Bella rejected his advances, he would lie for hours wallowing in his shame. He worshipped Bella, and access to her body was a privilege he never took for granted. It was a gift the goddess bestowed upon him at her whim. Kneeling at her bedside was utterly appropriate.

He felt a slight arching of her back, and eased his finger into the slit, and found her clitoris. She turned on her side, away from him, and he feared he had failed. She was ovulating and she desperately wanted another child. Her 'yes' was so softly sibilant that it took a long moment to register. He slipped under the covers and folded into her contours. He parted her vagina and inched slowly into her. He burrowed his head under her wild curls and bit lightly into the back of her neck. He moved slowly inside her, exploring, roaming. He had learnt not to progress to faster strokes unless she signalled her need. Here, more than anywhere, he was required to respect her privacy. Suddenly her cunt tightened, she gasped, and came in a rush, and he spurted into her and bit harder into her neck.

They lay still and his penis shrank out of her. She turned her face to him. It was wet with tears, as it always was. She kissed him lightly.

'I love you, Jack. I love you so very much.'

He had no words. He was far beyond them. She turned away again, and fell instantly into a fathomless, dreamless sleep. Jack lay awake, keeping vigil at the altar of his love, as the last echoes of his orgasm rippled through his body, and he felt, as always, unworthy and blessed. He lifted his head and reassured himself that Orson was still asleep. He liked the thought that perhaps the boy had been present at the conception of his sister.

TWO

Daniel fell under the spell of a recurring dream. He was a child actor in a movie and was approaching a closed door, the camera tracking behind him. He reached out to open it, but it filled him with terror. He looked back. The director was Daniel's adult self, and urgently demanded that the boy open the door. He reached for the doorknob, but the terror was overwhelming. He woke with a cry, drenched in sweat.

He looked at his watch. It was 8.55 AM. He had agreed to do an interview at 9 AM, followed by others for the rest of the morning. He pulled on white linen pants and a plain white T-shirt. He had an aversion to wearing messages or promoting makers' names on his apparel. His quest for no-logo trainers was becoming more and more difficult. It had finally driven him back to those blue canvas shoes with a yellow rubber sole that he had worn as a schoolboy. He couldn't afford to wait for the Carlton's notoriously sluggish lift, so he dashed down the six flights of stairs. Each landing announced the presence of film companies whose film posters cried out for his attention. How depressingly unoriginal they were. Star with a gun. Star in a clinch. Close-up of star staring out at the viewer, expressing strength, resolve. Whatever happened to clever graphics, the surreal Polish posters of the seventies? Where was the contemporary version of Saul Bass? These present images expressed the dim naturalism of modern movies. Movies are not real, movies are metaphors, he shouted at them.

In the lobby, he snatched *Variety* and *Screen International* from the piles of copies that were freely distributed in the hotels. The magazines relied on income from the ads: hundreds of movies begging to be made, to be seen, to be loved. He flipped over to the reviews of *Shadow of a Smile. Variety*: 'Will need careful marketing to find its audience. Absorbing drama but takes time to build up steam.'

Screen International: 'Great display of British acting talent, but the American star Alison Mulhoney seems to be in another movie. Daniel Shaw's direction is assured as ever. The gay bar scene is the steamiest ever shot, but for the wrong reasons: you can't see anything. It looks as though the studio was worried about the rating and added CGI steam to cover up glimpses of genitalia. And what about that tear?'

The twenty-one-year-old New York director Sidney Abel, whose low-budget horror film, shown in the movie market, had been discovered and lauded by the critics, was preening himself with admirers when he spotted Daniel buried in the trades.

'Mr Shaw,' he called out respectfully to the ancient forty-four-year-old Daniel. 'I'm your biggest fan. Would you do me the favour of watching my movie? It's on again tomorrow at midnight.'

'Thanks, I will if I can.'

Daniel tried to slip away.

'Mr Shaw, I love your trainers. What are they, sneakers? Do they still make those? So cool.'

He himself was dressed from tank-top to toe in regulation black Nike. Daniel waved and smiled and jogged away backwards, to make his escape onto the Carlton Terrace, where the distinguished French critic and editor of *Positif*, Michel Ciment, was waiting.

Squinting at the blinding sun and the aggressive blue of the Mediterranean, Daniel ordered a double espresso and a croissant. He gulped down a glass of water and yesterday's alcohol jumped out of his pores. *Positif* had championed his films, and Michel, to Daniel's relief, liked *Shadow of a Smile* very much.

'The surreal edge you put on the suburban scenes reminded me very much of Stanley Spencer,' said Michel, 'and the last scene was clearly influenced by Francis Bacon. Just as one could say that the puerile Damien Hirst attempts to be a sculptural version of Bacon, so you have achieved a cinematic Bacon. I like the way you deal with very mundane subjects but shoot them in a heightened fashion. All those oval shapes in the decor are clearly eggs to go with the Bacon, so to speak.'

Michel's mastery of English was often demonstrated by some very good puns. Many of his questions, Daniel had learned from the past, thankfully did not require answers. They were rehearsals for his review.

'I was going for the metaphor, not the real,' Daniel said, regretting right away how pretentious he sounded. He hadn't thought about Francis Bacon at all, but Stanley Spencer had always been an influence on him – and not necessarily for the good.

'You recall that Magritte painting of a pipe under which Magritte writes "This is not a pipe"?'

'Yes, yes,' said Michel, picking up the reference, 'exactly. It is not a pipe, it is a painting of a pipe, just as your film is not attempting reality, but a metaphor for it.' These little cultural connections between critic and director cemented the relationship.

'Your work has always had a strong narrative drive,' said Michel. 'So how do you sustain pace in a film like this, where there is very little narrative.'

Clearly Michel thought he had failed to do so.

'I was hoping the film would be driven by the emotional dynamics of the characters.'

It was suddenly clear to him that he should have edited the film with that in mind, that the cutting was too conventional; maybe he could do some re-editing before the picture was released; there was still some money in the contingency fund.

The purpose of these interviews was to publicise the film and get the maximum number of column-inches and pictures as possible, so as to make the film sound attractive. Most regular movie-goers do not read reviews, but they read interviews and gossip, and sniff out from these whether they want to see the film or not. Most people who read reviews, read them *instead* of seeing the films.

Telling enthusiastic lies about the film was exhausting, and Daniel was too tired to be mendacious.

'Michel, making a film is always a process of discovery: it shifts and alters at each stage, as new elements enter. You hang on to your vision, but it gets kicked around, and you never know quite what sort of animal it is,' he said, mangling his metaphors, 'until you have it in the cutting room, and even then . . . ' A great weight of weariness was upon him. 'I got the dynamics wrong, Michel. It doesn't work, does it?'

Father, I have sinned. He looked up to meet Michel's eyes, and saw horror there. His confession was unwelcome. In fact, Michel was indignant.

'You're wrong. The film has an inner force. If anything, the pace is faster than it needs to be. It is about characters going through human emotions without feeling them – which is a very contemporary issue. In emotional situations, we replicate scenes we have seen in the movies. The Japanese novelist Osamu Dazai, in *No Longer Human*, argues that we have lost our humanity and are merely acting out emotions that we no longer feel.'

Daniel laughed. He was feeling much better.

'That is a very kind way of saying that the acting was unconvincing.'

It was Michel's turn to laugh.

'It always astonishes me how little directors understand their own work.'

The waiter appeared. 'Another coffee?' Michel offered.

'Fuck it, Michel, let's have a beer.'

His next interview was with a young German woman who was more hung over than he was. She asked lazy catch-all questions that meant she probably had not seen the film. He could see she was clutching the synopsis from the press kit.

'Why did you make this film?'

It was a question that always emptied his mind, made him a blank, a nothing. He looked at her dead eyes and was animated by anger.

'I made it for people like you, people who have lost their connection with nature, with authentic feeling. Have you read Osamu Dazai's novel *No Longer Human*?'

He was shocked by his own facile ability to use secondhand ideas and parade them as his own, and he realised that his anger was largely because she was very attractive and clearly had no interest in him as a man.

'I thought it was about love,' she said, 'about how stupid it is to fall in love.'

Her eyes filled with tears. Daniel's anger ebbed away, and he felt ashamed. She had seen the film.

'Are you in love?' he asked.

'Yes, with a horrible man.'

She buried her face in a tissue. Daniel sighed; his weariness returned.

'OK, turn on your tape-recorder and I'll give you some quotes, and then I'd advise you to get some sleep.'

He dictated, giving her the standard stuff, while she yawned and searched the tables and the people strolling on the Croisette, clearly looking for the horrible man she loved.

He stood up to conclude the interview. She switched off her recorder and gathered her things.

'I ask you one more question for me,' she said. 'The plastic tear, is that a metaphor for – what you say – the loss of authentic feeling?'

Daniel winced, hoist by his own petard. She walked off without a word. What a bitch, he thought . . . No, what a pompous arse I am.

There was to be a late lunch at the Hotel du Cap, a strategy meeting with Fred, his agent; Jack, his producer; and Pierre, the press attaché. The festival provided a car and driver for directors and actors in the competition. The cars flew the official flag and were manned by volunteers, usually young men in love with the movies. Daniel had finished his last interview with a Swedish journalist, who, like most of the others, wanted to know if the teardrop was CGI. With the alcohol sweated out, he fell into the cool soft leather of the back seat of the car lent by Peugeot to the festival. He hoped to be able to have a snooze. The driver was a pale young man with a chauffeur's hat that fell into his ears. When he turned to speak to Daniel, the hat wobbled and tipped over his face. He shook it back, revealing eyes gleaming with intent.

'Traffic very bad, it will take more than one hour to the Cap d'Antibe.' He picked up a script from the front passenger seat and waved it in Daniel's face.

'Plenty of time to read my script. It would be an honour for me. Someday I hope to make great movies, like you.'

Daniel took it, and his heart sank. He opened it up.

'It's in French.'

'You can read French?'

'Well yes, but I was hoping to sleep.'

Daniel caught the boy's disappointment in the rearview mirror. He was on the point of tears. Everyone can cry, he thought ruefully, except my star. He relented.

'Look, why don't you pitch me your story as we go along.'

'Pitch? What is pitch?'

'Just tell it to me.'

The driver's name was François. He began his story as they nosed up the coast. It was Sunday morning, hot for May, and the beaches were filling up.

'It's about a boy in love with a beautiful girl. She love him but she don't want to make love with him. He can kiss her, but no feel. He can hold her tits but only with bra on. He can't believe she is so old-fashioned, but she is religious and she has a confessor, this old horny priest. She tell him everything. OK, boy say, at least suck my dick. She cry and cry but in the end she does it, but he push it in a bit far and she throw up all over his dick. So she tell her priest and he starts to laugh and laugh so much he has heart attack. She calls 'help help' and she puts him on the floor of the church and as he dies he puts his hand up her skirt and grabs her pussy.'

Daniel winced at the crudeness of the story, but it evoked Hope and her New York lover, and his imagination threw up images of them coiled together.

François droned on with his story.

'This priest makes her not so sure about religion. Maybe she change her mind. But the boy is driving movie star at festival who is very, what you say, piss-ed about her husband who cheats her, so she takes boy to her bed.'

They were passing Tetou, the famous fish restaurant. Daniel salivated in honour of past meals eaten there on the beach.

'Girl fed up with church, goes to boy ready to make love now, but finds him in bed with movie star. She so sad she jumps out of window. Great story, yes?'

Daniel had faced these situations many times. How to let him down gently but firmly enough to shake him off.

'Not yet, François. You have an idea and a situation, but you need to develop it. Why not have the movie star help the boy get back together with the girl.'

'Yes, maybe.'

'And don't you need a few more characters, friends, family? And weave in some festival event; after all, the movie star must have a picture in competition if the boy is driving her.'

'Maybe,' said François defensively.

'And the boy seems a complete asshole. I mean, there is nothing about him that would make a nice girl and a movie star want to bed him, and very little that would interest . . . an audience. You might be better off making it as a farce. Farce is never far away in Cannes.'

They were crossing from a congested Nice into the narrow gridlocked streets of the Cap. François was scowling at Daniel in the rearview mirror. Daniel smiled back.

'How a farce?' said François.

'Well, maybe the girl jumps out of the window but she forgets it is on the ground floor, and the boy crashes the car and injures the movie star. The star is so depressed she takes barbiturates, and the boy has to drive her to hospital to be pumped out. Her husband has a heart attack while making love to a young girl. The star wins the best-actress prize and arrives on crutches with a Venetian mask, and so on.'

'Now you make laugh at me.'

'No, I'm serious, think about it.'

François scowled.

'How much of this happened to you, François?'

'The first part only.'

'Up to where?'

'Up to when she throw up on me.'

'And the priest?'

'No, he didn't die, but I know he want to fuck her.'

'Did you get to drive a movie star?'

'Not yet, but tomorrow I have your comedienne, Alison.'

They pulled into the great white arch of the Hotel du Cap.

'Well, good luck, François, you have a lot to do on your story.'

François opened the door for him.

'I think I know better than you what story young people like to see.'

'I'm sure you do, François. Now get to work while you wait for me. Two hours at least.'

Daniel got out and was drenched in the perfume of the hotel's rose garden, out of which emerged Irwin Wilby and the Russian oligarch billionaire Vladimir Bradavitch, their white shoes pink from the brick dust of the tennis courts. Irwin gave Daniel a sweaty hug. Irwin had been the head of Traction until it went bust. He found himself a studio head without a studio, so he set up his own company, which, with commendable irony, he called 'Ashes Pictures'. He raised a lot of money, much of it from German tax shelters, which for several years had kept the Hollywood studios precariously solvent. The big hits had eluded Irwin, his taste being alternately too high or too low. Irwin had a wicked charm and a raunchy laugh that signalled to the recipient that he was aware that the whole business was based on bullshit, and not to be taken seriously. He knew everybody, was a buddy of Bill Clinton, and Daniel was not surprised that he had found a rich Russian. Irwin grinned and put his arm around Vladimir.

'I'm open for business again, Daniel. Come on in.'

'I will, Irwin, I will.'

'I hear great things, Danny.'

Daniel knew that Irwin had not been at the screening the previous night. Part of the Cannes Festival ritual is that American studio executives stay at the Hotel du Cap, confirming their importance by paying US$2,000 a night for their rooms, and in cash, since the hotel does not accept credit cards – thus proving itself as arrogant as its guests. The studio executives are able to demonstrate their power by holding court at the Cap and obliging supplicant filmmakers to make the pilgrimage. Fred had insisted on meeting here – where, of course, he was also staying. It was important for him to demonstrate his status as a senior agent, that his company was willing to pay these prices, and that his clients valued him so highly that they were ready to make the journey.

The chastened trio, Jack, Fred and Daniel, sat by the pool hollowed into the rocks at the very tip of the Cap and ordered $30 hamburgers. Pierre came by, and his tense and gloomy presence dampened their light-hearted gossip. He was pressing Daniel to do more interviews. Alison was giving him trouble. By the time she had finished her make-up, half the day was gone and many of the journalists had given up and left. She was having tantrums with her boyfriend, Lance. She had stormed back to her room, and Lance had taken the makeup girl to lunch.

'Any leaks from the jury?' Jack enquired of Pierre.

'I heard that this jury, after each film, they vote, and if not more than one person supports the film, it is eliminated. Well, apparently we are still in there, but the press is so-so. We need one or two rave reviews.'

'What's your take, Fred?' Jack asked.

Fred's eyes surveyed the Mediterranean, sweeping the horizon, searching. Will our ship come home? They waited respectfully on his silence. Finally he declared himself.

'We're not commercial enough for the mainstream, and the picture cost too much for the art market. We're stuck in the middle – which is not a good place to be, because the middle has gone. There is no middle any more. There's a hole where this picture sits, a black hole, and we're in it, the middle of the middle.'

'Fred, this is a great movie. We busted our asses to get this on the screen, and Daniel has surpassed himself,' said Jack.

'It's a very good movie. It's not a great movie, and only greatness can break this market open – and not always then.'

Daniel mused that Fred was looking and sounding more like Henry Kissinger every year – without the accent, of course.

'So what do we do, Fred?' Jack asked.

Fred threw him one of his long, eight-months-pregnant pauses, then leaned forward, glanced around to make sure no one was in earshot, and said, conspiratorially: 'We market the shit out of this baby. We need a great "must-see" quote, and I think we have it. Today's trades.'

He pointed up, as though it was written in the sky: 'Steamiest scene ever shot.'

'But Fred, he was making a joke, it was sarcasm,' Jack protested.

'So who the fuck cares; we have the quote. And that quote can market us right up into the mainstream.'

Daniel laughed out loud.

'You can be such a pompous old fart, Fred.'

Fred flushed and stiffened with indignation. Jack was in convulsions, trying to stifle his laughter. Daniel was approaching hysteria, all the pent-up tension erupting at the expense of Fred. Even Pierre was sniggering behind his hand. Fred was trembling, mortified, his dignity punctured, and then he too exploded in a paroxysm of laughter.

'It's Cannes,' said Daniel. 'It's just Cannes. Nothing means anything.'

The hamburgers arrived. Pierre left, mobile phone clamped to his ear.

The two Americans – the cultured Jack, the patrician Fred – buried their mouths into the hamburgers and became, in Daniel's imagination, the schoolboys they once were; mouths bulging greedily, biting too deep into the greasy minced beef, gulping their ten-dollar cokes. An enforced silence fell on the table until Fred finished his burger and resumed his adult life.

'Daniel, if this movie bombs, then the next one better work, because it's been two turkeys in a row for you. Three strikes and you're out, in this business. You'd better make a genre flick next.'

Jack sprung to Daniel's defence. 'Those pictures will all turn a profit after DVD and pay-TV. They will all break even, or better. No one has ever lost their shirt on Daniel – or me, come to that – and I'm talking films made with conviction and good taste.'

Fred didn't like Jack: much too high-minded, and a bad influence on Daniel, encouraging him to be arty.

'Daniel's an artist, Fred.'

There you are, right on cue. Fred leaned across the table, now the head-banger from the Bronx, the accent slipping.

'You want tuna with good taste, or tuna that tastes good?'

Jack flared up. Daniel laid a restraining hand on his arm.

'Fred's right, Jack. We have to make a movie that makes some money if we want to stay in the game.'

'And I don't need to remind you,' said Fred to Daniel, 'that in the teeth of my opposition, you have been deferring most of your fees. You have a big loan on that house I advised you not to buy, a wife who is a pathological shopper, ridiculous school fees, and *me*. You know what 10 percent of nothing is?'

Fred took a deep breath and tried to recover his lofty dignity.

'So, let's do a commercial picture and get it financed before this one is released,' he said, a note of resentment in his voice. How dare Daniel threaten his 10 percent.

Jack was flushed with anger. He pushed the remainder of his hamburger away and took a hard swig at his Coke.

'Your client is an important artist, Fred. You should respect that.'

'You want to be an artist? Paint a picture, write a poem. This is a business, an industry, and the law of the balance sheet rules.'

Jack was exasperated but tried to sound jokey.

'How can you have this monster as your agent, Daniel?'

Daniel got up and put an arm around Jack. 'Because even when I slip off the "A" list, being Fred's client ensures me access to the studios, guarantees that they will read my stuff, and because he is brutally honest without actually being embarrassingly truthful . . . .'

Daniel petered out as he saw that he had lost Jack's attention. Jack had followed Fred's eyes to the pool, where a beautiful girl had appeared. They were bedazzled. It was as though nature, after endless experiments, had finally achieved perfection. The rocks framed her as though it was their sole purpose. This place, this hotel, this Cap were put there to await her. Too unaware to be an actress, without the haughtiness of a model, she had the poise that a bikini strips most women of. Daniel was entranced by the sensual grace of her movement. She was careless of her beauty. She felt their eyes, and turned to face them, and fearlessly faced them down. The three men, having gazed upon her and paid tribute to the mystery, dropped their eyes, humbled.

THREE

The next morning, Daniel again left Hope sleeping and went down for breakfast and consulted the trades. Both magazines had a panel of international critics rating the pictures in the competition from nil to four stars. He was surprised, and relieved, to see that *Shadow* had as many stars as the two front-runners at this halfway point in the festival. No film had broken away, and there were complaints, as there were every year, that the films in competition were the worst ever. At least, Daniel thought, we are not out of it yet, and we can always hope that the notorious unpredictability of juries can work in our favour.

It was 8 o'clock Monday morning, so 7 in London. He called the Technicolor lab on his mobile. It was a good time. The nightshift was still there, and the day people had already checked in. He spoke to Les, the day manager, who asked if the screening had gone well. Yes, the screening had gone well, and the print looked good, thank you. Had they heard from Nigel? Daniel had failed to find him in Cannes and he felt a nagging need to apologise. No, they had not, but they weren't expecting to, since he was now officially retired. Daniel's eye fell on a piece in *Screen International* about Sidney Abel and his horror film. The gist of it was: why had it not been in competition? Not even selected for the Directors' Fortnight or the Critics' Week. So much better than the films in competition.

How the critics loved to chide the selection committee and poke around among the two hundred films in the Cannes market to find some undiscovered masterpiece. He had slipped into Abel's midnight screening and had come away dispirited. A neurotic handheld camera swirling and jerking in nausea-inducing pirouettes, or bewilderingly fast cutting, dressed up a derivative slasher movie. It was the new primitivism, abandoning the grammar of film, the conventions developed over a hundred years between filmmaker and audience since Griffith and Eisenstein, a universal language. Was this what audiences wanted today? It made him feel old and redundant. He reflected that the very first films made by the Lumière brothers were all ninety seconds long – which was roughly the length of films on YouTube. Perhaps the internet would kill off the two-hour movie altogether.

He had crept back into his room and the bed of his sleeping wife, and wondered if he really wanted to go on, or, even if he did, whether there was any longer an appetite for the movies he wanted to make. It had always been a youth thing: Welles made *Citizen Kane* at twenty-five. His own first film, at twenty-six, had been a kinetic road movie. He lay awake. Sleep was hard to come by in Cannes: the hyperactivity, the all-night parties, sent their charge into the soft May nights, sustaining the high voltage generated during the day.

Bella came out of the 8.30 AM press screening at the Grand Salle. Michelle, the au pair, was waiting with Orson. They walked over to the British Pavilion, the press credentials hanging from her neck gaining them access, and sat down to breakfast. Orson demanded *pain au chocolat*. She capitulated. There were no rules in Cannes; all disciplines abandoned. Michelle was a film student and wanted to hear about the Iranian film she had just seen. 'It was a surprise,' Bella said, 'not one of those quiet, understated films the Iranians do. It was about the twelfth-century Persian king Assan, who gave his name to the word and practice of assassination. He invented a new form of warfare. He arranged for powerful young soldiers to be drugged and awoken in a beautiful Persian garden surrounded by willing nubile young woman. The men assumed they were in paradise, so did not fear death. Assan sent them stealthily into the enemy camp with orders to plant a note pinned by a knife at the bedside of the sleeping king, demanding that he retreat or die. If the warning was ignored, an assassin was sent back to kill him.'

'Cool,' said Michelle.

Philip French, the *Observer* critic, sat down at their table. He was thrilled with the movie, a metaphor for today's suicide bombers, who were promised virgins in paradise.

'But what about those crude colours and all that posturing?' said Bella.

'Matches the Mongol war paintings. The detail is exact, and it connects to the Persian films of the fifties.'

Thank God for Philip, she thought. Who else can we go to when he stops? Who else knows everything about every movie ever made, and its connection to the larger culture? Well, perhaps David Thomson.

'How can you be so enthusiastic, Philip, after all those years reviewing? What is it, forty years? Most of your contemporaries are jaded, and deeply resent having to watch movies; I saw them in there this morning, trapped, no other job they can do, tortured by the avalanche of bad movies they have to watch each week.'

Philip laughed. It was a question he was often asked.

'I've never got over my good fortune that I am paid to watch films.'

Harold Evans clapped Philip on the back.

'Old film critics never die,' he said, 'they only fade out.'

Philip smiled. He could never resist a pun himself. As William Blake said of Shakespeare, he betrayed his art by his love of the pun.

The British Pavilion's raison d'être was to provide TV screens for Englishmen to watch the Cup final, which always occurred during Cannes. *Shadow* was the only British film in competition. A number of others were in the market: judging by the air of gloom, the sales were not going well. Bella had a theory – well, a whimsical notion – that everything in Cannes could be understood as metaphors for sex. Here were rejected suitors, and since they were English, they became bitterly supercilious, and affected to be above all this French nonsense. A failed film was like a failed marriage, whereas a new project was like falling in love.

In Daniel's sixth-floor suite at the Carlton, the saturnine Brad Tullio was sprawled on the sofa, notebook in hand, staring at the ceiling. Jack sat stiffly on an upright chair. Daniel paced, the bridegroom in an arranged marriage: he had to forget about his lover and find a rich woman. For the moment, he was still hanging on to his beloved, a wry comedy based on the making of his own first film. He had written a treatment. It was sensitive and quirky, the sort of picture a director gets to do after making a big hit.

'What if we beefed it up?' he asked. 'Somebody is killed, could be murder, the police investigate, they allow shooting to go on for the moment, but . . . '

The idea petered out.

Jack had been lighting his pipe, that lengthy contemplative process that lends the smoker an air of wisdom. Emerging from a fog of smoke, he said: 'Daniel, it's a tender funny piece, don't vulgarise it. Put it aside. I know it's tough but it won't go away, it will wait, it will be your *Nuit Americaine*, an English *8 ½*. No one loves it more than I do.'

Brad, who was too much of a realist, too Italian, to hold strong convictions, was ready to run with anything.

'How about the producer wants to fire the director,' said Brad, 'so the director kills the producer? Or the picture is going badly, so the producer kills the director to get insurance money and stop another bad movie getting made, and the producer becomes the hero.'

He grinned at Jack. Daniel laughed. These early script sessions always flew off into tangential anecdotes.

'John Hurt told me this story,' said Daniel. 'When he was very young, John Huston cast him as the lead in *Sinful Davey*, which they made in Ireland. After a week or two of shooting, Huston realised that the picture was a dud. There were a number of dangerous horseback scenes, and Hurt was convinced that Huston was trying to kill him, or at least severely injure him, so that he would not have to finish the film. It would be abandoned. Huston forced him to ride mettlesome horses through treacherous terrain – bogs, up on the Wicklow Mountains – and jump high hedges. Even when he wasn't riding, he was on the lookout for other ways Huston might find to kill him off.'

A little shadenfreude was what they all needed, and the laugh did them good.

'Come on, guys,' said Jack at last. 'We've got to find a straight commercial piece that Daniel can give a little class to.'

'But not too much,' said Brad, returning to his study of the ceiling. Jack pulled on his pipe. Daniel looked out of the window at the Croisette below, and caught a glimpse of Bella and Orson.

The posters roared at Bella as she approached the Carlton. James Bond was two storeys high, and blocking the entrance. And there was *Matrix 4, Exploded* – men in sunglasses staring down at her sightlessly. Give them white sticks, she mused. And there was *Die Harder Still*. And above all that, up in one of the windows, her husband was coaxing Daniel to make a commercial picture.

Orson was looking at a statuesque mime frozen in a posture of surprise. Orson was trying to stare him out. Bella kissed her son, left him with Michelle and crossed the road. Only 11 AM but traffic was already snarled. Paparazzi were swarming at the entrance of the Carlton, and she caught a glimpse of Alison climbing into Francois' car, the photographers shooting to kill. Alison looked distraught, covering her face, gang-rape being the metaphor. As François went to the driver's door, Bella observed that he had a plaster over his nose and a black eye.

Silence in the sixth-floor suite as the three men pondered the possibilities. Their meditations were disturbed by the arrival of a tray of coffee and croissants. Since it was a legitimate distraction, Jack allowed himself some gossip.

'We had a nasty problem last night. Pierre got me out of bed. It seems Alison had a spat with Lance and he went off to lunch . . . '

'With the make-up girl. I heard that,' said Daniel.

'Well, Alison was so ticked off she took our driver François to bed. Lance burst in and beat the shit out of him. Pierre is trying to keep it out of the papers. I offered François money. He wouldn't take it. He demanded that I produce a script he's written. I said I would read it.'

Daniel roared with laughter.

'Why is that so funny, Dan?'

'His script's about a movie star who takes her driver to bed.'

'That's not all,' said Jack, at his most gloomily rabbinical. 'I get François out of Alison's suite and into his car, nose still bleeding. And there's your Timer guy from Technicolor, stoned out of his head. He grabs François through the window and demands to know where you are. Well, I calmed him down and . . . '

'And then he gave you his script.'

'How did you know that, Dan?'

Bella was to meet Betty Latimer at the Carlton Terrace. Betty admired Bella's journalism and had been pressing her to do a book for some time. Betty was a famously glamorous publisher: authors craved her flattery, and once they had earned her genuine admiration, could no longer live without it. She wore a pink silk petticoat dress that offered no resistance to her demanding curves. Bella was in jeans, flat heels and a plain white shirt, with a small canvas rucksack on her back. They ordered salads and Evian and exchanged news of their children. Betty had twin girls. Her husband was a dashing TV war reporter. She had a top job, a beautiful family, great looks and a sense of humour. There must be a flaw somewhere, thought Bella – and was on the lookout for it.

'Here's the idea,' said Betty, lowering her voice. 'You know those dreary "making of" stories that everybody does about movies in production. They spend two or three days on the set, do some interviews, run it in the culture section of the paper with a couple of pictures.'

'I've done them myself,' Hope admitted.

'Well, what I'm interested in is a book that follows a film from conception to marketing. You remember Lillian Ross's book *Picture*, about the making of John Huston's *The Red Badge of Courage*, a classic. It's still in print after fifty years; and Isherwood's *Prater Violet*, which many people believe is the best "making of" novel ever. Both great books in their own right. That's what I would like you to do. Does it appeal?'

Bella was aroused by the idea, but her native caution and scepticism held her back. Her peripheral vision informed her that all the men at the neighbouring table were watching these two beautiful women, resentful that they were absorbed in each other and unresponsive to the testosterone vapour wafting over to them. They will write us off as gay to rescue their pride, thought Bella with one side of her brain, while the other side rapidly contemplated the possibilities of the book idea. She remembered the Isherwood book as being very funny on the writing of the script, and that it had ended with the wrap party. *Picture,* she recalled, had penetrating visual sketches, and didn't MGM cut the film to ribbons while Huston went off to make *The African Queen*?

'It's intriguing,' she said. 'Big commitment. And who is going to allow that kind of access?'

'Your husband. Isn't he producing Daniel Shaw's next movie?'

Bella smiled.

'You've got it all worked out.'

'Well, it would be a comfortable arrangement.'

Bella contined to turn the idea over in her mind. Those books worked because the films had failed. Her thoughts broke into words.

'Did you see that documentary about Werner Herzog's *Fitzcarraldo*? Stunning. Better than the film itself. And that one about *Don Quixote*, the movie that collapsed? Riveting. Disasters, all disasters. It only works if the movie doesn't. I can't go into Daniel's film hoping it's going to bomb.'

'But aren't all movies disastrous in one way or another?' Betty asked. 'I mean, *Apocalypse Now* was a huge success, but Eleanor Coppola's book about the making of it was a catalogue of fascinating disasters.'

A tanned, blond American in his thirties with a wide grin, which exposed blazing-white predatory teeth, was the first man to venture to their table.

'Monty Harris, Miracle Pictures. The guys over there . . . we've been kinda taking bets on you two. Are you actresses? Can't be. If you were, we'd recognise you. Producers? I say producers' wives. No? Ex-wives?'

Betty tried to shrug this off with a smile and turned her attention back to Bella. Not so Bella, the New Yorker. Her face hardened.

'Get lost, buster.'

He returned to his pals with a 'What bitches!' gesture.

'God, I wish I'd said that,' whispered Betty, noticing that Bella was trembling.

They got up, kissed the air and strolled out together.

'I'll talk it over with Jack and Daniel.'

Mobile numbers and e-mail domains were exchanged, linking them in cyberspace forever.

Daniel was still pacing the room, wound up now.

'So what is a genre movie? It's nothing more than a formal structure that the audience recognises. It's predictable; it's inevitable. It's just a matter of how well you do it, and the small variations you are allowed. Originality is the enemy. It confuses. You can't market it.'

'Remember,' cautioned Jack, 'it's got to attract a male star, preferably a twenty-million-dollar player.'

Daniel clenched his jaw, in a gesture of decisiveness.

'OK, let's work it out. Sequels and remakes are out. I won't do them. So what have we got, Westerns? No one wants them any more. Why? Who knows? Comic strip? Spend $30 million on CGI and eighteen months of post-production? No thanks. Let's get in and out fast with this picture. And I'm not going back to Bulgaria. Love story? Too dicey, totally dependent on getting two top stars to like it and be available at the same time. You could spend years waiting to cast it.'

'What about a road movie?' said Brad, still getting his ideas from the ceiling.

'What was the last road movie that made it big?' asked Jack.

'*Thelma and Louise*,' said Brad.

'And broke the mould. Two female stars,' said Daniel.

'What was that, ten, no, twenty years ago? And since then?'

No one could come up with another. Then Brad saw one on the ceiling.

'*Lord of the Rings* – the ultimate road movie.'

'How about a great horror movie? A *Dracula*?' said Jack, reading the smoke from his pipe.

'No thanks,' said Daniel.

'Detective story?'

'Not cinematic,' said Daniel. 'Essentially, they deal with events that have happened already. As Hitchcock said, "I'm not interested in whodunnit, I'm interested in who's going to do it."'

'Then it has to be a thriller, a film noir,' said Jack. 'Safest bet. Never lets you down, if you do it right. It attracts stars. It doesn't need a lot of CGI, necessarily. Let's check with the literary agencies to see if there's a hot thriller in the pipeline. If it's a Michael Crichton or a Stephen King, a recognisable name, it could jump-start the project. I'll get on it.'

Jack sucked harder on the pipe and inhaled – which he only did when he was excited. He went into the bedroom and started to work the phones.

'Why don't we just do an original – I know it's a dirty word – an original thriller,' said Daniel.

Brad held up a warning hand and unwound from the sofa.

'Remember *Simple Plan*?' he asked. 'This kid writes a screenplay, a thriller, goes to Hollywood, spends months trying to get someone to read it, goes broke, rewrites it as a novel, gets it published. Scott Rudin buys it. The kid sells it, on condition he can write the screenplay, waits a few weeks, then pulls the script out of his drawer and hands it in. The picture gets made. They don't trust a story that hasn't been a book.'

'Let's do it anyway.'

'Your call,' shrugged Brad.

It was three months since Hope had moved back from New York to her London home and put the children back into their old school. She promised Daniel she would not see her lover, Paul, again – which was scarcely possible, since he lived and worked in New York as an engineer for the city. He told people he dealt with water, but in truth he specialised in sewage. Paul was a powerful fellow who kept himself in shape, and her body ached for him. She loved the way he lay across her and crushed her against the mattress. It was as though her body had stayed loyal to him through all those years since their first affair, and welcomed him back with orgasms of a different order.

No longer able to endure the separation, Paul had told his wife he was being sent to France to advise on drains, and met up with Hope in Cannes. She had managed to slip away three times. They had made love in his rackety little hotel room in the back of Old Cannes. He had sat in a bar and watched her on TV going up the red carpet with her husband. He mooched about during the days and nights, could not get tickets for the movies, found everything shockingly expensive, and spoke no French. He complained about it all as they lay on the narrow bed. She realised, with a hollow feeling, that he had no sense of humour, and she saw how hopeless it all was. He begged her to leave her husband, but he had no money. So they cried a lot, made love again and cried some more.

Throwing caution to the wind, she called François on his mobile and told him to take Paul to the airport. At the last moment, she jumped in the car with him and held his hand all the way to Nice. She went with him as far as the barrier, and watched him until he disappeared. Her legs would barely support her. She collapsed into the back of the car. François looked at her disdainfully through his black eye.

'Hotel?'

Through the mists of grief, she was surprised to feel a relief, an attendant lightness. She put on her lipstick and saw in her mirror what a mess her hair was.

'No, François, the salon: hairdresser.'

FOUR

Bella's Notebook

So it was agreed. Jack is happy about it, Daniel wary. Feels that because this is a blatantly commercial venture, his reputation could suffer. But the context makes it work. Has to save his career, make a commercial hit to give him the muscle to do his more personal projects. Jack has not come up with a book anyone likes, so they are going for an original. I sat in on one of their story sessions. Fred came by and pontificated. 'Set it somewhere exotic that hasn't been seen too much,' he said. 'A male hero in his late thirties. A beautiful woman in trouble.' Daniel dredged up an appropriate quote, 'Jean Luc Godard said, "All you need for a movie is a girl and a gun."' 'Fred snarled, 'What does he know? When did he last have a hit? A girl and a gun is a start, but you gotta have' – he ticked them off on his fingers – 'A great villain. Violence. Fear. Death. Great costumes. Snappy dialogue. And more violence.

'Three acts. One: There's a serial killer out there. Two: Our guy is trying to get him before he nails the beautiful broad. Three: Hero saves broad, beats up killer and gets the girl. What's so tough about that?'

Brad jotted this down ostentatiously in his notebook. 'Mind if we use that, Fred?' said Brad innocently.

Fred was sufficiently self-aware to recognise sarcasm.

'Don't knock clichés. They got to be clichés because they worked. Over and over. Don't knock them.'

Watched three more sessions with Daniel and Brad. D seems to be forcing the pace. I get the feeling it is too soon for him to be thinking of a new film while he is still dragging the old one towards its conclusion. But when he gets going, images fly off him like sparks, and you can see he has a dozen unmade movies inside him. It's like sublimated sexual energy. He seems to grow in power and size. Brad takes notes and draws diagrams. It is a shapeless process. Self-indulgent. Irritating. They are both performing for me, of course. When I come into the room, they perk up. They are like those sub-atomic particles that alter when they are observed. They kicked around thriller plots, revenge being the laziest option. Most of the ideas sound trite. A man's wife and kids killed, he hunts down the killer – The Searchers. Or mistaken identity. Man on the run for something he didn't do – North by Northwest. What do they say? There are only eight plots? D and B have rattled through them all twice over. A child kidnapped; a serial killer; a bank heist; trapped coal miners. That was Ace in the Hole, *wasn't it? Kirk Douglas. And up to the minute - a terrorist has planted a bomb in New York. It will go off in seven days unless all the Hamas prisoners are released – Seven Days to Noon by the Boulting Brothers. D won't do remakes but, since everything has been done, why not? D wants a female lead but Jack resists, says a girl in jeopardy is horror, not thriller, but D is adamant. Jack fears a plot that will drag it away from the mainstream. The aim is to do a treatment, get it to Angelina Jolie, and go to the studios with her attached. Daniel got to know her when he was doing a movie with her father, Jon Voight. Jack caves in. They are working away at it, but tonight is the prize-giving and we have to get scrubbed up. I promised Jack I'd wear something off the shoulder. Just a little cleavage, he begs. He's so sweetly proud. The jury is deliberating this morning. I'm off to buy a dress. Jack has asked me to stroke Alison, and Hope has been calling me, wanting to unload on someone.*

In one of the festival's dramatic gestures, limos with smoked-glass windows and a police escort swept the jury members up to a villa belonging to the city of Cannes, where they were to have their deliberations. Mobile phones had to be surrendered, security guards patrolled the grounds, and the doors were locked. The ten jurors sat around a table in the Italianate reception room. Gilles Jacob hovered in the background while Thierry Fremaux gave the jurors a brief lecture on procedure and made them swear to keep their decisions secret, especially from the press. He pleaded with them not to give more than one prize to each film. When Roman Polanski was president, the Palme d'Or went to the Coen brothers, and Joel Coen then also got the Best Director prize. The president of the current jury, John Boorman, notoriously provocative, quoted this case in challenging the rule.

'Surely logic would insist that the best film was made by the best director,' he said.

'In French, a distinction is possible,' said Thierry. '*Prix de mis en scène is abo*ut the look, the style, the ambience.'

Boorman wasn't going to let it go.

'As the winner of two Best Director prizes at Cannes, it would suggest that I am a great director who does not make great films.'

'*Exactement,*' said Thierry.

They all laughed heartily at Boorman's expense.

'Touché, Thierry,' said Boorman ruefully.

As juries do, they had become very close over the two weeks, doing everything together, and a warm glow of affection pervaded the room. However, in evaluating the films, they tended to divide along Franco- and Anglophone lines.

Boorman suggested that they should decide on the Palme d'Or first, then move down the prizes in order of importance. They had already eliminated eleven films in their earlier discussions. Boorman listed the remaining nine in contention. Bruce Henderson, the Australian director, was the first to venture a view.

'Let me come right out with it. I go for the Iranian film, *Assassins*.'

'Me too,' said April Cassidy, the American actress who was having a passionate affair with Bruce. In consequence, they tended to fall asleep in each other's arms during the screenings. He would start to snore, which would wake her up, and then she would wake him up. The French critic from *Libération*, Didier Clement, shook his head in disgust. 'Impossible. It is vulgar and melodramatic, and also political propaganda to justify suicide bombings. We would be ridiculed in the French press. It is already a disgrace that it was selected.'

'Be fair,' said Steve Woolley, the English producer. 'It is a beautifully crafted movie. The British critics won't ridicule it: Philip French raved about it in the *Observer*.'

'Let's not be concerned about critics,' said Boorman. 'Didier, what is your choice for the Palme d'Or?'

'It must be the American film *The Wise Fool*.'

Vladimir Erenko, the Russian film historian, agreed, as did the French producer, Claude Vincent.

'I can't believe the French are all fighting for an American movie,' Boorman joked.

'It is a matter of aesthetics, not nationality,' said Didier sniffily.

The jury was split right down the middle. They argued for an hour, and Boorman had to remind them that there were five other prizes to be decided. Still they could not reach a consensus. Neither side would concede.

'Is there another film that we all like that we could agree on as a compromise?' Boorman asked.

'We all got off on *Shadow of a Smile*,' said April.

They tossed that one back and forth for another half an hour. There was no great enthusiasm for it, but little by little it gained favour, as a way of breaking the deadlock.

The festival organisers knew from experience that such intractable problems would often arise. They had a strategy. A great chef was recruited to make lunch for the jurors at the villa. As it got later and the jurors got hungrier, delicious aromas drifted into the room, and suddenly it became easier to make the choices.

'I thought we had put *Shadow* down for the Best Actress prize,' said Vladimir, the Russian. 'If it gets the Palme d'Or, it cannot also . . . '

He made an elegant spiral gesture with his hands, letting the thought float up to the ornate ceiling.

'Just as well,' said Bruce. 'That tear at the end was CGI; I mean, it makes the performance fake.'

People were shuffling their notes together: they thought it was all over. They were punched out and famished. Boorman asked quickly, 'OK, Palme d'Or for *Shadow*?'

Nods and shrugs of concession.

'Best Actor: Sean Penn for *The Wise Fool*. Best Actress?'

'It has to be Meryl,' said Woolley.

'Here we go again,' said April, cattily. 'She wins everything.'

'Probably because she is always the best,' said Woolley.

They quickly settled on the lesser prizes. To be awarded one of these was often seen as an insult by the more arrogant directors.

'What about *Assassins*?' said Didier.

'The Grand Prix?'

Boorman looked around the table.

'It should be called the Petit Prix,' said Didier bitterly. 'It means nothing.'

The others were already shuffling off to lunch in the next room. Didier followed them in. At least he felt entitled to the last word, and shouted in Gallic indignation, 'How did we manage to give the Palme d'Or to a second-rate, pretentious film like *Shadow of a Smile*?'

'Try the langoustine, Didier,' said Boorman.

Didier's eyes lit up.

'Ah, langoustine.'

Thierry was on his phone, the only one allowed to use it, calling the winners to make sure of their attendance. They would be told they had a prize, but not which one. When Jack got the call, they were all assembled for their drinks party. Alison lit up: since she had been hotly tipped, she knew it had to be her. No one believed they could give it to Meryl yet again. Alison called her publicist, her voice quivering.

'It looks good, real good.'

'That could help us,' said Jack. 'People will go and see a great performance.'

Lance hugged Alison, and she kissed him.

'And guess what,' she said. 'My agency has signed Lance.'

'Well, isn't that a surprise,' said Fred.

Bella was in a corner with Hope, who was pouring her heart out.

'I was a young single girl in New York. Paul was married, and much older than me. I spent my life sitting by the phone waiting for him to call, getting mad at him and tossing away the dinner that I'd made for him. And then he would hammer on the door at 2 AM in the morning, once his wife was asleep. I'd scream at him and cry, and we'd make amazing love and I'd forgive him. Oh God, I loved him so.'

She caught her breath and a single sob surfaced, alarming Bella.

'It was the aggravation that gave it the edge. I was addicted to the pain. And when I went back last year, we started up where we'd left off. He was sixty; still married, but to a different wife. It was the same thing: skulking and hiding, keeping me hanging around. It gave the sex the same frisson, plus it was revenge on Daniel, who had left me stranded.'

'Does Daniel know about this?' said Bella.

'Most of it. I wanted him to know. I wanted to hurt him. What he doesn't know is that Paul was here.'

'When?'

'He left today. He was here all week. And you know what, it was role-reversal. He had to hang around and wait for me to call. He couldn't call me, and you have no idea how he bitched about it, got into jealous rages. What a nerve. The sex was as exquisite as ever, and I was still madly in love with him. Except, when he left, I felt this weight lifting. I almost levitated. It was like my body always belonged to him and yet I realised I had never really liked him. You know what he works with? Shit. And he is one.'

When Meryl got the Best Actress prize, Alison shed real tears just when she desperately didn't want to. There was applause when Daniel collected the Palme d'Or, but also booing. The critics were mostly hostile to the results, so the award had a negative effect.

Francois drove Daniel and Hope to the airport and handed Daniel what he claimed was a completely new draft of his script. It turned out to be the old one with indecipherable handwritten notes in the margins. There was no sign of Nigel. Fred, instead of going to London as planned, went back to Los Angeles. There had been a putsch at his agency and he needed to defend his corner.

Assassin opened the next day in Paris, to rave reviews and sell-out business. 'LA PALME DE LA PRESSE' ran one headline. Another deplored the fact that two American actors had been honoured. Daniel left Cannes feeling like a thief. One British tabloid referred nudgingly to Boorman's friendship with Daniel Shaw's wife. The obsessive politics of Cannes, which had held them all in ferocious thrall, faded as quickly as it had arisen, and within a week most of the participants could hardly remember having being there.

FIVE

Although Jack and Bella lived in a Manhattan brownstone on Twelfth Street, they kept an apartment in Chelsea, where they stayed when Jack was working with Daniel. This would be their third collaboration. Daniel lived close by, on the Kings Road, in a house once owned by his hero, Carol Reed: it had a plaque on the wall to prove it.

Bella put Orson to bed while Jack prepared dinner. He enjoyed working in the kitchen and they both welcomed a home-cooked meal after a week in a hotel. He made a puree of parsnips and carrots, a favourite of Bella's, crunchily roasted potatoes and pork cutlets. Eating pork was one of the ways that Jack had of reconfirming his estrangement from Jewish tradition. They drank a bottle of Chateau Leoville Barton. She drank one glass, he the rest. The papers were spread over the sofa, opened at the Cannes reports.

'So like the English,' said Jack, 'berating one of their own for winning one of the great prizes in cinema. Here's a guy who's made seven movies, brought poetry and beauty into millions of lives, and they're down on him. Crazy. I mean, is there another director who can do women characters like he can, other than Almodóvar? He even made Alison look good.'

'If he's so good with women, why is his own wife such a mess?'

'That's not fair, Bella.'

'Jack, you're always telling him he's an unappreciated genius. I'm not sure it's good for him.'

Jack looked hurt. He swallowed what was left of his glass, and tried to squeeze a few more drops out of the empty bottle.

'So,' he said casually, 'how's the script coming along?'

Her turn to feel hurt.

'Jack, I told you. I can't talk about that. If they think I'm spying on them, this thing won't work. They'll show you the treatment as soon as it's ready.'

'I'm just concerned they're taking it left-field,' he said, aggrieved.

Such a little thing, yet for the first time, here was something they could not discuss: a hairline crack.

Daniel's office was at the top of his house, the windows facing onto the distractions of the Kings Road. Brad sat at a small table with his notes. Daniel paced. He was agitated. He glanced at the door, hearing movement in the house below. Brad picked up on it.

'Is she coming today?'

'I don't know. Where have we got to?'

Brad shuffled his papers and read from his notes.

'Well, we've got four storylines we kind of like.'

'The last one. Just read out the last one.'

'OK. Number four. We have a female lead. She's in jeopardy. She's running away from something. Or she's caught up in something. She must be an athlete. She's a musician. She's not a musician. She has a twin sister, they were separated at birth, her sister is involved in a murder, and she gets arrested for it.'

Daniel waved it all away. Brad tried to gauge Daniel's mood.

'Are you going to be negative today?'

A knock on the door. Bella put her head into the room, seeking permission to enter. Daniel nodded her in. He had talked long into the night with Hope, trying to understand what had drawn her back to her old lover, a man she claimed to despise. Shadowy images of them rutting followed him into an uneasy sleep, and he woke up with an idea.

'Brad, did you ever read *Letter from an Unknown Woman*, or see the movie Ophuls made of it?'

'Yeah. This officer gets a letter from a woman he screwed years ago – can't remember her – one-night stand.'

Daniel picked up the story.

'In the interval, she had become a great courtesan, pursued and worshipped by men because they could make love to her but never possess her. Her body was in thrall to this handsome but stupid guy.'

'So?'

'So, that's the story I want to do. But I also see her as Lulu in the Wedekind story. You know, spontaneous, vibrantly alive, causes havoc wherever she goes.'

He was not able to resist glancing at Bella to assess her reaction.

'And what genre would that be?' said Brad.

Bella's Notebook

I try to be totally self-effacing and not show any reaction to their ideas, but in a sense I'm their audience and they hungrily devour my slightest response. I was unable to completely suppress my shock at Daniel's idea, after what I knew about Hope. Daniel interpreted my reaction as approval. Obviously, he has no idea that I know what I know. My unguarded reaction seemed to galvanise him. He sketched out a story, extemporising dialogue and playing all the roles. It was extraordinary, it touched me deeply in some way, and I had to suppress an impulse to applaud. I realised I had almost fallen into Jack's role, that of cheerleader.

Because Brad was bilingual, he had fallen into screenwriting by helping Italian directors who wanted to make pictures in English, essentially translating their scripts, but also altering their sensibility. He was passed from Italian directors to American directors and somehow became essential. He worked on two studio pictures that went through the roof, and built a reputation as a script guru. He was hired when a picture was in trouble. His price climbed ever higher, and because he was expensive, studios told themselves he must be worth it. Nobody knew precisely what he did – or wrote – but whatever it was, it was somehow vital. He had worked on Daniel's last two pictures, and his complete lack of conviction was a perfect foil to Daniel's ungovernable imagination.

Daniel and Brad fleshed out the idea during the next few days, typing it up and handing it to Bella to give to Jack. She stopped off at the Bluebird Café, ordered a latte and read it. She took it home, and watched Jack's reactions. He held it in the crook of his arm, his head bent over it as though protecting it, or perhaps containing it, concerned that if it contained pernicious ideas, they might escape and get into the air.

Untitled Treatment
by Daniel Shaw & Brad Tullio

First Draft, for Jack Diamond's Eyes Only.

A girl running through the woods at night, moonlight. By her posture, we know her to be an athlete. She is sweating. She comes to a rocky pool, kicks off her shoes, strips out of her tank-top and shorts and dives into the cool black water. She hears men's voices. She hides under an overhanging rock. The voices get closer. There are sounds of effort, grunts, curses. Only inches from her face, a body is being lowered into the water; first the feet, then the torso, with metal weights tied to it. Finally, the face. She recognises it. She breathes the name: Lionel. Water shimmering over it distorts the features.

Fade to black.

Flashback

The girl, Heather, is in bed. A man (Dean) is beating on the door, begging to be let in. She looks at the clock, 2 AM, tells him to go away. He gets angry, shouts. She is worried about her neighbours in the apartment house. She lets him in. He is good-looking, with a flashing smile. She tells him it is finished, doesn't want to see him ever again, tells him to go back to his wife. He takes her in his arms, she pushes him away, but when he presses himself against her and kisses her, she offers no resistance. They make passionate love.

Dean tells her he will never let her go. He says, 'There is nothing we can do about it, we're meant for each other.'

'But there are other bonds, even stronger,' she says, 'like your two kids, and your wife's father, who owns the company you work for.'

A montage of Heather packing her suitcase, leaving her apartment, changing her car, driving away, crying at the wheel.

Dean lets himself into Heather's apartment. It is empty. He sits on her bed and cries.

On the soundtrack, Lucinda Williams' song '*I changed the lock on my front door, so you can't see me any more*'. She is driving across open country, the desert, the American South-west. The song continues.

A trucker stop. She is eating. Several truckers eye her. They can smell the sex on her. Threatening. She leaves, one guy blocks her way, she pulls a gun on him, he moves aside.

New Mexico. An eco-hotel. She asks for a job. The owner, Lionel Kraken (the body in the pool), likes the look of her. She becomes a guide, taking guests out into the woods and desert. Lionel hits on her. She turns away. He grabs her. He tries to kiss her. She is too strong for him. She knees him in the groin.

Lionel bullies his staff. Like her, many of them are fugitives from other lives. She befriends the night porter, Joshua, a dignified old man, who is mercilessly insulted by the owner. His age prevents him from getting another job. She meets Lionel's fifteen-year-old son, Mike, who lives in fear of his father and lacks self-esteem. She becomes their champion. They admire her resilience and her refusal to be browbeaten.

Lionel collects information on people in the town, whatever dirt he can find, all under the pretext of developing this ghost-town into a tourist haven. He is hated but admired, seen by many as a saviour and giver of employment. The sheriff, Jake Bradshaw, is a personable man, a man who knows the desert, a hunter. Lionel seems to have some kind of hold over him too.

One night, Heather sees Lionel brutally beating his son, Mike. She dresses his wounds. The boy is obsessed by his father. His mother died when he was four. He tells Heather that he spies on his father and keeps a secret journal about his father's activities. She takes him into her bed. She shows him how to make love.

Lionel wants to get something on her, a hold over her. He makes enquiries and tracks her down to the office where she worked. He speaks to her former lover, Dean.

The old man is told to leave by the end of the month. Heather consoles him, kissing and holding him. He has not touched a woman in the ten years since his wife died. She undresses and lets him touch her breast. (This is lifted from the Wedekind.) The old man is bitter at the pressure Lionel puts on her, grinding her down and piling more and more work on her. She won't complain or give in.

The sheriff, Jake Bradshaw, takes Heather to dinner. They start an affair. He insists they keep it secret from Lionel. Jake becomes besotted with her. He senses he cannot possess her, that she does not wholly give herself. It maddens him. He gets angry. She tells him about this other man and how she is somehow bonded to him.

She is out running in the woods at nightfall. She undresses, and bathes in the pool. The body lowered past her face is Lionel. She cannot make out the identity of the other two men. But they find her clothing and search with flashlights. As they come closer, she submerges. A face leans into the pool. The other man's torch illuminates it. It is Jake. They leave, carrying her things. She gets out, naked. She runs to the edge of the woods, where she can see the hotel. There is too much activity for her to slip in. She turns back to the woods.

She comes to a wooden cottage in the woods. The window is lit. An old woman sits looking out. Heather moves closer, trying to see if the woman is alone. The old woman sees her, comes to the door, invites her in, gives her clothes. Heather is sitting by the fire with a coffee in her hand. She does not tell the old woman what she has witnessed, just that someone ran off with her clothes while she was bathing, and obliquely she says that she thinks the man that she is in love with has done something really bad, and should she tell the police. How bad? As bad as can be. Well, how much do you love him? Heather hesitates. Not enough. There is another man. The woman instinctively understands Heather's predicament. She describes her good, solid marriage built on trust and affection, and how one day a man came to her door, a fine, gentle guy – a poet and a painter – and how they made love for a week of afternoons, and how, although she never saw him again, she still thinks of him every day, and her heart and body belong to him. She never told her husband, but on his deathbed he said, 'I knew I'd lost you.' The old woman looks up from her memories and says, 'Now you finish your coffee and go tell the police.'

Heather, of course, cannot go to the police. She returns to the hotel. Lionel's absence has been noted. His son Mike tells Heather that he saw his father leave the hotel with two men but could not identify them.

She has a date with Jake that night. They go out to dinner. She is on edge. He says if she can forget this other guy, he wants to marry her. She says how little she knows of Jake's past, which he never speaks of. He has told her his wife died, but little else. She asks him if Lionel has some kind of hold over him. He is evasive. She wants time to think about his proposal. She avoids sleeping with him that night. As he leaves, he produces her running shoes, shorts and tank-top. Are these yours? Her mind spins; if she says no, he will know she is lying. If she says yes, he will suspect she saw what happened. Where did you find them? Someone handed them in. You were swimming? Did you see anything suspicious? No, she says. I swam, and I ran naked in the wood to get dry. When I came back, my clothes had gone. He is suspicious. She is in a dilemma.

Next day she confides in Joshua. Should she call the FBI? Joshua considers the situation. Lionel had many enemies; he was hated; he was evil. Perhaps rough justice has been done. Does she really want to send Jake to prison or the electric chair for this evil man? He advises her to do nothing.

Lionel's son is worried about his father's absence. Heather realises that although the boy fears Lionel, he also loved him. Mike pleads with her to ask Jake's help in finding his father. Reluctantly, she takes the boy along to the police office and the boy tells Jake he saw two men take his father towards the woods. Jake asks if he could identify the two men. The boy can only describe their build and clothes. Was he coerced? No, he seemed to go willingly. Jake makes a missing-person's report. His suspicions about Heather grow. She is afraid and torn. Again, she seeks advice from Joshua, who urges her to forget the whole thing. He says that Lionel had dug up something in his past, which he was threatening to reveal, and he had something serious on Jake. If the FBI came in, all this would come out, and many lives would be destroyed.

Jake takes Heather for dinner. They park out on the edge
of the woods. He raises the question of his proposal again,
and says ominously that a wife cannot testify against her
husband. He then asks her if she knows who the second man
was. She says not. He says, I guess I believe you on that count.
You wouldn't have confided in Joshua if you knew he was my
partner-in-crime. What we did was rid the world of an evil
man, he says. If you really love me I can trust you, but I don't
think you love me enough to cover up for me. She tells him
that she couldn't do anything to hurt him. She asks him what
it was that Lionel knew about him that was so important. He
tells her that Lionel had some information that accused him
of being involved in his wife's death. Jake tries to kiss her but
she turns her head away. She cannot conceal her disgust. He
tells her to get out of the car. His gun is pointing at her. She
gets out, she runs, he fires as she passes behind the trees. He
misses. He runs after her. She goes towards the old woman's
cottage. She almost makes it but he is upon her, throws her
to the ground. She can just glimpse the cottage between the
trees. She cries out for help. He is standing over her, he is
crying, telling her that he has never loved any woman as he
loves her, but he cannot let her live. He tells her to undress, he
fucks her, the gun held to her temple. The old woman comes
through the trees with a shotgun. Heather's eyes meet hers.
She sees the gun pointed at Heather's head. Jake is reaching
his climax. The old woman shoots him. Jake fires his gun and
it grazes Heather's skull.

Divers raise Lionel's body from the pool. Joshua is led
away in handcuffs. Her former lover, Dean, is there. He comes
over to her, tells her he has left his wife and wants to be with
her. Her look to him is cold and distant. It's too late, she says,

and walks past him into the forest. She starts to run. She leaves it all behind, and gradually the pleasure of the scented air in her lungs and the aliveness of running, the sense of being in harmony with the forest around her, brings her back to a semblance of life.

SIX

Exhilarated by his work on the treatment, Daniel burst into the kitchen like a marauder, playing havoc with homework. Andrew, aged seven, catapulted out of his chair into his father's arms. They punched each other to confirm their love, as people pinch themselves to prove they are not dreaming. Five-year-old Rose screamed at her exclusion, rage and charm being her weapons in the struggle to compete with her larger, quicker, noisier and stronger sibling. Daniel hoisted her up with his free hand and she abandoned despair in favour of ecstatic joy. Hope was making a smoked-salmon sauce for the pasta, and the French au pair Sophie was left stranded with Andrew's history project: a model of a Roman aqueduct. Hope faced the invader defiantly. This was her territory, her routine – and her rules applied. She stood defensively in front of her friend and ally, the Aga. When she was busy with other fractious matters, it consoled her to think of her food cooking slowly and gently in the arms of the Aga. Daniel said, 'Show me a professional chef who cooks on an Aga', but she was adamant. Just as she had said after two years of marriage, 'Daniel, I want a baby', so, with the same voice that brooked no denial, it was, 'Daniel, I want an Aga.' This kitchen, this big wooden table, the meals she laid upon it, the children who sat at it; this Aga, big, solid, anchored to the floor, these were her things, and they kept her from flying apart.

She commanded Daniel to put the children back the way he had found them and to abandon his attempts to breach her defences.

He gave her a hug and lifted her off her feet. Her body stiffened in protest but he made her laugh and she identified his mood. He was coming to her having made something fine, laying it at her feet.

'You found your story,' she said.

'I think so, it feels good, but, as you know, tomorrow it may all fall apart.'

'No, I can tell from your tone. It's working.'

'It needs to marinate for a day or two.'

She had fallen in love with the tumultuous energy he generated when he was on a roll, when the juices were pumping, but she resented it too, because it broke over her like a wave and wiped her out.

'By the way,' she said, handing him a script, 'our postman left this for you. It's about a postman who screws bored housewives and makes them feel better. It's called *The Postman Always Comes Twice*.'

*

Bella loved Jack's pipe. It reassured her, and the aroma charmed her. At their first meeting, its scent had enveloped her, an erotic potion she had succumbed to. Jack had lit up his pipe to read the treatment, but had let it go out, and as he put down the last page, he tapped out the spent tobacco. He looked up at her. She could see that he was conflicted. She felt that this was a crucial moment in the project, and she began making notes in her mind.

'Jack Diamond put the treatment aside, moved by the power of the story but concerned that it was not the big commercial thriller he was hoping for.'

His own words cut across her thoughts.

'Great, but it's an "R". We'll never get a "PG" in the current moral climate: Hollywood is running scared of eroticism. More violence and less sex would help.'

She could see him getting gloomier.

'What do you think?' he asked.

'Well, the notion that a man has to kill the woman he loves because she is a witness to a murder is intriguing, although it could be melodramatic in the wrong hands,' she said carefully.

He was disturbed by the story.

'It always makes me queasy, equating sex and death. There's a hint of the pornographic.'

Bella did not respond. He sucked his dead pipe, seeking wisdom from it, but finding only ashes.

'There is a lot of Hope in the woman, in both senses of the word,' he ventured.

Bella had told him of Hope's confession of her New York lover.

'I wonder,' said Bella, 'is it culture or physiology that makes a woman surrender herself to a man. We still talk about "belonging" to a man.'

Again, she was trying out phrases for her book. Jack smiled, aware of her process.

'But isn't love an act of giving; and to give oneself totally is surely absolute love?'

'If the giving is equal on both sides – which it can never be,' she said.

'Never,' he said ruefully. 'That's bad news for an old romantic.'

She relented.

'Well, seldom.'

They became circumspect as they realised they were now talking about themselves, approaching a delicate subject which they had left unarticulated – and which they both knew should remain so. She kissed him, as a farewell to the subject.

'I'd better write up my notes,' he said.

'And I mine, after I put Orson to bed.'

'I'll come up and read to him later,' he said. 'Toad has just stolen a motor car.'

He chuckled at the thought of it. 'It's the greatest English novel ever written – by a country mile.'

She made a face, but was glad to be safely back with metaphors.

'It is so cosy and smug, and God-is-an-Englishman. We're Americans. You should be reading him Mark Twain.'

'*Wind in the Willows* made me an Anglophile.'

'England isn't like that any more, Jack. The Wild Wood has won. It's all weasels and stoats: greedy, thuggish and paranoid.'

Daniel was reading Philip Pullman's *Northern Lights* to Andrew, who lay in his bed clutching the threadbare teddy that had belonged to his mother. Daniel stopped as he saw that Andrew was crying.

'It's very sad, Andrew. Maybe you're a bit young for it.'

'I don't understand it,' the boy sniffed.

'Well, the idea is that there are lots of worlds just like ours, but each one develops in slightly different ways. In the one we're reading about, everyone has an animal that is connected to them: their daemon. Imagine if your teddy could talk to you and went everywhere with you.'

'We're not allowed to take them to school – which is why school sucks,' Andrew said, smiling in a teary way.

'These bad people have cut off the little boy's daemon, and he's dying of sadness. In our world, we don't have daemons, so when we are small we find "pretend" ones like your teddy, and all our lives we search for the daemon that we never had.'

'Do we ever find one, dad?'

'Yes, we do. When you grow up, you'll meet someone, and fall in love, and you'll have the feeling that you were joined to that person in another life, or in another world, and you will feel so happy that you found them again.'

'Was it like that when you found mum?'

'Yes, it was.'

'But not any more, because you shout at each other.'

'Well, it's sad to be alone, but it's also hard to be joined to someone.'

Daniel went downstairs. Hope was making herself a vodka tonic. He suspected it was not the first of the day. She handed him a single malt in the thick, heavy glass he favoured.

'So what's it about, your story?' she asked.

'It's about a woman.'

'As ever.'

'A thriller.'

'Murder?'

'Naturally, that's part of it. But under it, is something else. Remember *Letter from an Unknown Woman*? Well, it's about a woman who's sexually bonded to a stupid married man.'

He watched her reaction. She gulped her vodka.

'So, it's about me.'

'You're not the only woman in that kind of relationship.'

'Who gets killed? Paul, I suppose. Or me? You want to kill me off, deep down?'

He had hoped they would not fall that fast back into combat.

'Instead of being eaten up by it, I decided to use it.'

'Like you use everything. Don't you see what a betrayal that is? You turn all your life into story, so you don't have to live it. Then you can control it, and make it come out the way you want.'

They were both on their feet, facing up to each other.

'No, writing this story has made it clear to me. When you went back to him, I realised he had been significantly present throughout our marriage – which was why you could never entirely give yourself to me.'

She flared up.

'Give? I gave you two beautiful kids. I gave you my devotion. What did you give me?'

'I could have had dozens of women. I only wanted you.'

'What about all those actresses you work with. All right, you didn't fuck them – or so you say. But you fell in love with them, and that's a betrayal. Worse than fucking.'

'Fictitious emotions! The business of art is falling in love.'

'What about Alison? You didn't fall in love with her.'

'Which is why the picture didn't work.'

They were toe to toe, glaring at each other. Daniel turned away, back to his corner; she to hers.

'Same old stuff,' she sighed. 'Raking it over and over.'

'I'm sorry, Hope.'

I'm the cuckolded husband, he thought, so why do I always end up apologising?

Jack's Notes

Well, my dear Daniel and Brad, you have come up with one great story. As you know, I was sceptical about having a female protagonist, for shameful commercial reasons. Thrillers are almost always led by men, but you have created a fascinating character that is both victim and hero. As always, I have a number of points – for instance, taking the boy to bed is a hot potato in this paedo-phobic world – but I'll leave them aside at this stage because I want to address the one big issue I have. The opening flash-forward is brilliant. It grabs you; it holds you; it haunts the first part of the movie. You then go back and establish Heather as helplessly in sexual bondage to this guy, and she runs away. This is your 'Letter from an Unknown Woman' theme. When you finally bring Dean back into the story, the movie is already over. We have forgotten about him. Now, either he has to come in earlier or – and this would be my inclination – you drop him altogether. Isn't it stronger if she is really deeply in love with the sheriff, rather than still pining for the other guy? If she is strongly attached to the sheriff, her dilemma – should she finger him or not – becomes much more acute. If you would consider this point and resolve it one way or another, I think the treatment is strong enough to take to Angelina Jolie and hopefully, with her support, go to a studio and get the deal done fast. Congratulations.

Daniel read through Jack's notes. The treatment was too fragile, and Daniel too vulnerable, to deal even with Jack's gentle criticisms. He screwed up the pages and threw them across the room. Lacking weight, they hovered in the air, and floated back accusingly at his feet. It was why Jack sent written notes rather than having what in Hollywood they call a 'flesh meeting', where Daniel would put up such an obdurate defence that he would be unable to retreat from it. In the filmmaking process, the transitions from the personal to the collaborative were always painful.

Next morning, Daniel woke up with the bitter ashes of his fight with Hope still in his throat, and with Jack's criticisms turning in his mind. He levered himself out of bed and left the house feeling sluggish, turned from the Kings Road on to Oakley Street, and walked over the fragile Albert Bridge, where a sign demanded that troops break step when they cross it. It was a glittering, backlit May day and, in Battersea Park, the new grass struggled through the winter mud; the weary plane trees were managing a fresh coat of leaves. The soiled Thames ebbed tamely between the severe embankments as the ancient city strained to respond to yet another spring – as did Daniel himself. He started jogging, and soon ran the anger out of his blood. By the time he'd reached the incongruous Buddhist pagoda in the park, he felt appropriately Zen and tranquil. It was 9 AM. Brad was due at 10; Bella too. He doubled back along the Embankment, thick with urgent rush-hour traffic, and up into Old Church Street. He rang the bell of his mother Jenny's flat. She fluttered moth-like at her door, while he jogged on the doorstep. As always, his heart ached for her lack of substance. It was a duty call with no content.

'You look well, Jenny.'

'I can't tell how you look, with your face going up and down.'

'Anything you need?'

'How are the children? The trees are in leaf at last.'

'Hope says come to lunch tomorrow. . . . You can't? The day after, then.'

She swamped him with a smile that carried too much love for early morning, and he trotted off, hand waving back, high in the air, drowning.

He took a shower and was ten minutes late. Daniel watched Brad read Jack's notes.

'Well?' Daniel asked.

Brad shrugged. Shrugging was what he did; his eyes, his shoulders, his mind – they all shrugged, much of the time. This irritated Daniel, and a quotation popped unbidden into his head, reprovingly: 'The best lack all conviction, while the worst are full of passionate intensity.'

'Do you want to try bringing Dean back in earlier?' said Brad.

'Why not?'

They chewed that over. Brad was there to offer solutions to problems as they arose.

'What if Dean is an insurance assessor, tracking down false claims,' suggested Brad. 'Maybe Heather was his assistant. So he is, like, a detective, and uses his skills to track her down.'

'What then? What does he do when he finds her?'

They fell silent. Neither could follow it up. Daniel was back at the window watching the firemen across the street washing their engine. A woman handed them a bunch of daffodils. Had they put out a fire in her house? He decided not. Her movements were too light and easy. Her cat from a tree, he decided.

How much more attractive just about any story seems compared with the one you're working on, he thought. These speculations pushed the problem further back in his mind. Another story floated across his imagination. The woman with the flowers falls in love with a fireman. He rejects her, and she sets fire to her house to get his attention. Better still, she sets fire to his house. *Fatal Attraction 2*.

'Should we even consider losing Dean altogether?' said Brad, tentatively.

'I'm not going to lose the *Letter from the Unknown Woman* idea.'

'Well, in a way the Wedekind Lulu theme suits our story better,' said Brad. 'A woman generous with her love, a bit reckless, full of life. Gets her into trouble.'

Daniel pondered that. Then . . .

'If we lost the notion of her running away from her life, it would be hard to make that flash-forward work, and without that, the first part of the picture would be flat. You remember what Hitchcock said: "You start a movie with a man getting out of bed, showering, shaving, dressing, getting into his car: it's boring. Insert a shot at the beginning of a rifle aimed at him, and all those trivial actions become absolutely fascinating."'

Brad quietly pressed his case.

'OK, what if we jolt the whole story forward and start right in the middle, go from Heather in the pool, seeing Lionel lowered into the water. Cut straight – or dissolve, maybe – to Lionel hitting on her. She has been working there for maybe a year.'

Daniel could see where this was going, and caught the idea as it floated into the stale room like fresh air.

'So the sheriff is the guy she is sexually enslaved to. He's married, and all that. We come right in on the resort where the guests are meditating and getting in touch with the planet. And the people running it are writhing in a snake-pit. They all hate Lionel and wish he was dead, and there's a deadly atmosphere, and . . . '

Daniel stopped short, having regrets.

'I hate losing the song.' He started to sing *'I changed the lock on my front door . . .'*

'Well, couldn't she be planning to run away from the hotel?' said Brad. 'Use it there. We crash straight into the middle of the story and let the audience catch up.'

It was a breeze.

Bella's Notebook.

Daniel says it's always like this: stepping stones. Jump to the next, narrowly avoid falling in the water and being swept away, and you think you've done it, and reached the far shore. But then you're aware there's another stone you need to jump to. You grope and fumble. It's as though film is a foreign language that everyone can understand but no one can speak.

Brad had left, and Daniel started musing on the writing process. He said that film writing is about compression. It's much more like writing a poem than a novel. Every word, every image, every gesture must be made to count. You have two hours to tell your story, develop characters, resolve the issues. Everything unintended or inessential must be stripped away. Daniel quotes Sam Fuller's quest for "The One Thing": the extra ingredient that transforms a photographed scene into cinema. There must always be at least two things going on in the scene, he says, and they should each resonate or enlighten the other. He has this mantra: 'Metaphor. Film is not real, it's metaphor. Find the metaphor.' He has a picture on the wall of Magritte's Painting of a Pipe, *under which is written: 'This is not a pipe.'*

This breakthrough, this idea of starting in the middle of the story, has got them fired up, and they are applying this pressure to each scene, cutting the first part. It is jagged and abrasive; it is all beginning to feel edgy. I strive to keep my distance but I feel myself being caught up in it. Daniel says the film process sucks people in. The unmade film is a huge black hole of negative energy that devours actors, crew, bystanders (me), people, money, locations, sets. It is rapacious and insatiable. It consumes everything, and all you are left with at the end of the day is a light flickering on a wall. In a great film, the transformation is alchemical. All the matter, the dross, the banal, the solid, intractable waking world is transformed beyond light, into spirit.

'Don't use that last bit,' says Daniel, 'it would look so fucking pretentious in cold print.'

I'm beginning to understand how Brad functions. He is careful not to impose, not to run away with ideas, but he is clever at pulling Daniel back from tangents and blind alleys. He never falls in love with his own ideas, but always has a suggestion ready when Daniel is stuck. He watches me a lot; whenever I look at him, he is looking at me.

Jack was delighted with the new treatment, though still wary about its commercial possibilities. He decided to go to LA and hand it to Angelina in person. They e-mailed it to Fred, who responded, saying, 'Promising, the agency will get behind it. I'll take a look at the production slates of the majors to see which of them has a hole in their release schedule.'

He pointed out that the big five – Universal, Paramount, Sony, Fox and Warners – had all cut back from twenty to ten pictures a year, and were mostly concentrating on blockbusters and franchises, leaving the lesser pictures to be made cheaply by their subsidiaries: Sony Classics, Fox Searchlight, and the rest.

Jack met with Fred in LA and, despite the coolness between them, figured out a strategy as to which studios they should target. Fred brought two young agents into the meeting, and they briefed Jack on what Angelina was doing, her love life, her state of mind. All the major stars are monitored in this way. Fred had heard it rumoured that Ms Jolie had gone cool on her agent: he saw the treatment as a way of poaching her from CAA.

'Better I give it to Jolie,' said Fred. 'She'll feel pressured if you do it, and she'll back off.'

Jack laughed.

'Your agenda is showing, Fred. No, I'll do it myself, but in recognition of your sterling contribution, you can come to the follow-up meeting, if there is one.'

Bella's Notebook

Jack is in LA. It's waiting time. Daniel is shooting a commercial to make some money. Brad asked me out to lunch. Very charming and easy, but didn't want to talk about his process. He made me laugh a lot and, having softened me up, said my presence at the meetings was creating sexual tension that was stimulating but also inhibiting. He suggested – with his Jack Nicholson grin – that I could solve this by sleeping with him. I said I was a happily married woman. He said, 'What has that got to do with it?' It was my coolness, my remoteness, that was driving him crazy, he said.

He took rejection in his stride. He smiled and shrugged in that Italian way that says, it was worth a try. It was simply opportunistic: Jack away; me here. Behind his smile there is something coldly predatory.

Jack met Angelina in her agent's office and handed her the treatment. She had agreed to read it right away. She said how much she admired Daniel's work and how wonderfully he directed women. Jack agreed to meet her the next morning at her house. He came away so buoyed up by the meeting that he felt strong enough to call his ex-wife, Helen. To his surprise and horror, she invited him round.

He drove up to the house in Beverly Hills and rang the bell. The door was opened by an English butler, who showed Jack into the drawing room. At the time of the divorce, Jack had just finished a picture, which had not yet been released. His ownership rights were passed to Helen as part of the settlement. It turned out to be that one big hit of a lifetime. That was seven years ago. He still got the accounts each quarter. So far she had made $53 million. It had recently been released on DVD, and money was still flowing in. Helen entered the room, and relished the shock on Jack's face. She was fifty years old, without a line on her face. Her blonde hair was an oxymoron: windswept, but rigid with hairspray. Blue contact lenses gave credence to the hair colour. She had acquired Mick Jagger's lips, Jane Russell's breasts and the butt of a teenage boy. Jack's jaw dropped.

'Hi, Helen. It is Helen, isn't it? You look unbelievably . . . '

He couldn't find the word; maybe no word existed to express what he felt. Finally he settled on ' . . . well.'

'I've been working out a lot,' she said coyly.

She attempted a smile, but her new face would not permit it.

'You, on the other hand,' she added, 'have put on a few pounds.'

He patted his protruding belly in apology.

'How are the boys?' he asked.

'I don't think they would want me to talk about them. Call them yourself.'

'I do. I do. But they don't respond.'

'Well, that's not my business,' she snapped. 'The reason I wanted to see you was so . . . '

'I could see the new you . . . ' Jack interrupted.

'You haven't changed: you never let me finish a sentence. Are you still trying to humiliate me?'

'Sorry, go ahead.'

'I'm getting married.'

'Anyone I know?'

'Arnold.'

'Your divorce lawyer?'

'Yes.'

'Well, he got you all that money, and now he's marrying it.'

When she flared up, he noticed that her new skin flushed unevenly.

'He is marrying *me*, and the boys adore him.'

Jack stood up and went over to her.

'Congratulations, Helen. I wish you great happiness.'

He attempted an awkward kiss, but she turned away from him.

He got to Angelina's house ridiculously early and drove his rented car funereally around the block until the appointed hour, musing on all the Helens working out in their private gyms with their personal trainers.

Angelina loved the treatment but had decided to concentrate on her directing career, and she wondered whether it wasn't too erotic for the mood of today's audiences. Jack then met Fred for lunch at Morton's, an industry eatery. Hollywood people drive to their offices, talk on the phone, then drive home. At the weekends they sit by their pools and read scripts. They get up early, work out, and go to bed at 9 PM. Lunch, Jack thought, is one of the few opportunities Los Angelinos get to experience traditional human contact. They table-hop, shake hands, display teeth, tell each other how great they look, order salads, and drink Evian or San Pelegrino. And all conversations eventually decline into analysing the weekend grosses. Nobody drinks or smokes. Jack, the ex-New Yorker, the jet-lagged

Anglophile, the devoted wine drinker, the inveterate pipe-smoker, with the image of his reconstructed ex-wife burnt onto his retina, had a manic flash of insight: all these Hollywood toilers, Helen, Fred, were no longer human. They were digitalised. It was only when you came in from the outside, and then only by the subtlest of signs, that you could you tell. The acting was so brilliant, they were so cleverly constructed, that it was almost completely convincing. It was a bland version of *Blade Runner*. For a hundred years, Hollywood actors had been simulating emotions in a simulated city; now only the fake was genuine.

'That was our only chance of fast-tracking this movie,' said Fred gloomily. 'I told you. Have a guy in the lead. How many broads can open a picture?'

Jack felt alienated. This process reminded him of how the system forced you into rigid patterns – which was why Hollywood movies were so predictable.

'You want me to get you a development deal?' said Fred.

'I'm not going to play that game,' said Jack. 'I'll do it as a European film and go for the tax shelters, and maybe try for the UK Lottery money.'

'It's all set in the States, Jack. That won't fly.'

'I'll find a way.'

He was dispirited, and itching to get back to Europe, to stay in control and not get sucked into development hell.

Daniel seized the phone on its first ring. He knew it must be Jack, but it wasn't.

'Daniel, I'm in trouble, can I drop round?'

Jason Everly, a hot actor and an old friend of Daniel's, had been wanting to direct for some years, and had finally got his chance. Ten minutes later, he was at the door, looking drawn and grey.

'I start shooting next week, Daniel, and I'm out of my depth, fucked. As an actor, they pick you up in a limo every morning; someone dresses you; someone else makes you up; a girl brings you breakfast. Now I'm out there on my own, the crew asking questions I can't answer, and I'm not sleeping. And when I do, I have anxiety dreams and . . . '

'Have you done your homework, Jason?'

'Homework?'

'Broken the scenes down into set-ups.'

'I've tried, but I keep going round in circles.'

He was wild-eyed and distraught.

'I mean, how do you know where to put the camera, Danny?'

It all came down to that. When you have worked the scene through and have it thoroughly prepared, the camera positions choose themselves, but he could not say that to Jake. It was too late.

Daniel remembered a theatre director making his first movie. The director asked the great cinematographer Conrad Hall, 'How do you know where to point the camera?' 'I point it at the story,' replied Conrad.

If you have to ask the cameraman where to put the camera, you are not a director. How to advise Jason?

'You have a fine cameraman, Jason, and an experienced editor. Ask them to help you break it down. If the scene is right, the camera position will choose itself. If it won't, there's probably something wrong with the scene.'

Jason left feeling better. Daniel reflected that good films had often been made like that, with directors taking care of the actors and letting the technicians see to the rest; but a movie that is the vision of a single mind, where the content of every image is intended, and everything inessential has been stripped out, exists at a higher level.

Before flying back to Heathrow on the overnight flight, Jack called to arrange a meeting with Kieran Corrigan, an Irish producer and financial expert who was deft at putting awkward packages together, and asked him to think about ways of doing it. Jack didn't want to go home empty-handed, so he went straight from the airport to lunch with Kieran at the Ivy, where showbiz people were eating fatty foods, drinking wine and generally indulging their human frailties. They felt privileged to be there, since the restaurant always claimed to be full, 'But for you, sir, in recognition of your talent, we will find you a table.'

'Could you shoot Spain for New Mexico?' said Kieran.

'I guess so.'

'OK, under the European Co-production Convention, you can shoot anywhere in Europe and still get 20 percent of your budget through a UK tax shelter. We might also qualify for the Spanish Investment Incentive. With Daniel's stature, the BFI should put up some Lottery money. The most they give is £1 million. This is a repayable loan, of course. What is the lowest figure you can make the picture for?'

'If we don't have a major-major star, it feels like twenty US.'

'OK, we need a reputable sales agent to make estimates for all territories. If the estimates cover the budget and the agent has a trustworthy track record, the bank will put up 15 to 20 percent of the budget as a loan.'

Kieran produced a legal pad and began jotting down figures. His face lit up. He was a juggler. He started tossing balls in the air.

'OK, $20 million . . . less UK tax shelter at 20 percent, that's . . . $4 million. Now we have to find . . . $16 million. BFI hopefully comes in at £1 million . . . $1.8 million. Now we're down to . . . $14.2 million. The bank comes in for 20 percent . . . $4 million. So now, we only have to cover . . . $10.2 million.

'You need presales to cover the remainder, so either you sell four European territories – say, UK, France, Germany, and Italy or Spain – or you go for a big chunk out of the States.'

Jack was lighting his pipe, utterly absorbed in it. His cheeks were drawn in as he sucked deeply to get it going. Kieran's manic momentum was checked. Jack finally emerged from a miasma of smoke with his response.

'I'd like to cover the budget from Foreign and leave the US open,' he said. 'That way I can do a straight P&A deal with one of the majors. If they're not putting up money, I can negotiate their distribution fee down from 25 percent to maybe 17 percent.'

Kieran tossed up another ball.

'There are hedge funds in Germany that invest in Prints and Ads that we might get down the line. If you're putting up the P&A for America, you should be able to knock that 17 percent fee down to 12 percent.'

Jack puffed and considered.

'I guess that would work if the studio was strapped for cash, but surely they're as clever as you in getting these tax-shelter P&A deals too.'

But Jack's smoke could not diminish Kieran's fire. He was keeping all the balls in the air.

'The American P&A is going to be bigger than your budget. If you get a wide release, you will be looking at, say, $3 million in prints and $28 million in ads. So let's say the picture does $70 million – which would be very good for a movie without a major star. The theatres take half: that leaves you with $35 million. The studio takes its distribution fee of 17 percent, which is around $6 million. Now your $35 million is down to $29 million. That doesn't even recover the P&A, but your DVD, TV and video should match the $70 million you take in the cinemas. You get 20 percent of that, which is $14 million. Now you still owe $2 million from the P&A, so you're $12 million to the good. Out of that, you have to pay the bank loan and the BFI, which leaves you with $5 million, but interest on the loan will eat into that because the film will take three years to recoup. So you end up with $4 million profit, to be shared out between the profit participants. The investors will take 50 percent, the actors, probably 25 percent – leaving you and Daniel with a million. Not bad. You can expect this pattern to be repeated in the rest of the world, so you might get another million dollars to share between you.

'But if you only do $50 million theatrically in the States – still a good figure for this picture – you will make no profit. The studio, however, would have got their P&A back, and a distribution fee of $3.5 million. And they make 50 percent profit on DVD sales – which would be $25 million. There would still be some P&A owing to the studio to be deducted from your 20 percent of $50 million in DVD sales. Now you have $10 million, but the studio will point out that you owe interest and P&A of $7 million, so you're down to $3 million.

'So let's say you make another $3 million profit from foreign. Six million dollars will pay off the bank loan and half of the Lottery money. You should cover the balance of $4 million from Japan, Spain, Scandinavia and the smaller territories. So there you are: a $50 million theatrical take in the US doesn't even get you to breakeven.'

Kieran pushed the legal pad across to Jack, who studied the figures morosely.

'So if Daniel and I defer our fees, there is scant chance of ever getting them back.'

'Not unless it's a runaway hit.'

The waiter hovered, looking for an opening.

'Are you gentlemen not going to be eating?'

Jack blinked, momentarily forgetting which restaurant, and even which country, he was in.

'I seem to have lost my appetite.'

Kieran, a big man with a big laugh, roared across the table. Jack may have renounced his religion, but he had kept the melancholy of his race. Once in a lifetime, he pondered, you have a project that everyone wants: it clicks, you get paid, it sails through, and you might even make a fortune, as indeed had once happened – to the benefit of his wife and sons – but mostly you get beaten up. You have to defer fees, risk your own money, and end up losing. He recalled someone asking him at a seminar: how do you get to be a millionaire as an independent producer? He had answered with the old joke: 'You start off as a billionaire.'

'Jack, don't worry, we'll make it work,' said Kieran, collecting his balls from the air and stowing them in his briefcase. They had fishcakes and a bottle of Chablis, and soon felt better.

'Living well is the best revenge,' quoted Jack as they stepped out of the restaurant. Across the street, *The Mousetrap* was still playing at the St Martin's Theatre after fifty years.

'Imagine having a piece of that show,' said Jack ruefully.

'Did you know that Dickie Attenborough was in the original production? He was already a star, and they couldn't afford his fee, so they gave him a percentage, which he collected for fifty years – except I heard that he sold his points to help finance *Gandhi*,' said Kieran with another explosive laugh.

Jack slumped into the taxi: jet lag and the lack of sleep had sent the Chablis to his head, and the taxi was swimming pleasurably under water through Trafalgar Square.

Kieran dropped him off at Daniel's house on the Kings Road. Hope opened the door. 'You look wasted, Jack. I'll make some coffee.'

Jack gave Daniel an account of his forty-eight-hour trip, with its disappointing outcome.

'So we have to get a script before we can move on,' said Jack.

'We have to pay Brad.'

'I've decided to finance the script myself.'

'I'll go halves with you, Jack.'

'You're broke, Daniel. I'm the producer: it's down to me.'

'You're breaking the first rule of producing, Jack. Never use your own money.'

'I'll get it back. I believe in this project; I'm passionate about it,' he said wearily. Daniel laughed, and mimicked Jack's passionless voice.

' "I'm passionate about it." That's so fucking Hollywood. You were exposed to the virus out there, Jack.'

Jack grinned, caught out.

'What's to be passionate about?' said Daniel, unable to hide his disappointment. 'I mean, what's this fucking film about? What are we doing?'

Jack's thoughts were strewn across his mind like wounded soldiers on a battlefield. He gathered them up and brought them to attention.

'I'll tell you what it's about. It's about making an honest genre movie that will make money for people. It's about staying in the game, because you and I are addicts. We would die if we couldn't make pictures, and they won't let us if we keep fucking up. And it's about sex and death and how, in a godless world, sex fills the place of religion.' Hope came in with the coffee and caught the last line.

'Making love has become the only place where we can feel human,' said Jack, yearning for Bella and thinking of LA. 'Kids shoot each other in school because they can't feel anything. And you know, and I know, that movies made by good people are a way of making a shitty world better. And if we don't, who will?' His flurry of non-sequiturs finally petered out.

Hope put the coffee down between them, smiling and shaking her head.

'It's only a fucking film, Jack. Go home and get some sleep,' she said, kissing him. Daniel was amused at his friend's intensity. Steady old Jack letting rip.

'Don't you hate it, Jack, the way women shoot us down when we're flying with some lofty idea.'

'Bringing you down to earth,' said Hope. 'Which is where we all live, like it or not.'

Daniel gave Jack a bear-hug and a grin.

'I love you, Jack.'

Daniel turned up at the National Film School in Beaconsfield feeling fragile. He was to give a lecture on composition. Thirty aspiring directors, all in their early twenties, watched him resentfully. If only they had his resources, what great films they would make.

He sensed their mood and decided to use the Socratic method, leading them to understanding through questions.

'What is the purpose of composition?' he asked, surveying the blank faces.

No one responded. He pointed to a girl with red hair, wearing dungarees.

She shrugged. 'To make a beautiful image.'

'If it is very beautiful, do you have to hold it longer, so that the audience has time to absorb it and roam over its loveliness?'

'I guess so.'

'What if this holds up your story?'

'If it's that's great, I would hang on to it.'

'Did you ever hear the expression "kill your darlings"?'

'Ezra Pound, wasn't it?'

'Anyone else know what composition is for?'

A boy in glasses perked up.

'To draw the eye to where you want it to go?'

'And where is that?'

No answer. Then a boy at the back called out in a firm voice. 'To the story.'

'Yes, to the story. And be kind to the audience. Don't swamp them with too much information. Only include what is essential. Take them by the hand. Let your compositions seduce them into the narrative.'

He saw how Heather would have to charm the audience into her world, and he would have to frame her so that the audience shared her fragility and felt they were by her side.

Bella's Notebook

The dynamic has changed. Since Jack is financing the script out of his own pocket, Brad and Daniel have fallen into the role of employees whose purpose is to please Jack. Brad sits at the computer and types the words. This gives him a certain power. The computer is the surrogate camera, the neutral receiver, which will give substance to their random, scattered thoughts. Daniel moves from the centre to the periphery and takes on the position of pitching in ideas, making subtle changes, suggesting dialogue as he paces the room. The absent Jack is like Banquo's Ghost, hovering over the proceedings. The thought occurs to me: did Jack pay out this money subconsciously to gain a stronger influence over the embryonic film? Behind every movie, Daniel says, there is a struggle for influence, ownership, credit and money, and he quotes Hitchcock, who said that a successful film has many fathers, but a failure is an orphan.

Jack came back from LA diminished and depleted, but after he had made the decision to finance the script himself, he recovered, and regained his strength. He had agreed to pay Brad $100,000: $10,000 on signing the contract, $10,000 on delivery of the first draft, and $5,000 on first-draft revisions, the balance of $75,000 to be paid on the first day of principal photography. So if the picture *is not made, Jack will only lose $25,000 – still a lot of money. This is well below Brad's established price of $250,000, so various bonuses are built into the deal. If the picture grosses $50 million, he gets another $50,000. If it grosses $75 million, he gets a further $100,000. At $100 million gross, he collects $100,000 – making a total of $350,000, plus another $50,000 if he gets nominated for an Oscar. He also gets 5 percent of the net profits.*

Brad is working from a programme called Final Draft, poorly named in Daniel's view. 'There is no final draft,' he says. 'The script is constantly evolving and changing, right up to, and including, the editing process.' Brad says there are only two ways that he can convince himself that he is a proper screenwriter: when somebody is paying him to do it, and when Final Draft is laying out his chaotic words into a neat formula acceptable to the studios. He says he has tried to write screenplays on spec, but without success. They have so little chance of being sold, let alone made, that the process becomes dispiriting and his efforts simply peter out in fits of depression.

It appears that Daniel writes the subsequent drafts himself. I asked Brad how he felt about relinquishing his work. He shrugged, 'I am a craftsman, like a carpenter making a sofa. I make the sturdy frame, and Daniel puts in the springs and the stuffing and chooses the material and the colour and covering. But he always brings me back in to attend rehearsal with the actors. When we hear the dialogue spoken, we do a lot of fast revisions and I do a draft based on what we've discovered.'

Another day: Daniel is addressing the issue of sex scenes in movies. He says they only work if they have narrative, otherwise they ask the viewer to be a voyeur, and to watch simulated sex is to be a voyeur faux, *which is a humiliating thing to be. Brad said he likes sex scenes. It is always interesting to undress the stars, see their breasts and get to know their bodies. Daniel talked about* Ai No Corrida. *He got the DVD from his library and we spent the afternoon watching it. I found it very disturbing, and hid behind my hair. Daniel said the film worked for two reasons. First, the sex was real, not simulated: Oshima showed the erect penis and penetration. Second, the story is about sex: sex itself is the narrative. The Japanese merchant casually fucks a serving maid. Something happens: a bond, a need is met. They quickly become obsessed with each other. They give up all other activities and ties and travel across Japan, literally fucking themselves to death. Brad doesn't like the film. He says sex should be fun – which it only is if you avoid obsession and, especially, falling in love. Daniel is shocked. 'But you love women, Brad,' he says. 'Yes, I do. I also love wine, but I'm not an alcoholic.' Daniel laughs and said, half-mocking, half-serious, 'But to make love, when you are in love, is transcendent. You both escape the self and you enter another. Never felt that?'*

Brad grinned and shook his head.

'Believe me, sexual obsession is very unhealthy and, as old Oshima shows, it leads to madness and death.'

'You've never been in love, never told a woman you love her?'

'Nope.'

Brad became aware that we were both staring at him, wanting a fuller explanation.

'I make them laugh. I laugh them into bed,' he said. 'The secondary benefit is that I have never slept with a girl without a sense of humour.'

He gave me a sly look to see if I was laughing. I was, and it made me blush.

'Brad,' said Daniel, 'our movie is about sexual obsession. Maybe you're the wrong writer.'

Brad pointed out that he had written about gays, transvestites, serial killers and impotence, without being any of those, so he could imagine sex that gets out of hand. Daniel winced at the expression. It demeaned what he felt was a notion that got to the very centre of being human. I also felt instinctively that dealing with this subject was a way for Daniel to vicariously experience Hope's adultery. Brad constantly tries to read my reactions to the discussion of sex, but Daniel never looks at me. He looks past me or through me. He thinks of me only as an adjunct to Jack. With a lot of circumlocution, they finally got back to the problem of how Daniel would stage the sex scenes, given his reservations. Brad's solution was to leave it and solve it on the set. But Daniel said no, it had to be story. The scenes have to be about her wanting to resist him because she is victimised by her feelings, but she cannot. She despises herself for her weakness. She is humiliated, feels she has lost her identity and wants it back. That's 'story', he says. There is no 'story' in consensual sex.

'OK,' says Brad. 'We'll do it your way.'

Bella glanced at her watch: it was 6.30 PM. She had promised to collect Orson from a friend's house at 6. Watching *Ai No Corida*, and the talk of sexual mores, had been awkward and disturbing, and it had eaten time alive. She was sure that Brad had been indirectly repeating his proposition to her, because he had made her laugh – which she now knew was his preferred method of seduction – and she thought of Jack's solid, sacred approach: he the priest, she the goddess. She imagined, with a shudder, how Brad would scoff if he ever learned the secrets of her marital bed.

She hurried out of Daniel's house, her hair making waves in the wind. She felt dirty and compromised in some way she could not define. She hailed a taxi. Outside the window, people streamed by, going home, doing some late shopping, holding hands, drifting in to the Chelsea Cinema, buying shoes at R-Soles. She thought of them all making love in different ways, or wanting to, or wanting not to, or tiring of their lovers, or besotted by them, betraying them, loyal to them. Her sexuality occupied a private box which she kept locked away, and she was resentful of it being tampered with.

She held Orson tightly to her breast.
'Why are you crying, mom?'
'Because I'm so happy to see you.'
She wanted domesticity, normality. She craved the mundane. Movies existed at the neurotic edges, the emotional extremes. It was late opening at the toy shop. She swept Orson in and bought him a Sylvanian car.

Daniel had stood by the window and watched Bella climb into the taxi.
'She drives me nuts,' said Brad.
Daniel looked over at him sharply.
'The way she watches us. So fucking cool, like we're two stupid pricks goofing off.' Daniel laughed.
'She's become our audience. I find her presence stimulating.'
'Yeah, instead of writing a movie, we turn cartwheels for her.'
Daniel saw the truth in that.
'OK, she's seen the script process. I'll tell her to back off until we get into casting or budgeting, or whatever.'
Brad turned back to his computer. The programme offered him several choices: *Action, Dialogue, Parenthesis, Scene.* He selected *Scene* and typed in *Int. Lobby – Day.* The computer self-selected *Action.* He wrote: *In her borrowed clothes, Heather moved quickly through the lobby. Joshua, behind the desk, raised an enquiring eyebrow.* The programme offered him the names of the film's characters. He selected *Joshua* and then *Parenthesis* and typed '*mockingly*'. The computer centred it

and put brackets around it. Brad then selected *Dialogue*, which the computer neatly centred under the *Parenthesis*: '*What have you been up to? Nice outfit.*' He hit *Action*, and wrote: *She gave him a cold glance and stepped through the door marked 'Staff Entrance'.*

Daniel leaned over Brad and looked at the result.

'Do you know what bothers me about this programme, Brad? It makes everything look so final.'

'But it's piss-easy to revise.'

'Yes, but it intimidates. Once it's in there, all perfectly laid out, it kind of defies you to cut or alter it. Maybe that's why movies get longer and longer. Same as novels. All down to the computer.'

'Do you want to go back to when we cut up scenes with scissors and pasted them together for the typist, waited three days for her to finish, and then spent a week weeding out the typos: no spell-check, no nothing? Then a week to get the script to LA. Now we press a button and it's there by e-mail in seconds.'

'Brad, have you ever wondered why the movies they made without computers, without CGI, without mobile phones, without Final Draft, were better than the ones we make?'

They fell silent. Brad's eyes drifted to the chair that Bella habitually occupied. Her departure had sucked all the energy from the room.

'Fuck it, let's pack it in for the day,' said Daniel.

As he let Brad out of the front door, he was confronted by Nigel Bateman. He had recovered his obsequious self.

'Sorry to bother you, Daniel. I was passing by and just wondered if you had had a chance to take a look at my script?'

Caught off guard, Daniel blustered, 'Ah yes, well, not really.'

Despite Nigel's meek manner, Daniel nervously recalled the violent episodes in Cannes. 'Come in, Nigel. Have a drink.'

Nigel backed away.

'No, I won't trouble you, Daniel.'

Daniel opened his arms in a gesture of abject apology.

'Nigel, I have a confession: I left your script at the hotel in Cannes. I'm so sorry.'

'Got another one for you, Daniel.'

He slid it out from under his coat. He passed it over solemnly, holding it with both hands. Daniel thought of a priest offering the chalice at communion. The lab was Nigel's sacred church. And now he was unfrocked. He backed away to the gate, bowing, as you would from an audience with the Queen. He waved, he nodded, he smiled, he almost touched his forelock.

When faced with the chore of reading a script, Daniel's solution was to put on some music that could occupy his spirit while his mind was reluctantly engaged elsewhere. If it was a tough read, he would listen to something light: Vivaldi, perhaps. In this case, he was anticipating that Nigel's script would not be too taxing, so he picked one of the late quartets of Beethoven. One day, he promised himself, he would make a film like that music: something pared down, utterly simple and true.

Nigel's script was called *Negatives*, and was set in a film laboratory. It sprawled over the pages with none of the neat constraints of Final Draft. It had a manic energy. It was about a downtrodden man called Norman (Nigel), who spent his life working nights in the lab, being bullied by his boss and disdained by the wife he scarcely saw, since she worked during the day. They were childless, the characters barely spoke – and when they did, only in clichés – yet they felt alive.

Night in the lab was a kind of hell, developing thousands of feet of negative to the shrill roar of the machines: the gloom and shadows of the lab, the smell of the chemicals, and the ghostly figures of the white-coated operatives, who seldom spoke to each other: like vampires, they were creatures of the night. Daniel was shocked by the chemical waste and pollution involved. He knew that the manufacture of film stock was a major pollutant, but he could never have imagined this laboratory nightmare. All our hopeful films about the human condition, thought Daniel, had passed through this Hades. Our liberal pleas for ecology, our satires on pollution, were themselves causes of pollution. He turned off the music and read on.

Norman, following in Nigel's footsteps, has just come off night work. Digital grading has made him redundant. Exposed to the light of day, he discovers that his wife spends her nights sleeping with another man, an old school friend of Norman's. He uses his knowledge of chemicals to poison them both. He dumps them naked in his bathtub. He goes on living alone in the terraced house. He finds he can only sleep during the day, because he has became allergic to light. He wanders the streets at night, witnessing crime and poverty and loneliness. He starts returning to the lab, concealing himself by crouching in a corner, seeking solace in the throb of the machines. Each night he steals a litre of acid and takes it home and pours it into the bathtub.

He haunts the archives deep underground, where the negatives of innumerable films are stored. In the innermost sanctum is a sealed steel room that Norman longs to enter. He imagines it as the very soul of the lab, a place that must surely contain the mystery of the place. The bullying night manager holds the keys. Norman stalks him and murders him too. He opens the forbidden door and finds it full of old, flammable silver-nitrate films. He recalls the beautiful black and white tones it produced: the silver screen of old. Safety film took out the risk, but something indefinable was lost. He goes there each night and inhales the sweet-sour smell of the nitrate film. Many of the films are well preserved, but in some of the cans he opens, the film has turned to dust, and he sprinkles a pinch into his tea. There is an ancient Moviola, and he laces up the old films and watches them in negative; all light reversed, black skies at noon, eyes blind and white. Phantom actors, silent ghosts. He understands the properties of nitrate film, the silver it contains, and why it is so highly flammable: as it burns, it produces its own oxygen, so that it cannot be smothered or doused by water.

He is visited by the police and questioned about the disappearance of his wife. He tells them she has run away with his friend. After they leave, he goes up to the bathroom. The flesh has been dissolved and the enamel eaten away from the bathtub. He puts the bones and skulls into a suitcase and takes them to the lab. He empties them out behind a pile of rusted film cans.

As Daniel turned the last page, Norman was immolating himself and the lab was burning to the ground. With a nice ironic touch, Nigel described the new building housing the digital lab escaping the fire. Daniel found himself moved by the loneliness and nihilism of the story, and noted how compelling it always was to be taken into the authenticity of another world. It made his own story feel contrived and empty. Yet his film was based on some kernel of his own experience, or at least his wife's. Of course, Nigel's script would never be made.

SEVEN

Bella made beans on toast for Orson and Jack, and they ate it in front of the TV watching the Japanese animated movie *Spirited Away* for the fourth time. Jack claimed it was one of the greatest films ever made.

'No, dad, *Lord of the Rings*,' said Orson.

He had not been allowed to see Peter Jackson's trilogy, although many of his class had, and he could not understand that his parents, who claimed to love him, could deny him the greatest joy that a child could experience.

'When you're older, Orson. It would give you nightmares.'

'I asked my friends at school, "Did you have nightmares?" They all said no, they didn't, they just had these great dreams.'

'Well, it's really scary,' said Jack.

'*Spirited Away* has monsters.'

'Not scary ones.'

'Yes, they are.'

'Do you dream about them?'

'No, 'cause I dream about Frodo and Gollum and orcs.'

'You haven't seen them.'

'Well, you can't stop me dreaming about them.'

Jack was weakening. He looked at Bella. Shall we? She shook her head firmly. Jack had loved the trilogy. He was in awe of the craftsmanship. He watched it like a wondering child. He said it was an achievement comparable with the building of the medieval cathedrals. Bella found it tedious and repetitive, and the endless slaying of mindless orcs revolting. She thought that the computer-generated spectacle swamped the wonderful central concept that the Ring of Power corrupted its possessor and only one as simple and good as a hobbit could withstand its allure.

Bella swept up the plates and clattered them into the kitchen, closing the issue.

'Bedtime, Orson.'

Orson sunk onto his haunches and gave his version of Gollum.

'Nasty mummy says bed, bed.'

Then, switching to the good Gollum.

'Gollum must do what mummy says.'

'No, mummy must let Orson see *Lord of the Rings*. No bed.'

Jack was enchanted, and he threw the boy over his shoulder and marched him into his bedroom. Bella watched them go, and for the first time felt Orson to be 'other', not part of her, but belonging to the larger world.

The babysitter arrived from next door. Bella and Jack left the house and walked up to the Chelsea Cinema.

'How does he know about Gollum?' Bella said. 'I found that display alarming.'

'It's in the air. The zeitgeist. It's irresistible,' he said with a sigh. 'Imagine having a movie like that. The marketing guys talk about the "want-to-see" quotient, but now and then, along comes a picture with "must-see", and this is one of them.'

'Bertolucci is a must-see for me,' said Bella.

'Me too,' said Jack, happy to be in accord with her.

They met up with Daniel and Hope in the foyer, as arranged. *The Dreamers*, set in Paris in 1968, was about a French brother and sister who invite an American boy to live with them in a ménage à trois. They are besotted with each other, and ignore the raging student rebellion in the streets below.

The two married couples spread themselves out on the spacious Pullman seats that made the Chelsea such a luxurious experience.

They went back to Daniel's house for a drink afterwards.

'The sex was so sweet and innocent,' said Hope, 'that it wasn't erotic at all.'

'That was down to the girl,' said Daniel. 'She was so unselfconscious about her body that you didn't feel embarrassed about watching Bertolucci's lens exploring every inch of it.'

'They had to cut the shot of the penis and the front-on vagina for the States,' said Jack, 'and still only got an NC17 – which a lot of theatres won't take.'

'I've got to find a love-making language for our movie,' said Daniel, 'and we can't afford an NC17, so goodbye vaginas and penises.'

'Just show the before and after,' said Hope. 'Unless you can wire the audience to the actors' orgasms, what's the point?'

Bella was still relishing *The Dreamers*.

'I was swept away. I became that girl, wished I had been her, not the stiff, inhibited, cold bitch I was. I lost myself in her. That's what I want from a movie. *Lord of the Rings* I admired, but I wanted it to be over.'

Jack was touched, and took her hand. It was so seldom that Bella would reveal herself like that. Daniel was amused to see that she was blushing.

'Do you recall that line of Truffaut's?' said Jack. ' "I don't like films where the hero has a best friend. *I* want to be his best friend." '

Daniel had opened champagne. It was a celebration, but of what?

'All great movies,' said Daniel, 'whatever else they are about, they are about the movies. When the impossible happens and the limitations of that light flickering on a screen are transcended and you fly with it, you understand the magic of the movies and the process that makes art out of light.'

He was directing this at Bella, to let her know what his deepest aspirations were, and she caught it and understood it.

'I'll drink to that,' said Jack.

And they all touched glasses.

'To our new movie,' he added.

'And to Bertolucci,' said Bella.

Daniel let them out of the front door. He embraced Jack, and as he kissed Bella, he said softly in her ear, 'Bella, Brad is feeling a little inhibited by your presence, so if you can gather what you can about the script process by the end of the week, well, we'll then go it alone for a bit.'

Bella stiffened and drew back defensively.

'I'll stop right now.'

'No, please see the week out.'

Bella lay in bed staring at the ceiling. Jack sensed the negative signals and lay on his side, watching her. An orange light from a street lamp filtered into the room through a gap in the curtains, and lit her profile.

'What is it?' he whispered.

She shut her eyes, feigning sleep.

'You upset about being shut out?'

'I got my period.'

'Oh, I'm sorry.'

It wasn't that, of course.

'What makes me angry is the way we get sucked into this movie process. It's so needy, this unmade movie. It's like a monstrous child. It has to be fed, and we all become like doting parents. I mean, I'm just an observer: it's ridiculous for me to feel wounded about being excluded. I feel like dropping the whole damn thing and going back to interviews.'

A car went past, with a rap song roaring. Jack took her in his arms, and when he kissed her he tasted the salt of her tears.

Bella's Notebook

I hid my face under my hair and sat half-turned away. I couldn't be more self-effacing unless I was in a coma. They worked on yesterday's scene. Brad had written it up. Heather, after witnessing her lover's involvement in the hotel owner's death, has borrowed clothes from the old woman and sneaks back into the hotel. Joshua mockingly says 'Nice outfit' as she hurries through the lobby. Daniel wants it to have more resonance. Brad says it's just a linking scene; don't make too much of it. Give the audience a break. They have just watched some strong scenes. But Daniel wants it to say more. It should tell us something about the hotel, he says, and we don't know at this point that Joshua is involved in the murder, so there has got to be a subtext in what he says. Brad says that if we put too much in, it will slow the pace. 'No,' says Daniel. 'What I'm adding will all happen on the edges of the frame; it's texture.' More density, more compression.

After several versions, the scene goes as follows: Heather enters as a couple – in walking boots and carrying rucksacks – leave the hotel. They greet her warmly. Heather goes to the desk, nervous, pale. Joshua looks concerned. He smiles, and hands her a bunch of keys. She looks past him at the TV. A man and a woman are stuffing a body into an oven. Joshua follows her look. 'Torn Curtain,' he says. 'Not one of Hitchcock's best, but . . . ' She hurries into the door marked 'Staff Only'. Brad advises Daniel to shoot an alternative version where Heather simply hurries through the lobby: a seven-

second link. 'Hey,' said Daniel, 'let's see how it holds up ten drafts down the line.' I begin to see how they function: Brad simplifies, Daniel complicates.

On Friday, my last day, Daniel takes me (took me – scripts are written in the present tense, and it is getting to me) to lunch at Thierry's, a tiny French brassiere on the Kings Road, where the small tables are pressed so close together that intimacy is unavoidable. It was the first time we had ever been together without others, I realised. I had loup de mer, while Daniel ate liver, medium rare. I have never got used to the European custom of eating organs. Americans mostly confine themselves to animal muscles. Daniel saw the distaste in my face, and ascribed it to my being bumped from the writing process. I told him it was just the liver. That lightened up the occasion, and we began laughing about everything and nothing. Then I asked him who Heather was based on. He said, 'Haven't you guessed?' I pretended I hadn't. He said, 'I'm sure you have.' I told him that Hope had complained that he lived his life through his movies in order not to have to live it in life. 'Not just me; we all do it,' he said. 'We can no longer respond to grief or any highly charged emotional situation in a spontaneous way, because we've seen everything, been everywhere, made love with beautiful women, killed in every imaginable way. The stars have done it all for us, so no experience comes to us new. Well, with me it's the reverse. When I was at my father's bedside and he was dying, I was taking note of the scene: how different it was from the cliche. How he didn't want me there. Cursed me. I wasn't upset, I was exhilarated, because I recognised it was a great scene and I put it into my next picture.'

I replied, 'Jack thinks that too. He says that we are secondhand people, no longer human in the fullest sense. He says the reason we cry in the movies at stuff we're dry-eyed for in real life is that we are more human watching a good picture than living life.' 'Yes,' Daniel

said, 'movies and sex are all we have.' 'And kids,' I said. 'Yes, kids,'
he agreed.

*We thought of our children, and how they came between us.
'What about this lunch?' I said. 'Can you use it? Are you taking
notes?' 'Are you?' he asked. I pointed to my little tape recorder next
to the wine bottle. He laughed. 'It always depends on where you
put the camera,' he said. 'If it was their point of view' – he indicated
a couple a few tables away – 'they would note our intensity, our
constant laughter. They'd know we weren't married because we're
talking too much. On the other hand, we know they're married,
because they have said nothing to each other for the last half an hour.
They could tell we're not lovers: not intimate enough, no accidental
touching of hands, not holding each other's eyes.' 'So what would
they or the camera conclude?' I asked, not really wanting to know
the answer. 'There you are,' he said. 'It's an original moment, to be
stored away and used later.'*

While Daniel and Bella were having lunch, Hope was following a
regular ritual, which involved Harrods and the Brompton Oratory. In
the food hall, she never failed to be thrilled by the exotic profusion.
The best of everything from the far corners of the world gathered
together for those who could afford it. The plethora of cheeses, each
with its own texture and smell, the cornucopia of fruit and vegetables,
the game and fish. She lusted after it all and, in a flurry of sensual
excitement, bought more than she needed: mangos and passion fruit,
organic chocolate, Bath Olivers, quails eggs, kangaroo steak. And
she did not need to carry it. It would be delivered. She had once
bought a T-shirt that proclaimed, 'I want everything and I want it
delivered', which she had never dared wear. As she paid, horrified
by the bill, guilt settled upon her: it had always been in her nature
that, having sinned, she was impelled to sin further, to be hung for a

sheep rather than a lamb. So she hurried into the cosmetics hall and bought a lipstick. Although she had several unused ones at home, the colour spoke to her. It was a deep dark red, secret, mysterious and dangerous. Then she cast her eye over the glittering produce in case there was a new night cream or moisturiser that would do what all the others had failed to do, despite their claims.

To expiate her guilt, it was her custom to walk the length of Knightsbridge to the Brompton Oratory, resisting the siren calls of the dress shops. If she achieved it, she would feel purified. But often a certain something would catch her eye and her little demon would say, What harm can it be to try it on? You're not going to buy it, only admire it. But once it was on and clinging to her, she knew . . .

She had been brought up a Catholic, and missed the spiritual ardour and transcendence that she now only approximated in the arms of Paul. Secretly and shamefully, she had started going to church again, knowing she would be ridiculed by her circle of friends if it came out. She pretended she was going to the gym, or to yoga, both of which were acceptable. She believed that lying about going to church was a sin automatically forgiven.

She loved to be swallowed up in the vast, dark emptiness of the Oratory. She always fined herself 5 percent of what she spent in Harrods and put it in the poor box: £10 today. She lit a candle for her dead mother and one for Paul in New York, who was a heavily blaspheming lapsed Catholic. She started thinking about him, got angry with herself and blew out his candle. She felt imprisoned and constrained by the kids, duties, obligations, Daniel. Here, in the Oratory, she expanded. She could feel her spirit filling the cavernous church, and wallowed in the mystery. She never spoke to God. She felt that He was much too busy to bother with her. She liked making confession, however. She never admitted to her real sins: adultery, and thoughts of murdering her husband. If it was an old priest, she would admit to a harmless lie or taking God's name in vain. To a young priest, she would find herself inventing outrageous sins to embarrass him, claiming to have masturbated in her pew during the Eucharist.

She stepped out of the confessional. A man was sitting in a pew, writing in a notebook. He turned and looked at her. It was Brad. She felt his eyes scanning her breasts and neck.

'I write in here sometimes. It reminds me of my Italian boyhood: the smell of incense, and so on. The usual.'

'And me of the convent.'

'Your secret's safe with me,' he said.

'And yours with me.'

She felt herself blushing. He smiled, awkwardly.

'We are both Daniel's creatures,' he said, 'but he doesn't have to know everything about us, does he?'

She left the Oratory saddened that her secret had been discovered and uneasy that, somehow, she had entered into a conspiracy with Brad, whom she did not like or trust.

Jack took Bella to the meeting. The alpha males – and one alpha female – were spread out around the conference table at the office of Phyllis Silverstein, the sales agent: Kieran Corrigan; Herbert Moss, the media lawyer; and Sid Evensong of Labyrinth, the company that raised tax-shelter money.

'What are your sales estimates, Phyllis?' said Sid.

'Well, we don't have a script yet, only this treatment, and of course no cast and no budget, so there is a big margin at this point between low and high.'

'What's it going to cost, Jack?' Sid pressed.

'Between $20 and $25 million, depending on the cast.'

Kieran weighed in. 'Phyllis, the banks trust your estimates, and they will come in for 20 percent if you can nail two major presales, say Spain and France, or Germany and the UK.'

'What about the tax shelter, Sid?'

'Well, it has got a lot tighter, as you know. At one time we could raise 40 percent of the budget, but that involved double-dipping.'

'Double-dipping?' Bella asked.

'Using more than one tax shelter,' Sid explained. 'We have another mechanism that can get it up to 23 percent.'

'But you want back-end points for that, and a bigger fee,' said Herbert.

Sid bared his chest, offering it to whomsoever wished to stab him.

'I have to live too.'

They all had their notepads and calculators out. It became a blur to Bella. She wrote down: *the EU Media Programme Development Fund – back-end escalators – above-the-line deferrals – inter-party agreement. Mystifying. They use euphemisms to dignify what look to me like scams.*

Their faces are flushed with pleasure, eyes flashing as figures fly. They are high on numbers. In a Ken Russell movie, he would have them break into a tap-dance routine and leap onto the table.

Phyllis surreptitiously lit a cigarette. She held it beneath the table, but a whiff of smoke caught Sid and Herbert. They demanded cigarettes from Phyllis, and sucked in, with the greedy inhalations of people who have given up and no longer buy cigarettes. Jack interpreted that as permission, and pulled out his pipe. Soon the air was thick with smoke; Bella found it unendurable and slipped out, unnoticed.

On the way home, she asked Jack how many lawyers would be involved. He counted them on his fingers.

'Ours, the sales agent's, the bank's, Labyrinth's. The Spanish co-producer will have two – a Spanish and a UK one. If we get Lottery money, the BFI will have one; so seven at least.'

'And their fees?'

'Quarter of a million. And then there are what are called "finance" costs, which all have to come out of the budget. Labyrinth will insist on a fee of probably half a million.'

'They put money in, and take some of it out again right away?'

'Yeah, they're taking big bucks from us for finding investors who want a tax break.'

'So it's the government that pays, finally? It's money that would otherwise go into hospitals or roads.'

'Supposed to stimulate the economy,' said Jack, without much conviction. 'The sales company will ask for $350,000 from the budget for expenses, so that's $1.1 million spent before we start, and they all want executive-producer credits.'

'What about the bank?'

'Yes, the bank will want a fee, probably $100,000, and the interest will cost us around $300,000. Now we are up to $1.5 million in dead money. Then we have to buy insurance, which costs 2 percent of the budget – say, $500,000 – and the completion bond will be twice that. I make that about $3 million out of the $25 million.'

'I find it all so depressing,' said Bella, 'but you seem to love it.'

Jack grinned, opened the window of the cab and relit his pipe. Bella pointed at the sign in the cab. 'Thank You for Not Smoking'.

'Do you remember that cab scene in *To Live and Die in Long Island*?' said Jack. 'The cab driver says, "Didn't you see the sign, mate?" and John Hurt replies, "And since I am smoking, I do not expect to be thanked."'

The cab driver's voice came over the intercom.

'You know how many people have pulled that one? I had John Hurt himself in the cab one night – picked him up from the Ivy.

Started smoking. He told me about the film. I got the video out. It was the only joke in the picture.'

Jack leaned back in his seat laughing, and pulled on his pipe.

'My dear Bella, I have never ceased to wonder that it is possible to get people to invest huge sums of money to make movies. All they've got at the end of the day is light, light and shade . . . '

'I know,' she said, 'light flickering on a wall.'

He looked sheepish. 'Yes, Daniel's line. I borrowed it.'

She was always touched by his honesty. She kissed him. He was wily and shrewd and obdurate, and it was all in the service of his romantic, spiritual aspirations. She leaned her head on his shoulder, happy and safe, melting into him. She kissed him again.

'You have the power of transformation too,' he said. 'All it takes is a kiss like that and a middle-aged, short-sighted Jew becomes a slim, young, blond guy, like Robert Redford in *The Way We Were.*'

'No. That was so mawkish.'

'OK, in *Out of Africa.*'

'Better, but I prefer my Jew the way he is.'

EIGHT

Bella's Notebook, 20 June, Wiltshire

Tomorrow is the summer solstice, and the script is finished. The first draft, at least. We are staying the weekend at a stately home converted to a country hotel. The idea is that we can all read and discuss the script away from distractions. The hippies and the druids and the new-agers are assembling at Stonehenge, up the road. Daniel comes every year, apparently – not to Stonehenge but to Avebury, which is where the really hip pagans go. We'll make our pilgrimage there to witness the dawn. Jack excited; me sceptical. We had dinner at the hotel last night, and Hope got drunk and said she did not intend to hang around shivering and looking at a bunch of stones, and why was it all right to be a pagan and worship nature, and why, she asked Jack, was it morally acceptable to sneer at Catholicism but anti-Semitic to criticise Judaism, with its cruel god. Jack tried to head it off.

'You're right,' he said. 'It's all superstition. I hold no truck with any of it; a pox on all their houses.'

'Then why did you have Orson circumcised, which is barbaric?'

Jack went pale and said nothing. Stupidly, I said, 'How did you know?'

'Because I saw his poor little penis.'

Jack recovered and spoke very quietly, trying hard to keep his cool. 'It's a tribal thing, not a religious thing. It was a powerful message from my ancestors passing through my genes. Bella hated the idea. I'm ashamed to say I insisted.'

119

Daniel looked daggers at Hope. The air was thick with accumulated recriminations. Hope said, 'I'm sorry, too much fucking vodka.'

I spoke to her afterwards, when we were on our own.

'It had nothing to do with you or Jack,' she said. 'I was getting at Daniel.'

It seems Daniel's way of dealing with their problem is to faze her out.

'He acts as if I'm not there,' she said.

So she was ready to do anything to get his attention.

Jack and Daniel had a drink in the lounge after the women had gone to bed. It was their droll notion on these occasions to drink Jack Daniel's. Daniel was relieved that the hotel did not stock it. He had a Morangie malt instead, and inhaled the peaty vapour. The silky liquid steadied him. Jack was clearly shaken by the episode. Daniel groped for a way of apologising.

'She is going through a bad time, Jack, but it was inexcusable – none of her business.'

'I've turned my back on the whole damn thing – Judaism, Zionism, all of it – but I guess at bottom I'm still a Jew, whatever that means.'

Jack fell silent, disappearing into some gloomy inner place where his friend could not follow. Daniel's need to heal the breach led him to a painful confession.

'When she was in New York, Hope had . . . '

'I know.'

Daniel was startled.

'She told Bella, and Bella told me.'

'We're both off balance,' said Daniel, peering into his whisky. When he looked up, he saw such warmth and understanding in Jack's eyes that he got a lump in the throat.

'She's a good woman. It's hard on her. You get buried in your work.'

In the morning, Daniel took Orson, Andrew and Rose off to an adventure playground while Hope, Jack and Bella read the script. They gathered for lunch. Jack ordered a bottle of champagne and they touched glasses. Daniel was on edge, nervous about how Hope would react to elements of her character that had been shoehorned into the story, but Hope was aware of Daniel's concern and was determined to be gracious.

'Let me jump in,' she said. 'I think it's great: it's passionate and sexy and daring. You never know what's coming next.'

Daniel leaned over and kissed her.

'Wonderful, gripping,' said Jack, 'exactly as a thriller should be. It works. It works, but . . . '

'But,' said Daniel. 'Oh, those buts.'

'We gotta believe that she wouldn't go to the FBI. We know she can't go to the police, but what's to stop her calling the Bureau?'

'That's the challenge,' says Daniel. 'She loves the guy. Lionel was hateful and deserved to die, yet for the boy's sake, justice is required – and for her own conscience. We have to hold these all in balance, so the audience is always unsure of what she's going to do next.'

'When the police investigate the missing Lionel, perhaps they should find clues that point towards Heather as a possible murderer,' said Jack.

'That's the idea. If she goes to the FBI, she might incriminate herself,' said Daniel. 'We don't want the audience to guess correctly what she would do.'

'There could be something in her past she's running away from that you don't reveal until the point when you need it,' said Jack. 'Maybe some other guy she knew, who died in weird circumstances.'

It was what Jack was good at, being engaged but objective. Daniel kept glancing at Bella. He had got into the habit of watching her reactions. Following her policy of self- effacement, she volunteered no opinion. Finally, Daniel asked for her verdict. It gained value from being withheld.

'I find scripts hard to read. I'm not very good at visualising them. It's such hard work and I don't feel qualified to make a judgement.'

Jack remonstrated with her.

'Come on. You must have got a sense of it as a story – its tensions, and how convincing it is?'

If she refused, it would be taken as a negative reaction, so she spoke carefully.

'Well, I felt you were so anxious to make her behave rationally and logically to each turn of events that I sometimes wished she would act, as it were . . . intuitively.'

Jack started to put up a defence of the script, but Daniel stopped him.

'You're right, Bella, but that's second-, third-draft stuff,' Daniel said. 'At the moment, the characters are following the plot rather than the other way around.'

'Speaking of which,' said Jack, pulling out four pages of tightly written notes. 'Here's my usual offering of nitpicking.'

Daniel gave a mock groan and stuffed them in his pocket. A thought was welling up in Bella's mind – or in her body, more precisely. She found she was trembling and her hands were moist with sweat, all from the effort of trying not to say something which demanded to be said. She was like a Quaker when the spirit moved. Finally it forced its way out without permission.

'Heather is . . . at least what I get from the script . . . is so open and honest, even pure . . . she could never conceal this thing . . . it would destroy her.'

The others were startled by her intensity. Jack took her hand to steady her.

'She was following her heart, not her head,' said Hope. 'She was in the grip of passion. Not everyone can be cool like you, Bella,' she added ironically.

Daniel and Jack could see that Bella was anything but cool, and so could Hope, but her irony was well concealed.

The longest day stretched on, usurping the territory of the night. Hope decided to go with them after all. They drove past Stonehenge, which was besieged. Avebury was a disappointment to Jack. The outer ring was ten times greater than Stonehenge but the stones were like stumps of worn-out teeth, and with no horizontal cross-pieces. The great ring had been brutally bisected by a modern road.

'I have to say, Daniel,' Jack said apologetically. 'I prefer Stonehenge. It is an image, a shape, but this is like a map. It's kind of academic.'

'No, no,' Daniel protested. 'Use your imagination. Look at its scale, its vastness. Compared to this, Stonehenge was a' – he searched for an appropriate metaphor – 'a garden shed. And what about the road, cutting it in half? How about that for a visual metaphor?'

'A metaphor for what?' said Jack.

'Wholeness severed by ignorance. The blindness of the material world. Rape. Take your pick.'

'The sperm entering the ovum,' said Bella softly.

Jack took her hand. Daniel caught their looks to each other.

'There was a belief, probably still is,' Daniel said, carefully, 'that if you made love under the stones of Stonehenge, or here, on midsummer night, you would surely conceive.'

'Shall we give it a try?' said Jack, intemperately, earning a scathing glance from Bella.

A scattering of pensive folk wandered aimlessly round the stone circle. It was overcast and a grubby grey light suffused the sky, a disappointing dawn. A warm breeze stirred with the light and folded around them, connecting them to each other. It brought a memory to Hope.

'This leathery old nun told us girls that the early monks believed that the wind was the Holy Ghost. I used to have an image of her pulling up her habit and opening her legs, no knickers, and letting the breeze blow up her, having it off with the Holy Spirit.'

As they drove back, a gap appeared in the north-eastern sky and a blazing sun dramatically illuminated Stonehenge.

'Awesome,' said Jack. 'Screw your metaphors, now that's an image.'

'A cliché,' said Daniel, but he stopped the car and couldn't tear his eyes away from it. Bella watched him, and grasped how deeply this landscape affected him: she sensed that it took him to dark and mysterious places.

It was five in the morning before they got to bed. Jack and Bella made love, not under the stones, but in the faux-antique four-poster bed. The sun slid in through the window from the north-east and anointed their bodies with a soft light diffused by an early mist. Bella's labyrinth surrendered its secrets without protest. Jack missed the slow rituals conducted in total darkness, but there was such a sensuousness in the air, and she was so open, that he soon began to emit his moaning cries.

'You make me feel like the Wailing Wall,' she had said once, hurtfully.

She, as ever, was silent.

When Daniel entered his room, which was next door to Jack's, he found Hope leaning against the connecting wall. She held her finger to her lips to silence him. They listened to Jack's moans and tried to stifle their laughter. Hope took his hand. He kissed her. She responded. It was a hard, angry fuck, fast and furious, but afterwards tender, as they held each other. It was the first time they had made love since her return from New York.

'I'm sorry,' she said.

'Me too.'

They lay there quietly, listening to the sated silence next door.

'Why is she so silent?' Hope whispered. 'Does he stuff a sock in her mouth?'

Daniel laughed. The earthy, irreverent Hope was, however temporarily, his once more.

They slept late, walked over the barren Salisbury plain with the kids, and drove to Salisbury Cathedral for evensong. The voices of the choir rang out against the implacable stone, as they had every day for eight hundred years, a liturgy yearning for a response but dying against the obdurate limestone. Billions of sea creatures had lived and died and donated their bones to make these stones, and the dreamers, the master builders, had arranged them so that they seemed as light as air as they soared up to the improbable spire, reaching foolishly for heaven, dangerously unstable, rescued from collapse by another painter in stone, Christopher Wren. Jack, the lapsed Jew, Hope, the closet Catholic, Daniel, whose work was prayer to an absent god, and Bella, the devout atheist, all felt a deep harmony with the church, the music and each other that they would never quite know again. As they left, Jack admitted to an epiphany.

'Know what hit me in there? Darwin was right. There never was a God, a creator. Only chance; but little by little, through need, we're creating one. Not the old adage, you know, if he didn't exist we would have to invent him, but actually creating him, her or it through prayer, and by building cathedrals; and now finally science

– with the help of a massive main-frame, all-knowing computer – will make the god we're looking for. It's all backwards. That's the purpose of evolution: starts with a bang and ends with a god.'

'And what will he, she or it be like, this god of yours?' said Bella.

Jack was burning with the fervour of the converted.

'Why, it's us. All of us, merging together. You know the ecstasy of becoming one with a lover. Imagine becoming one with seven billion.'

'Some orgy,' said Hope, who knew God had always been there, and that fanciful notions like this would only occur in arid minds empty of spirit. Bella recalled from her philosophy courses at Harvard that Teilhard de Chardin had proposed a similar notion, but she kept silent, not wanting to take away from Jack's sense of discovery.

From Daniel's rattle-bag of quotations, one popped out.

'Bertrand Russell was asked what would he say as a lifelong atheist if, when he died, he found himself in the presence of God. He replied, "Sir, what possible reason could you have for concealing all evidence of your existence?"'

Jack was still enjoying his epiphany. 'You see, it's all reversed. Instead of starting with God, we end with him.'

Bella's Notebook

Jack says one of the reasons why movies fascinate is that they touch the world in so many ways. They deal with multinational conglomerates, large sums of money, technology, honest crafts like carpentry, actors, art, and finally the public. That may be true, but I am beginning to realise how unglamorous much of the process is. Jack and Daniel met with Kevan Barker, an Irishman taken as a lad to London. His exaggerated cockney accent must have been acquired to camouflage his Irishness from jeering English schoolboys. Jack has an affinity with him because he is a fellow pipe-smoker, but I notice that Kevan also smokes cigarettes and cigars, and drinks beer and wine and whiskey, all to dampen down his huge energy, which would otherwise overwhelm him. Daniel had already gone through the script working out how much time he needed to shoot each scene. He came to a total of forty-seven days, plus two travel days. He also marked the number of extras he required, and wrote it down on the bottom of each page. Kevan sat at his computer with a budgeting programme called Movie Magic. The above-the-line costs – script, director, producer and principal actors – they put to one side for the time being. Jack and Daniel calculated that they needed four weeks' location shooting in Spain, standing in for New Mexico, including the hotel exteriors and lobby, and six weeks of interiors in Pinewood Studios back in England. Kevan had the crew rates from a recent picture and was able to put in the camera, grip and electrical packages.

'How much film stock do you shoot, Daniel?'

'Put in four thousand feet per day.'

'The bonder will want more.'

'Let him look at my record: I seldom go over two thousand.'

Daniel explained to me afterwards that the camera would only be running for twenty-two minutes each day, which was the equivalent of two thousand feet. The rest of the eleven-hour day would be spent in lighting and rehearsing the actors and the camera moves, or moving from one set or location to another, or waiting for the sun to come out, or for an actor to be dressed or made up, or for the generator to be fixed, or for flags to be set against flares, or a thousand other snags and embellishments.

Daniel quoted Billy Wilder, who complained that making films was mostly about waiting around. He said, 'In fifty years of moviemaking, do you know how long the camera was running? Maybe two weeks.'

'So,' said Kevan, 'sixteen days' shoot in Spain, two days' travel, thirty-one interiors at Pinewood, twelve weeks' pre-production,

twenty weeks' post-production.' Kevan and Jack stepped back, lit their pipes and disappeared in smoke. Kevan smoked a black tobacco that smells of peat fire and Meadowsweet. The two aromas swirled around me and undid me. The figures and calculations melted into the mist. When I came round, they were working on the above-the-line costs, and put in $1 million for Daniel, $500,000 for Jack and $5 million for the female lead, $350,000 for Brad and $2 million for additional cast. Selfishly, I wanted to know why Daniel got twice as much as Jack. Daniel went through it with me. A producer could have several projects going at one time. He was not committed on a day-to-day level. Jack was more involved than many producers, who would often develop a project, package it, put a star and director together, take a fee and move on. An A-list director in Hollywood could command $5 million a picture, but in independent films $1 million was the upper limit. Daniel only managed a film every three years. 'Once I finish a film,' he said, 'it takes a while to shake it off and decide what to do next.' Very often he developed several ideas, which did not work out, for one reason or another. Between writing a script all the way up to promoting the finished film around the world, three years would pass. Of the $1 million fee, 10 percent went to his agent, another 5 percent to lawyers, accountants and business managers, leaving $850,000; $300,000 went in tax, leaving $550,000. So $180,000 a year clear, not enough to maintain his lifestyle; so he was obliged to shoot three or four commercials a year.

The budgeting process went on for three long days, Kevan plying Daniel with questions and considering options and alternatives. The Spanish location shoot was expensive. The crew and cast had to be flown out and housed in hotels. Kevan thought it would be cheaper to charter a plane, but on closer analysis found that actors were going and coming at different times and it would only work if everyone went out and came back together. There was night shooting and day shooting in Spain, so an extra turnaround day had to be allowed in the middle for the crew to recover.

Kevan said, 'Look, you need eighteen days in Spain over four five-day weeks, plus a turnaround day. If you could lop a day off and shoot six-day weeks, we could be out of there in three weeks.'

'What would that save?' Jack asked.

Kevan hit a button and the programme deducted the week's costs for hotels, per diems, equipment hire and local labour, and automatically reduced the insurance, completion bond and contingency by corresponding amounts, giving him an instant answer. 'Two hundred and fifty thousand, three hundred dollars.'

Daniel winced.

'Too tight. We are outside; there are weather considerations. I would sooner squeeze a week out of Pinewood if we must.'

'Will you do a digital grade?' said Kevan.

'Absolutely,' said Daniel, thinking of the absent Nigel and reminding himself to call him.

'If you are going that route, have you thought about shooting 16mm instead of 35mm?' 'I've thought about it a lot,' said Daniel. 'Sixteen-millimetre gives you deeper focus, which I like for this picture, and Kodak has developed a new stock especially for digital grading. I want to shoot the film high-contrast, with velvet-black shadows and de-saturate, which I can only do by going digital.'

'What are the savings?' said Jack. It was his perennial question. Kevan didn't leave the computer. He grinned.

'What you save on film stock and lab charges by shooting on 16mm is soaked up by the cost of a digital grade.'

'Let's do it,' said Daniel.

They were shuffling the schedule to make it more time-efficient.

'One day,' said Daniel ruefully, 'I want to shoot a movie in sequence.'

He looked through the schedule pages that Kevan had printed out.

'The Hotel Lobby in Spain: two days' shoot. Opening scene, a middle scene and an end scene. We are going to be jumping all over the story, and the actors will have to make these great emotional leaps. It can't be helped. That is why rehearsal is so important.'

'How much rehearsal do you need?' asked Kevan.

'Two weeks.'

'You have a couple of actors who don't play in the first four weeks. You will have to make some tricky split deals with them.'

At the end of the three days, they had a preliminary budget based on the first-draft screenplay. The budget and script would go through many drafts before it was finalised.

NINE

London to LA, the polar route. Daniel had made the trip countless times, and invariably fell into a long reverie. Liberated from phones and family, it was a kind of aerial Ashram. He thought of it as a semi-colon in his life, a parole in the middle of his life sentence, eleven hours crossing the icy no-man's land between Europe and America. He took a window seat and watched the ice below. It was a clear day, and at 35,000 feet the glaciers were so sharply defined that he felt he could reach down and touch them, and burn his fingers on their permafrost. He searched for evidence of global warming, ice flows breaking away from the frozen mass, but even in midsummer it looked reassuringly solid. Greenland, Nova Scotia, the Great Canadian Tundra, over the Rockies, then the hot desert of Las Vegas, across the San Bernardino Mountains, to the hundred-mile city, with its yellow pall of smog and its hundred thousand swimming pools flashing smiles up at the 747 gliding down over the freeways and flopping onto LAX.

Jack and Bella had gone to their home in New York and would follow on and meet him in LA. Jack had a play running on Broadway and told Daniel that he needed to tend to it for a day or two, but the detour was really to allow Bella to visit her doctor at a fertility clinic, in her ongoing quest to get pregnant. Jack was required to go along and give sperm in case that was the problem. They both found the experience deeply disturbing, in that it took their sexual relationship from the sacred and secret to the public and statistical. Jack was sent to the bathroom with a jar, and several *Playboy* magazines. He turned their pages morosely, failing to find stimulation. All he could think of was Bella's vagina and her womb being clinically investigated. He found a pouting nubile creature and tried to fantasise about her giving him a blow-job, but then he imagined Bella discovering them at it, and his nascent erection flagged. He opened his wallet and took out a photo of Bella and tried to conjure in his mind their coupling in Wiltshire. He felt furtive and guilty about using her in this way, even though it was in her interest, and at her behest.

They went to lunch afterwards, at Pastis in the meat district, which was close to the clinic. Bella could sense how the experience had upset him, however hard he tried to conceal it. She hated making him do it. They each felt they had committed a low-level betrayal of the other. They treated each other carefully, like invalids, much too solicitously for married people. Bella was thinking of Daniel's observations on the behaviour of couples and wondered if people at other tables could tell they were married.

On arrival, Daniel spent an hour in Immigration waiting to be fingerprinted. He was taken to one side, body-searched and interrogated. They had information that he had once had a private pilot's licence and was a member of CND. The conjunction of these two pursuits profiled him as a possible terrorist. When he pointed out that CND was about stopping people blowing things up, he was accused of being a 'smartass' and was treated with bristling hostility. These security jocks had been given power over others, and relished it. They were desperate to find an enemy, and angry with him for not being one. A director friend of Daniel's, when asked the purpose of his visit to LA, said he was here to 'shoot a pilot'. He was clapped in irons.

Daniel checked in to the Chateau Marmont, feeling intimidated by the billboards he had passed along Sunset announcing the big upcoming studio pictures. They made his project seem frail and anaemic. He was already seeing things through Hollywood eyes. He took a shower and looked down the front page of the *LA Times*. A couple of paragraphs of seven stories, and then you are required to turn to page something-or-other to read the rest of the piece. None of the offerings interested him enough to warrant searching through the advertising-heavy inner pages. He flicked over to the Calendar section to see what movies were playing. Nothing much of interest there either.

Fred Schneider, his agent, picked him up at seven to go for dinner. It was 3 AM London time. He felt that his density had increased in the course of the journey, or that gravity had doubled. The physical heaviness was matched by a light-headedness. His spirit couldn't keep up, and was still somewhere over Greenland, and his higher brain functions had drowned in the jetstream.

Fred had booked a table at Michael's in Santa Monica, where expensive Nouvelle California food at its best was reliably on offer. But Daniel did not want to make the tortuous thirty-mile journey down Sunset, and suggested Musso and Frank, just up the road. Fred agreed, with some reluctance, since the restaurant was frequented by what he called secondary-industry types – screenwriters, cameramen and ADs – but the food was honest and there was a European quality about it, which was almost convincing.

Fred was preoccupied with his own problems at the agency. He was the old bull elephant and the young males were gathering to depose him. He had been forced to give up some of his privileges. Most of the agency's income was from TV, which Fred felt was unworthy of his attention. The young agents had had the temerity to point out that his commissions over the last two years had been less than his salary and expenses. They were demanding that he abandon some of his prestigious but unprofitable clients. Daniel bridled.

'So you want to drop me?'

Fred shook his head, smiling.

'But I might drop all of *you*.'

He confided that he had been offered a job running one of the major film studios.

'Are you going to take it?'

'It might be a poisoned chalice.'

'How so?'

'They've had a bad year and they have another bunch of turkeys waiting to be released,' he confided. Then, with his characteristic grimace that masqueraded as a smile, 'When John Calley took over at Sony, he inherited *Men in Black*. It was a monster hit. He said, "When you take over a studio, it is very important to choose your predecessor."'

'So you're concerned that you'll be associated with these bad movies?'

'Yeah, I think Tannenbaum wants to put someone in there to take the heat for a year, and fail. Then he can bring in the guy he really wants; but nevertheless, if I lose the battle at the agency, I might do it.'

Fred cast a suspicious eye over the nearby diners, and leaned forward.

'Strictly between us, Dan. Nobody knows about this. If it gets out, I'll know who let it out.'

Daniel was struggling with terminal fatigue. The top half of his skull was anaesthetised. Fred fell into a gloomy silence, munching his dry lettuce leaves. Daniel's digestive system had gone to sleep hours ago. The wine tasted harsh and acidic. Daniel tentatively introduced his own business.

'All the studios got the script and the budget?'

'Yeah. Better you had cast the girl.'

'Well, you know the problem.'

'Yeah, we bombed out on all the broads: Blanchett, Johansson. Busy, or won't do nude. Jolie we know about.'

It was the Hollywood thing to call the stars by their first names – Tom, Meryl, George – to imply intimacy. Fred only used last names. He turned them into commodities, slabs of meat. If there were two of them, he would still resist using their first names. 'Fat old Curtis,' he would say. Or 'the Curtis filly'. Then, out of the blue, he said, 'Tannenbaum wants to invite you to his place in Santa Barbara for the weekend; me too.'

' "In Xanadu did Kubla Khan, a stately pleasure dome decree". I heard about his place.'

'Wait till you see it. The guy pulls down a $100-million-a-year salary; forget his stock. He's got to spend it on something.'

'Why the invitation?'

'He wants you to do a movie for them.'

'He doesn't get involved in the movie division, surely? He's a conglomerate, he's in orbit, he doesn't get his hands dirty any more.'

Fred pushed his salad away in disgust, and ordered ice cream.

'The stock has dropped 12 percent in the last year. He had a messy divorce and a bypass – the usual rite of passage at fifty – but it hit the papers hard. Movies are only 5 percent of his business, but they're high profile. Those turkeys got noticed on Wall Street. They jeered at him: "Tannenbaum, beset by personal problems, has lost his Midas touch." '

'So he's going to prove them all wrong?'

'He's got this project he wants to make and nobody else does, but he won't let it go. It's kinda like Citizen Kane trying to teach that tone-deaf broad to sing.'

Profiteroles were delivered to the next table, and Fred's eyes rolled towards them, lusting.

'So he's been through the A-list directors . . . ' Fred started.

'And finally got down to me?'

'I told him I could deliver you, so do me this favour, play along with him, till I decide to run with this gig or not.'

Daniel's brain had just touched down, and he remembered that Jack and Bella were coming in. He couldn't abandon them.

'I'll call him,' said Fred. 'Maybe he'll invite them too.'

They got up to leave, and were greeted at several tables. A publicist, Harry Bitzberg, jumped up and hugged Fred, whispering in his ear, 'I hear you left the agency to take over a studio.'

Fred dismissed this contemptuously – which none of the several people watching the encounter believed for an instant.

'Are there no secrets in this town?' Fred grumbled to Daniel.

Fred dropped him off at the Chateau Marmont and waited while Daniel went upstairs to find Nigel's script. Fred had agreed to get the agency to cover it. In London, Daniel had invited Nigel home for a drink and told him gently that it was not a film he wanted to make, and warned him that it was a difficult subject and that he shouldn't be too hopeful. After a couple of drinks, Nigel switched from obsequious to belligerent, and had been plaguing Daniel with calls and notes ever since. Daniel handed the script to Fred, with a request.

'A really tough critique: put him out of his misery. It's got to say that there's no chance of it being made. Coming from a big agency, it might sink in and get him off my back.'

As Fred got back into his car, Daniel hastily remembered to ask after Fred's wife.

'How's Trudy?'

Fred gave him a blank stare. Like movies that fail, a wrecked marriage must never be acknowledged. Trudy? He'd never heard of her.

Daniel fell into bed, and into a deep sleep. It was 6 AM in London. He awoke an hour later, his usual getting-up time. He lay in bed watching the news: a drug ring arrested; Schwarzenegger talking about gay marriage; a Latino politician demanding that Spanish should be the official language in California since Spanish speakers were a majority; kids handing over their weapons as they entered the school, and collecting them at the end of the day; and a police chase on a freeway followed by a helicopter with that great giro-mounted camera that floated in the sky and could probe down to a close-up of a hunted man, and still be silkily smooth. He flicked channels and caught the end of an interview with a relaxed Jason Everly saying that, having acted in a lot of pictures, directing came easily to him.

Nothing would induce sleep. It was now 8.30 in London. He called Hope and spoke to the kids. He could hear Bob Dylan playing in the kitchen – always a sign of discontent, and yearning for her hippie days on the road.

'Your mummy loves Bob Dylan, Rose.'

'No, dad, she loves you, she loves the *sound* of Bob Dylan,' was the five-year-old's logic. Was there anxiety under it? How much had the kids picked up? He turned the bedside light off and practised his pitch to the studio: It's about a girl, about sexual obsession, a small town in New Mexico, an eco-hotel run by a man, Lionel, everyone hates. The woman witnesses her lover committing a murder, the murder of a hateful man. Should she turn him in or . . . It all sounded so trite. They had all read the script, so rather than telling the story, he should be bringing it to life, talking about the style, landscape, emotions and tensions. It all began to spin in his brain. He lay in the dark; still, sleep would not come. He tried to empty his mind, but anxious thoughts insisted on spiralling up from the depths and leaping into his consciousness like jumping fish. He knew he needed to be alert when he pitched his story, to display a youthful zest. If he gave the impression of aging and tiredness, he would be driven from the city of youth, his wings clipped, and his name would plummet from the 'A' list and tumble down into the 'B's and, once in freefall, why not into the 'C's and the dreaded 'D's, and perish there with all the other fallen angels, or worse, be obliged to make periodic television for eternity.

Fred had set up two meetings for him the next day, one in the morning and the other in the afternoon. Jack would only arrive in time for the four meetings on the following day. He drove his rented car into the studio of his first call, and was stopped by concrete blocks strategically placed to stop suicide bombers from crashing their way in. The studio's main-frame had been hacked, and they were paranoid. He was instructed to open his trunk and a guard looked under his car with a mirror on a stick. When they were satisfied that he was not prepared to give up his life for the pleasure of destroying the studio, he was allowed in.

Four very young 'creative' executives, three of them women, greeted him effusively, assuring him they were all avid fans. After a round of pleasantries – how great he looked, terrific jacket, was he jet-lagged, did it show – one of them assumed the role of spokeswoman.

'We have all read your wonderful script and it fell to me to correlate all the notes. We all agreed that we'd like to be involved, but the problem that we're all kind of stuck on is the sex. We feel she should be in love with the guy, plain and simple. Her sexual obsession with the sheriff makes her unsympathetic. I mean, we want the audience to root for her. We also felt that it would really help if instead of it being this upmarket eco-hotel, it should be a summer camp for deprived or, better, handicapped kids that she looks after. And we couldn't go along with her taking the boy to bed. We'd get an NC rating.'

She dropped her voice when she articulated 'NC', in case the obscenity escaped into the building and infected other scripts.

Daniel managed to keep a smile creased across his face throughout all of this, and held his anger in check. He addressed the spokeswoman.

'You must know women who are victims of sexual obsession.'

He looked from face to face, but none of the smiles flinched.

'My guess is that of the three of you in this room, one of you is with a bad guy that you want to leave, but can't.'

He flashed them a grin that said 'only kidding', then, seriously, 'Without it, the story collapses. The suspense is engineered around the concept of obsession.'

The male among them spoke up protectively.

'Well, we'd sure like to see the next draft, once you've cast it.'

They all stood up together, signalling the end of the meeting. Daniel remained seated just long enough to make them ill at ease, then got up and, with a display of humour and grace, shook each hand, and looked deeply into the eyes of the women, who fluttered. One said softly, 'We love how you direct women.'

Daniel drove to the museum downtown to lunch with his friend Bob Chartoff, the producer of the *Rocky* movies and *Raging Bull*, amongst others. There was an exhibition of David Hockney's watercolours of Los Angeles. They were so delicate and transparent that it seemed as though the city was fading back into the desert, its fictional nature finally found out, and it could no longer sustain the illusion of reality.

'It probably is disappearing for him,' said Bob, 'now he's gone back to live in England.'

'I went up to his house once,' said Daniel. 'His swimming pool was empty but on the bottom he had painted those little blue tics that looked like waves, just like the ones he has on his pool paintings. Hockney loved LA for all the reasons I can't stand it. Why would he leave?'

'He was hounded out, I believe,' said Bob. 'There was nowhere he could smoke any more.'

The afternoon meeting went much the same way, but for other, or additional, reasons. The executive there saw it as a take on Iraq. Lionel was Saddam Hussein. The sheriff was the American army getting rid of him. Heather was the feeble doubting European. He accused Daniel of attempting to infiltrate American society with subversive material. Daniel laughed. He thought the guy was being ironic. But he was quickly learning that many Americans who at one time saw a Red under every bed, now imagined a terrorist at every turn. Daniel had always loved the welcoming generosity of America after the negativity and mean-spiritedness of England, but now he felt himself under suspicion, an invader to be repelled.

He recounted his misadventures to Jack and Bella that evening over dinner. He was relieved that he would have moral support at tomorrow's meetings.

Daniel was comforted to have Jack with him. He knew how to appease these people; his manner was reassuring. But the sex issue frightened them all. It was the old story. Hollywood was self-censoring itself for fear of censorship being thrust upon it. All the gains that had been made since the demise of the Hays office, and the temporary setbacks of McCarthyism, were being eroded from within. Jack counselled him not to be too down-hearted.

'No one ever says yes right away, you know that. You have to keep going back, each time with an added ingredient: a rewrite, an actor, some of the money. It takes three "maybe"s to get to a "yes", and three "no"s to make a pass. When Harvey Weinstein dumped *Lord of the Rings*, he gave Peter Jackson and his agent, Ken Kamins, an impossible forty-eight hours to turn it around. If they failed in that time, they were dead in the water. Every studio, major and classic, turned it down, some of them twice. Kamins went back to New Line, a faltering subsidiary of Warners, with a passionate plea. In what the industry saw as a reckless decision, New Line not only took it on, but insisted that it be not one film, not two, but three. If the first one failed, the second and third would be unreleasable. It got made by the skin of its teeth. A salutary lesson.'

Bella had set up an appointment with Harold Witt, the head of marketing and distribution at Tannenbaum's studio. Witt was a stocky man with cropped grey hair, arms pushed wide by big biceps, and a shirt-stretching belly. He came into his outer office, where she sat waiting, and his strutting walk said, 'Don't fuck with me.' Harold waved her in.

'OK, shoot,' he said, signalling that his time was not to be wasted.

'Do you have any influence on what gets made, or do you make the best of what they send you?'

'Used to be like that; not any more. Nobody green-lights a movie in Hollywood any more without getting the nod from marketing and distribution. You know what they say about us? The marketing tail is wagging the creative dog. That was yesterday. Today that dog doesn't take a piss without our say-so.'

He was enjoying flexing his muscles and posturing in front of an attractive woman. He resented her coolness. If he couldn't fuck her, he wanted to hurt her, or better still, both. 'It's a jungle out there. Brutal. And you know who wins? The biggest, toughest honcho. Survival of the fittest, like this presidential election. You know who's gonna win? The bitch, or the son of a bitch, who spends most money on TV spots; the same with movies.'

She reflected that it was this species of man that kept America going and was finally responsible for its tragic flaw. He was a fighter. He was at war. It was all he knew.

'So tell me how it works; the economics. This picture, *Acid Murders*, you just released, for instance.'

'Yeah, *Acid Murders*: it's a serial killer. We got a major star to hunt him down. We got a sexy chick on his list of victims. You can get that over in a thirty-second spot.'

'Because they've seen it before?'

'Exactly. I keep telling them upstairs in Creative, when these guys come in pitching their stories, tell them to come up with the TV ad. If they can't put it across in thirty seconds, we shouldn't make it. Because that's how we sell movies.'

'It wasn't always so.'

'They used to open in the major cities and roll them out slow. That don't work today.'

She set her trap.

'*2001: A Space Odyssey* opened with two prints, one in New York and one in LA. It got poor reviews and the business was not good at first. It was so original that it took a while for word of mouth to get around. Eventually, it became a huge hit. If it had opened wide today, it would have had a bad opening weekend and disappeared.'

He glowered at her.

'In those days you were in a trench with a rifle; you could choose your targets and pick them off one by one. We don't have that kind of time no more. We have cruise missiles. They make big hits. Sometimes there's collateral damage. A few pictures die in the margins.'

'So you would say originality is the enemy?'

He gave her a hurt, suspicious look.

'Well, it don't help.'

'So tell me about *Acid Murders.*'

He brightened up.

'There're only four kinds of movie. You got to make 'em laugh, make 'em cry, scare 'em, or thrill 'em. And you've gotta make up your mind which one you're going for. So *Acid Murders* has got to scare 'em. So we make a scary TV spot. And when I see the picture, I realise it's weak: not bad, but it won't have legs. So I gotta get out there, grab my money fast before they catch on. I spend $30 million on advertising. I go out with three thousand prints. That's $5 million. I do $25 million on the first weekend. I have 90/10 deals with the theatres for the first week, so I get $22.5 million back. We know from the exit polls it ain't going nowhere, so it will only do another $30 million on the run, but now I'm only 50/50 with the theatres and I'm lucky if I get back another $15 million.'

Bella was jotting all this down and making some quick calculations.

'What did the picture cost to make?'

'$55 million.'

'So $55 plus $35 on prints and ads, that's $90, and you've only got $37.5 back. You're more than $50 million in the red.'

'Sure, but if I hit $40 million domestic, it triggers a higher rate for our cable and TV sales. I'll make another $15 right there, and DVD will match the theatrical take of $40 million and I take 80 percent of that, so $32 plus $37.5, a total of $69.5 million.'

'You've spent $90: you're still $20.5 short.'

'Then I've got the rest of the world. These kind of pictures play gangbusters in Japan. I'll pull in at the end of the day another $55 million foreign, gives us a profit of $34.5 million. Not bad for a dog.'

'You share that with the producers and star?'

'If the star has a gross deal, yes. In this case, 10 percent of the gross. We have already paid him a fee of $20 million, so he doesn't get any more until the picture grosses over $200 million, which it won't in our books.'

'But there's nothing in this for the net-profit participants?'

'$34.5 million is swallowed up by our own distribution fees, 25 percent in the States and 30 percent foreign. Then we charge interest on the money.'

'It's hard on the filmmakers.'

'Hey, they were paid their fees. They made a bad movie. They don't deserve shit.'

He gestured at the sound-stages and office blocks outside his window.

'Look at this place. They got two thousand people employed here; we spend half a billion every year on buying properties and developing scripts. We got offices all over the world. If it wasn't for German tax money and those crazy hedge funds, we'd be in the toilet.'

'As I understand it,' she said, 'it costs more to make and market mainstream movies than the audience is willing to pay. How long can this escalation of costs go on spiralling before the system collapses?'

No one in Hollywood wanted to face up to this, least of all Witt. He looked at his watch with a shifty eye.

'Nearly lunchtime. There's a gin mill across the street. I'll buy you a drink, and we can talk some more.'

They stepped out of the hot, bright sun into the cool, dark bar and sat on stools. As her eyes became accustomed to the lack of light, the shapes of still and silent men, intent on their drinks, emerged. He followed her eyes and looked at them contemptuously.

'Drunks. Those guys are in here drinking every lunchtime.'

'Now how would you know that?' she said.

He threw up his hands in mock surrender.

'Guess you got me there, lady.'

He'd sunk his martini and the barman slid him another, unasked. He leaned towards her. 'I've gotta have some way to relieve the stress of this job. There's no let-up. All week I'm running flat out to stand still, then at the weekend I'm so twitchy I call every hour to check the grosses. Only booze does it – well, booze and sex.'

He watched her reaction to the word 'sex'.

'I could see all those big numbers were turning you on in there. Movies and money, the best aphrodisiac known to man,' he said.

He put his hand on her knee.

'Wrong,' she said, 'it made me nauseous. And if you don't remove your hand, I'm going to throw up.'

She was angry, not only because he had hit on her, but also because he and men like him were raping the movies. And if Fred took over the studio, this is the person he would have to filter his films through.

She got up and left, trying to recall where she had parked her car. How do you remember what a hire car looks like? She walked through the five-acre studio car park zapping all the cars until one flashed a response. She dialled New York on her mobile. Only by talking to Orson, making sure he was OK, could she recover herself and return to who she was. When she got off the phone, she noticed that her hand was shaking. The car had burned up from the sun. She was drenched, her dress stuck to her skin.

Daniel woke up at 3 AM, the sheets twisted around him, pinning his arms like a straitjacket. Put on the TV. Turned it off. Picked up Joan Didion's *Memoir of a California Childhood*. Realised he had read two pages while turning over in his mind the meetings of the day before and had not taken in a word of a book that had completely absorbed him on the plane coming over. At 5 AM he called Hope: 1 PM London time. He told her about his jet lag, but not about the disappointing meetings. He had always feared that if he failed, she would cease to love him – if she loved him at all. He got her assurance that the kids were OK, safely at school.

'What are you doing?'

'I'm making lunch for Brad. He's here; speak to him.'

She handed Brad the phone.

'I was passing by, it was close to lunchtime, I had a nostalgia for Hope's lunches when we worked upstairs.'

Daniel told him about the sex issue. Brad made a characteristic suggestion.

'Take out the sex in the next draft, and put it back in the shooting script.'

Daniel hung up feeling a little put out by the thought of Brad having penetrated his citadel and, at this moment, having lunch with his wife.

'So what was it you were writing in the Brompton Oratory?' Hope asked.

'I'll tell you, if you'll tell me what sins you were confessing,' Brad said, making her laugh.

'I never confess my real ones.'

'OK, then I can lie about what I was writing.'

'I can guess. You are writing an original screenplay, but it would ruin your cynical reputation if anyone found out.'

They were eating pasta she had made with fresh basil and fresh tomatoes grown in the little fecund walled garden at the back of the house.

'No, I was working on my VAT returns,' he said, through a mouthful of pasta. 'You see, Daniel and I are total opposites. I write so I can eat well and drink good wine, and get up late, and live easy and make love. Daniel makes movies *instead* of doing all those things.'

'That's not fair. Daniel appreciates the good life.'

'But it's secondary. If he was here now, he would say, let's get back to work, while I would much rather make love after a good plate of pasta and a glass of red wine.'

'You get an espresso,' she said, 'then I'm going to kick you out.'

He sighed and shrugged in his good-natured manner, which disarmed offence.

'Well, let me ask you this, if it can't be you, do you think I have a chance with Bella? She's driving me crazy.'

'Not a hope in hell.'

TEN

Mark Tannenbaum had laid on his helicopter to take Daniel, Jack and Bella up to Santa Barbara. He had a landing pad in his garden, concealed by topiary in the shapes of mythological creatures. To get to the house, they passed the nine-hole golf course, tennis courts (one clay, one grass, one hard), and glanced at the colonnaded Roman swimming pool. None of these facilities were in use. The house was neo-Palladian.

They were shown to their suites in the guest wing. There was no sign of their host. They wandered through the house, identifying the paintings: a Picasso, of course, and one of each of the big five Impressionists, an overblown, muscle-bound Rodin in the garden, and the obligatory Robert Graham nude girl in bronze. They looked in on the library and pool-room, and then took a walk and inspected the stables, the falconry and the organic vegetable garden. They encountered no one, except for a distant glimpse of a gardener, and a butler slipping through a door. When Bella made a disparaging remark that they were being offered facilities instead of hospitality, Fred put his finger to his lips. He was convinced they were undergoing some kind of test and that their behaviour was being monitored. As if on cue, a CCTV camera came swivelling towards them.

Daniel realised that Fred wanted this job badly, and that perhaps he was on some kind of probation. They all began to feel ill at ease, and Jack got behind some bushes to have a surreptitious pull on his pipe.

When they got back to their rooms, they found that their luggage had been unpacked, clothes pressed, shoes shined. A gong-like sound came softly from the telephone. When Bella picked it up, a recorded voice advised that dinner would be served at 7.30.

Drinks were set out in an anteroom, and suddenly, and silently, Tannenbaum appeared from a hidden door. At fifty, he was still slim, with a thick head of black hair showing no hint of grey; he wore a carefully sculpted Clark Gable moustache. His face bore the mask-like aspect that several 'lifts' imparts. He had started out as an actor and still gave the impression that he was playing the role of a master of industry, rather than being it. His ego was so inflated, so all-consuming, that it seemed to create a magnetic field around him, an aura that vibrated with narcissistic self-absorption. He needed no one. And there was no one. No woman. No friend. No child.

He greeted each of them solemnly, looking into their eyes. The experience was papal in its intensity. Tannenbaum had a large diamond on his finger, and Daniel said afterwards that he felt a powerful impulse to kiss it. They were each presented with a menu with the date and their names in gold embossing on it. There was caviar, foie gras, chateaubriand and duck with truffles. Fred dumped his diet and ordered everything with high cholesterol. It was Tannenbaum who ate only dry lettuce.

Tannenbaum's soft, deep voice drew their attention. It felt so pre-scripted that at one point Daniel turned, looking for the autocue.

'I ran the studio myself some years ago, as I am sure you are aware, and with considerable success. You hear people saying it's all down to gut instinct or hunches as to which picture you make, that success is a matter of luck. We see people who should know better, nodding sagely in agreement when William Goldman says 'Nobody knows anything'. Not true. I ran the studio on rational grounds. Each year you need a tent-pole, an event picture, action-orientated, that will drag your lesser pictures along in its wake, so that the Harold Witts can say to theatre chains, 'If you want the big one, you gotta take the little ones. And Daniel, I want to speak to you about an event picture, a little later. Then we need a franchise, a Bond or a *Batman* or a *Men in Black*, that can come out of the traps every couple of years.'

He surveyed the table to make sure they had all absorbed his wisdom.

'You make one, and one only, serious drama for Oscar consideration; one thriller; one horror; two teen comedies; two action adventures; and a love story. Ten pictures. That is all we are going to make.'

He sent a questioning look across the table to Fred, who, after a pause to suggest that he was weighing all sides of the argument, nodded his considered agreement.

'Can I ask a question?' said Bella. 'I'm doing a book on how a film gets made. I understand how you define your categories, but surely what is important is not the genre but just how funny or thrilling or scary they are?'

Tannenbaum looked at her as though she had just shit on his Chinese silk carpet.

'I find that question somewhat patronising. There is no secret to it. You get the best writers, the best directors, and when the movies are made, you audience-test them. And if they don't work, you re-cut them, re-write them, re-shoot them, and you keep doing it until your scores are in the nineties, and then you release them.'

'What about the classics division?' Fred ventured.

'I shall close it down,' said Tannenbaum.

'What's your policy on budgets?' Fred asked.

'Whoever runs the studio has got to find the money to do it. I want it to be self-financing. He will have to get out there in the marketplace and find investors.'

Which meant he was strapped for cash, thought Fred. More poison in the chalice.

After dinner, Tannenbaum took Daniel to one side.

'You'll find a script by your bedside called *Other Lives*. It is big in every sense, an event. Yet I'm prepared to make it without a major star.'

Ah, thought Daniel. That means all the major stars have turned him down.

'I'm pretty far advanced with a picture of my own,' said Daniel.

'It can wait, can't it?'

'I guess so.'

'I want *Other Lives* to go into production this year.'

'I'll be happy to read it.'

Daniel finished it at 2 AM. The hero was a Tannenbaum figure, running a multinational empire. A terrorist is undermining the business, attacking it in various ways: a fire here, an explosion there, manipulating the stock, spreading rumours. His intention is to destroy the company and cause a Wall Street crash. So far, not too bad, but the Tannenbaum character goes to a guru who tells him that his is a great soul that previously inhabited other great men, including Alexander the Great, Julius Caesar and Napoleon. He is able to time-travel and get their help in solving his problems. It was clunky and turgid beyond belief.

Daniel had a powerful urge to flee. But how? They had seen the electrified perimeter fence; besides, he had no idea where they were.

Somewhere outside of Santa Barbara. Could he call a cab? Find the helicopter pilot?

At breakfast, Tannenbaum was absent but they confined their conversation to harmless topics, for fear of bugs. Only when they took a walk in the garden did Daniel let rip. 'There is nothing I can say to him. If this is an indication of his judgement, his state of mind, then he won't need a terrorist to destroy his company. Think hard, Fred, before you get involved.'

But Fred was in permanent pause mode.

'Let's get out of here,' said Daniel, 'I'm having a panic attack. I mean, what is this? I expected a house party, glamorous people, drugs, music, Gatsby. What we've got is this narcissistic paranoid.'

'He's in a lot of trouble,' Fred said in a low voice. 'If he wants me to find money, I want an option to buy the studio if I turn it around.'

Daniel was appalled.

'You're not going to take the job? You'll have to make *Other Lives*. And then you'll be laughed out of town. Let's go, for Christ's sake.'

Fred grabbed him by the arm.

'Tell him you'll think about it, stall him. I gotta get this job sewn up before I get dumped from the agency. I'm in trouble, Dan: give me a break.'

Daniel submitted, saddened to see Fred's power and presence so diminished.

Jack and Bella caught up with them. Jack suggested to Fred that they hit a few golf balls. Neither were impassioned golfers, but so many deals were made on the golf course that they were obliged to be players. They shuffled off, leaving Bella with Daniel.

'I dreaded coming here,' she said, 'but I never believed it could be this awful.'

She turned to a nearby bush. 'And I don't care if you're listening.'

They came upon a Japanese garden with patterned sand, a waterfall and a teahouse. They went inside. All the ingredients were at hand for tea: an electric kettle, tiny tea cups, Japanese green tea and an instruction manual on the subtleties of the tea ceremony. Daniel set about putting it all together. They touched cups and drank.

'A few Zen moments is what we need,' he said, 'to restore our karma.'

They savoured the tea in silence. Daniel reviewed in his mind the studio reactions to his script, picked away at their remarks and comments. Finally he allowed his thoughts to meander into spoken words.

'It's not just the sex scenes: something else bothers them. We've designed this as a commercial genre piece and yet there is all this resistance.'

She offered no response, mindful of her role as observer, but again she felt the spirit rising, welling up. Soon she was quaking, and out it came.

'I know what it is. It doesn't feel American. It's not the dialogue or even the sense of place. The sensibility feels alien to them, and so it threatens them in some way. You're threatening people who already feel threatened.'

Daniel was jolted by her intensity. He poured them more tea. He tested her thesis against scenes in the script and found virtue in it, but its implications were disastrous.

Bella watched him, wondering if she dared to go further. But there was no stopping. The spirit moved her, and moved her on.

'Daniel,' she said softly. Hope called him 'Dan' and Jack favoured 'Danny', but as far as he recalled, Bella had never used his name.

'Why don't you set the film in England? Use that hotel where we stayed at the solstice. You are so connected to that landscape, the cathedral, Avebury, and there's a dangerous kind of magic there that you understand, that would give your story something authentic and wonderful. Why don't you?'

His heart jumped at the prospect. He could see it instantly, the movie ready formed, shot, cut and scored. She saw the light in his eyes and it emboldened her to go even further.

'While I'm at it, one more thing. Why do you call it *Beyond Good and Evil*?'

'It's Nietzsche: "Whatever is done in the name of love is beyond good and evil."'

'Do you believe that?' she said.

'Lovers do when they are betraying their wives and husbands. Our characters do.'

'But it means something else to Americans right now. They see themselves involved in a war between good and evil, and beyond that lies uncertainty and confusion, the unknown. They don't want to go there. They fear "beyond". So there you are, I've said it.'

Daniel was amused to see that her hands were trembling and her face was flushed. She had truly lost her famous cool.

'You're supposed to be the neutral observer,' he said. 'Now I feel like those subatomic particles that change when they're observed. Come to think of it, I have been changing every since you started observing this process.'

'You said in an interview once that everything gets into the movie.'

'Yes, it picks up the zeitgeist. The movie *Cleopatra* tells you more about Hollywood in the sixties than it does about ancient Egypt. So be careful what you think and do. It will work its way into the picture.'

He got up.

'Let's try it out on Jack.'

'Don't tell him I suggested it.'

Daniel told Jack as they went in for lunch. He groaned. No English thriller was ever going to do $100 million at the American box office. They could wave that goodbye. Yet the script as it stood was not ringing bells either.

'How did this idea jump up on you?'

'Where's Fred?' Bella asked, to cause a diversion.

'At the third hole he was sent for, and never returned.'

'This weekend is getting more Agatha Christie by the hour,' said Bella.

There was a buffet and, in the absence of Tannenbaum and Fred, they helped themselves. Daniel noticed that there was no alcohol on offer. He needed a drink if, for Fred's sake, he was to find something positive to say about *Other Lives* yet not commit himself to having to make it, or even develop it. On second thoughts, if he was going to walk a verbal tightrope, perhaps alcohol was not such a good idea.

Tannenbaum entered through his hidden door, with Fred in tow. He raised a hand for silence, even though all three were fixed in frozen poses, and without a word passing between them.

'Fred and I have reached agreement. We've been talking to the lawyers. Fred will head up the studio and report directly to me. A press release will be in tomorrow's trades.' Jack got up and shook their hands, and Daniel gave Fred a hug.

'Can I come and pitch you a sexy thriller?'

Suddenly everyone was talking at once, tensions were eased and appetites expanded. When it had all settled down, Tannenbaum said, 'Well, Daniel, what did you make of my script?'

Daniel was relieved that now Fred had the job, there was no need for him to deceive or prevaricate.

'Well, I have to say the script has some problems. You have a great premise – a terrorist setting out to destroy a multinational and cause a Wall Street crash – but your character, the Boss, is so brilliant, so clever, so attractive, so rich, does he really need help from Julius Caesar and the others? Frankly, I found it preposterous.'

Tannenbaum stiffened, his magnetic field fractured.

'You found it what?'

'Just not credible. But, look, I don't want to be negative. Let me give you a take on it that would work,' Daniel continued. 'Let's revise this character. Supposing he is a guy who has sacrificed everything in his drive to get to the top. He has betrayed his fellow executives. His wife has divorced him because of his neglect; cocaine has made him paranoid; he trusts no one; he lives in a huge house with every toy imaginable, but he is alone. His grip is slipping; he is losing his hold on reality, and his fellow directors and shareholders, maybe even the big investment institutions, are after his blood because his business is floundering. His enormous ego will not allow him to admit to failure, so to distract from his real problems, he hires criminals to attack the company and he blames it on terrorists. If he is going down, he is going to drag the company down with him.'

Daniel regarded the faces at the table. Tannenbaum was ashen. Fred was looking daggers at him. Bella was trying not to laugh. Jack was alarmed.

'If we can get a rewrite along these lines, I'd love to make it. Can I get a drink? Malt whiskey?'

Tannenbaum was trying to govern his anger. He spoke very quietly. He was a snake about to strike.

'You are like every other two-bit director I've ever met. You all want to make your *Citizen Kane*. Well, let me remind you, *Citizen Kane* was a dud. It lost money, and I'm not going to subsidise your ego-trip. It's Caesar and Alexander and Napoleon that make this picture unique, that make it an event.'

'Fine, go ahead,' said Daniel. 'I'm just giving you my take on it. What do you think, Fred, you're the one who has to make it?'

Fred fell back on one of his famous pauses. He seemed to be contemplating and considering and, as the pause stretched out, possibly meditating.

'This is a movie. Unique. With its own voice. Maybe it needs a polish; a Goldman or a Stoppard. I've suggested that Mark plays the part himself, and he has graciously agreed. He was a very fine actor in his young days. You don't lose those skills.'

Fred managed to say this with a straight face. In fact, he gave the appearance of wisdom and confidence and sincerity. Years of agenting had stood him in good stead.

On his final day in Los Angeles, Daniel went to the agency on his way to the airport. Fred was packing his files into boxes and preparing to move over to the studio.

'You understand I can't take on *Beyond Good and Evil*, not after you pissed all over Tannenbaum.'

'I don't think you would have done it even if I hadn't. You don't like it any more than the rest of them.'

Daniel waited for the pause to play itself out. Was Fred going to abandon his principle of neither lying nor telling the truth, now that he was a studio head?

'It is what it is,' he said, staring at the wall over Daniel's shoulder, where the unmade film was being projected in Fred's head, 'and I'm sure it's evolving into what it will become.'

It was classic Fred. Daniel chortled with delight.

'Fred, I love you. Never change. And I expect an invitation to the premiere of *Other Lives*.'

'It ain't gonna happen,' whispered Fred, looking under his phone for a bug.

'Come on, Fred, you might as well tell me: it will be in the trades tomorrow.'

'I'll walk you out,' he said, sealing his lips with a finger. 'By the way, here is the report you wanted on that script.'

Daniel glanced at it in the elevator. Tag-line: 'Creepy English lab assistant murders wife and her lover, then kills his bullying boss, incinerates himself, and burns down the lab, destroying valuable negatives. Not recommended.'

They walked to Daniel's car in the underground car park. They were in a scene from *All the President's Men*. Fred's face was in shadow, his voice was Deep Throat.

'One of the big shareholders has been trying to oust Tannenbaum for a while now. I told him Tannenbaum wants to play the lead himself in *Other Lives*.'

'Did you tell him it was your idea?'

'I didn't tell him it wasn't.'

'He's going to use that to topple him?'

Fred gave something between a shrug and a nod – a carefully cultivated gesture that did not commit him. It had served him well in the past and would be useful in his second coming.

'Tannenbaum is on the slide. I didn't want to be seen as his boy, and I had to find a way not to make that turkey.'

They embraced. Fred was a creature of his times, perfectly adapted to the Los Angeles environment, a realist who knew how to survive in a fantasist society.

Daniel drove to Santa Monica, to Fred Segal's, and bought a dress for Hope. He knew exactly what suited her and what fitted her, and quickly found it. He was shocked by the price tag but bought it anyway. He had told Fred where he was heading and Fred said, 'Nobody shops at Fred Segal's except at the sales.'

'Yes, but I won't be here during the sales.'

Early in their relationship Hope had been entranced by Daniel dressing her. He made daring choices, things she would never buy for herself. It was as though he was discovering aspects of her she wasn't aware of. But more recently she found it oppressive. She felt now that he was imposing his view of her upon her, defining her in ways that she resisted.

As he was paying, a pale blue dress caught his eye. It was simple, waisted and with an elegant skirt cut on the bias. Boldly, he bought it for Bella. He had wanted to find a gift for her to express his appreciation for her idea. He was so relieved and happy to be adapting the script to England that it seemed appropriate. He made a quick dash to Toys 'R' Us to pick up gifts for the kids, then headed down Ocean Boulevard for the airport. It was a night flight, but he stayed awake and worked on the script, anglicising it, enriching it. The only sticky problem was that the CID seemed more accessible than the FBI, somehow closer to hand, so her decision not to report the murder had to be because of her loyalty to her lover; but later, when she felt trapped and threatened by him, it had to be clear that evidence was pointing to her as the murderer.

ELEVEN

The doctor had told Bella to take her temperature during ovulation and to be sure to have intercourse at the key moment. When she informed Jack that the moment had arrived, he failed to get an erection. It was just too clinical for him, especially since his libido had become so conditioned to the delicate and complex process of stalking her through her psychological maze. Did he really, in his heart, not want another child, she wondered – but said nothing, and nor did he. They made love successfully the following night, much to Jack's relief – though not at precisely the right temperature. The old joke had been nagging away in his mind: what's the difference between disappointment and despair? Disappointment is the first time you can't do it twice. Despair is the second time you can't do it once.

'You just sliced $5.25 million out of the budget. No more expensive fucking American actors, no first-class fucking fares from LA, no Spanish fucking locations,' said Kevan Barker, spouting smoke.

'But unfortunately,' said Jack, gloomily, 'Phyllis has lowered her sales estimates, it no longer being an American movie.' Jack noticed with disapproval that Kevan chewed his pipe.

Kieran Corrigan was there, juggling.

'We can go back to the BFI for Lottery money,' he said. 'They turned us down before because it was a non-UK subject.'

'If you can get $3 million from the Lottery, we're home free,' chortled Kevan between his teeth clenched around his pipe.

Jack left Kevan and Kieran grinning at the computer screen.

Hope dutifully tried on the dress and presented herself for Daniel's approval, while the kids ripped the wrappings from their gifts.

'Beautiful,' he said.

'It's the old me rather than the new me,' she said.

He was hurt, but made light of it.

'Well, wear it when you feel like the old you.'

There was a heap of mail next to the pile of scripts, including a letter from Nigel apologising for his rudeness, begging for another meeting and pledging to behave. Daniel pulled out the script report and put it in an envelope, together with a note: 'Dear Nigel, the Agency did this coverage of your script, which I enclose. Sorry.' Daniel read the report through for the first time and was satisfied that it was sufficiently dismissive: 'Too remote to have any interest for American audiences. The protagonist is dull and unsympathetic.' The only positive comment was 'fascinating glimpse into the arcane workings of a film lab'. Daniel filled in the address, which he now knew by heart, and sent it off. He climbed to the top of the house and went back to his script.

Hope invited Bella and Jack for supper and put a casserole to simmer in the Aga. Daniel tore himself away from the script to greet them. Jack passed on the news about the budget savings and enquired tentatively about the progress of the story.

'Do you want to get Brad back to help you?' Jack asked.

'I'll do this draft myself and then we can assess it. I'm getting a lot of resonance from the new settings. I've got Lionel involved in a secret satanic sect based around Stonehenge. It's a way of externalising his sadistic impulses. Now that the New Mexico sun has gone, it's getting darker, more mysterious.'

Jack feared the film was slipping inexorably from mainstream to arthouse.

They all sat at the big solid-elm kitchen table. Daniel poured wine and they waited for the Aga to complete its unhurried business. Daniel gave Bella her gift.

'For liberating me from America,' he said.

'You promised not to tell Jack it was my idea.'

But of course he had. She opened the package and the silk dress unfolded itself and flowed out as though it had a will of its own. She held it up, confused and embarrassed.

'It just caught my eye. It seemed perfect for you.'

Hope stood askance in front of her Aga, her backside warming on the rail.

'How do you know what's perfect for Bella? It's one thing to do it to your actresses: you're defining a character.' She put a sisterly arm around Bella. 'But we want to decide who we are and what we wear for ourselves.'

Jack was amused to see that Bella was so flustered.

'At least you should try it on, Bella,' he said.

She refused, and Hope defended her. They ate supper in good spirits and afterwards Hope left the dishes to the men and took Bella upstairs.

'Try it on. I'm curious to find out how he sees you.'

It was plain, with a high neck and long sleeves, and slim-waisted, but the skirt flared out at one side. The colour was so pale that it could scarcely lay claim to blue. In artificial light, it looked grey. They stood side by side in front of the wardrobe mirror.

'Plain, colourless and simple is how he sees me, apparently.'

'But the skirt's a bit hectic,' said Hope, 'and I have to admit you look stunning in it.'

Daniel woke early, his head full of the script. His unconscious had been labouring all night, and he dashed up to his workroom to put it all on paper before it faded.

He looked up with dazed eyes as Hope burst through the door.

'Snap out of it. Your mother walked in front of a car. She's in hospital.'

Shaken, he squinted at his watch. Three o'clock. He had been working since seven. No breakfast or lunch. On the table was a mug of coffee, untouched, that Hope must have brought in.

He jumped up and grabbed a jacket.

'Where?'

'Chelsea and Westminster.'

They sped through the bright murals and amusing mobiles. The hospital put Daniel in mind of an overblown kindergarten. His mother was propped up in bed, consoling the driver of the car that had knocked her down, who was weeping unashamedly.

Jenny greeted them with a fluttering wave.

'Danny, Hope, my fault entirely. This poor man is so upset.'

The driver looked up at them imploringly. His glasses were misted up, his bald head reflecting the harsh overhead lights.

'So very sorry,' he said, 'She stepped off the curb. I braked, but ...'

Daniel made a mental note of the scene. He loved the inversion of victim and perpetrator. Hope jabbed Daniel with her elbow. 'You're not shooting this. It's your mother.'

'Now off you go, Henry,' Daniel's mother warbled, her voice weak and tremulous. 'And stand up to that wife. Don't be – what's the expression – pussy-whipped.'

Daniel was shocked. She seemed to have shrunk. There were lacerations on her arms and head.

'Oh, Jenny. Poor you.' Hope kissed her, and she winced from that lightest of touches. Everything hurt.

'I want you home with us,' said Hope firmly.

'Very kind, Hope, but I will not give up my independence. I will just give up crossing busy roads.'

Every evening after his work on the script, Daniel walked round to Jenny's flat in Old Church Street and took her a light supper from Hope. There were no bones broken but she was covered in bruises. While the bath was running, he carefully peeled off her clothes, carried her naked, lowered her into the tub and gently washed her black and blue body.

'How often I bathed you as a babe. Now it's all turned on its head.'

Even as a boy he had felt fiercely protective of her, but seeing her so vulnerable made him weak with compassion and brought him to tears. Jenny captured a tear on her finger and put it to her tongue, something she had often done when he was a child.

For years they had kept each other at bay with banalities, but this enforced intimacy made confession natural and easy. He told her of his problems with Hope, and her affair.

'You hang on to Hope for dear life. She grounds you. You need her. So what, she had a fling. I had a lover once.'

The shock turned Daniel's knees to jelly.

'Who was it?

'No one you knew. A stranger. He turned up one day. It seemed ordained. It was very orgasmic. Then he was gone. It was nothing, just a physical thing, but it gave your poor father pain.'

Daniel tried to digest the implications.

'Why did Dad resent me?'

'He was jealous of my love for you. You were mixed up with that other man in his mind. A rival.'

'I tried so hard to make him proud of me.'

'Are you sure of that?'

'What do you mean?'

'He saw your often frantic efforts to succeed as an attempt to usurp his position.'

Daniel passed the sponge over that bruised and once-desired flesh, his mind reeling. He thought he would pass out. Had she died under that car, he would never have known all this.

He lifted her out and folded her into a sheet, less abrasive than a towel.

He had always thought of her as fragile, but he realised now, beneath the delicate surface, how tough and raunchy she was, and how like Hope.

Ten days later, Daniel had finished the new draft, now called *Crime of Passion*. Jack took it by hand to Ben Roberts at the BFI and pitched it with conviction, because he knew it had gained reality and originality. He suppressed his niggling doubts about its commercial potential. Ben was encouraging, and promised that he and his colleagues would read it immediately. Jack then hurried over to Phyllis's office in D'Arblay Street, Soho, for a meeting with a prominent French distributor who had done well with Daniel's films in the past. Jack loved Soho. It was the most New York part of London; in fact, it was several Manhattan districts jumbled together, jostled and confused, yet sure of itself. It was Little Italy and Chinatown, the garment district, the porn of old Times Square, and, of course, the home of the movies. A pole-dancer hurried past him, carrying her music from one strip joint to another. Resting her professional painted smile, she wore the frown of a businessman late for an appointment. Soho was changing, of course, he noted sadly; getting more respectable. Expensive apartments were towering over high-tech special-effects offices, commercials companies were blanding it out.

Jean Paul was already with Phyllis when he arrived. This was the sharp end of the business, Jack knew, where there was no sentiment and finer aspirations were irrelevant. If Phyllis could get a good advance from France, it would improve their chances of pulling in other territories at a similar level, and in convincing the bank to lend that crucial last 20 percent. Jean Paul had been given the script the night before.

'I'm disappointed,' he said. 'I thought it was an American movie. English films are . . . .' His hand spiralled downwards, indicating decline, insignificance.

'But now it is no longer American,' said Phyllis, 'it allows it to be made more erotic.'

Jean Paul looked up sharply and caught the fleeting but unmistakably needy expression on the faces of Jack and Phyllis. He knew in that moment that he could bid them down.

'How erotic?'

'Tastefully explicit,' said Jack.

'You mean, acceptable to the Americans,' he sneered.

Phyllis glanced nervously at Jack.

'If necessary, we will do a softer version for America, like Bertolucci did with *The Dreamers*.'

Jean Paul made his fingers into scissors and cut the air.

'*Coupe* the penis. A circumcision for America.'

He laughed heartily at his own joke.

'We want a million two for France,' said Phyllis. 'None of the other French distributors have seen the script. They will kill me, but Daniel only wants you.'

Jean Paul enjoyed the flattery without believing it, and jotted down some notes.

'I have to dub into French. With that, plus prints and ads, it will cost me two million. Too much.'

'It qualifies as a European film,' said Phyllis, 'so you'll get more for your TV sale. I know what your DVD deal is; you're covered, Jean Paul. You have no downside.'

His face hardened; he resented this intrusion into his domestic deals.

'Eight hundred thousand.'

'Oh, Jean Paul, be sensible.'

'*Non.*'

'All right, because Daniel wants you, one million one.'

'*Non.*'

Phyllis glanced at Jack but could not read him.

'I give you nine, and finish.'

He cut his throat with his hand. Jack's adrenalin came in a sudden gambler's rush. He got to his feet.

'It just went up. It's now a million two-fifty. You've got till the end of business today to make up your mind. Tomorrow, it will be a million three.'

He left the room. Phyllis smiled reassuringly at Jean Paul, who was a cipher of Gallic indignation.

'Impossible. I don't do business like that.'

He had intended to enjoy himself for an hour or so, bullying Phyllis and making her squirm.

'Is this the way you want to work?'

'It's his film,' she said sweetly.

He called his office in Paris, screamed at someone or other, then hung up.

'OK, I give you what you ask, million two, and fuck Jack Diamond and his million three. Because of Daniel. Tell him what sacrifice I make. Tell Daniel because of him, not Jack. And subject to casting. Must be a star.'

Jack called Phyllis on his mobile from a café in Greek Street. She told him the news. He invited her for lunch and she suggested Soho House, a club favoured by disaffected members of the Groucho Club.

'Why not Groucho's? I'm a member,' he said.

'No one goes there any more.'

'But it's always jammed,' said Jack.

'Nobody who is anybody.'

Daniel drove Bella down to Twickenham Film Studios, where the casting agent, May Tredegar, had her offices. May was famously fierce and earthy, and wore her heart precariously on her sleeve. She mothered her actors, loved them, but slapped them when they were naughty.

'Well,' she said firmly, 'you don't want a girl you have to plead with to get her knickers off, and if her agent wants her to have approval of the lover, he can fuck off' – thus identifying the problems they would face. They ran through the names, the Kates – Winslet and Blanchett – Rachel Weisz, and so on. And scored them: not athletic enough, too tough, too fragile. May would check out availabilities with the agents. They worked their way through the other characters, May closely interrogating Daniel about their characteristics.

'The policeman, is he tall?'

'No, I see him square.'

'Dark?'

'Yes.'

'How old?'

'Forty.'

'Really, he reads early thirties. Is he the kind of womaniser who loves women or hates them?'

'A bit of both.'

'What's his essence?'

'Control, which is why he does that job and why he never gives himself to a woman.' 'So he uses his dick as a weapon; I hate him.'

'No, he has a kindness which he is only able to show when he is not threatened. It makes him sympathetic.'

'Not in my book.'

May was working herself up.

'Arsehole, worshipped by his mother, like my mum with my brother. He turned out like that, always looking for a woman to be his slave.'

'No, I based him on a key grip I knew who was an orphan.'

'Looking for a mother, and when he finds her he is going to punish her for leaving him, by leaving her.'

On the drive back, Bella switched on the tape recorder and did her first interview with Daniel.

'You seemed on the back foot with May, defensive?'

'Yes, well, I feel I should know everything about the characters I've invented, I'm kind of responsible for them, but the truth is I know very little about them. I mean, how much do I know about you or any of my friends, but May wants to know everything about them, because the actors will.'

'Should the actor know everything about the person she plays?'

'I resist it, as you saw.'

'Because you don't know yourself?'

'No, because the actor should act out of imagination, not simply knowledge.'

'Do you think of a particular actor when you're writing?'

'No, and I never find an actor who is absolutely right.'

'So casting is disappointing?'

'Every time you cast an actor, you give away a piece of the movie.'

'Do they always fall short?'

'At first, but then you have to change the part to fit the actor. It never works the other way round. If you're lucky, the actor makes the role better than you imagined: different, but better.'

'I suspect you hate actors, deep down.'

'Wrong, I love them; I'm so grateful that people are prepared to expose themselves in front of a camera.'

'So why do they do it?'

'I don't know. I asked Lindsay Anderson once. He said, "They can't help themselves." With many actresses who are not quite beautiful, it's to attain beauty with the help of light and cosmetics and the right lens – which is why they spend so much effort in makeup. Truly beautiful actresses are usually careless of their looks.'

'People say you're a good director of women. Why?'

'I prepare them, help them build the role, try to provide them with a safe environment, and most importantly, love them.'

'Isn't that dangerous?'

'I love them as a father loves his daughters.'

'Oh come on, directors have affairs with their leading actresses, we all know that.'

'Well, I don't.'

'Never?'

'I did once.'

'And?'

'It was a disaster, I lost judgement.'

'So actresses only give of their best when they are loved?'

'There are two kinds of acting: defensive acting and daring acting. If an actor doesn't trust the situation, he or she will fall back on what they know they can get by on, but great acting is always about giving, exposing emotions, being vulnerable, daring to fail. It can only happen in a safe and trusting environment – and a loving one.'

'Do you find it easier to love actors than people?'

He laughed ruefully.

'Ouch. It is easier, but not the way I love Jack, you.'

'Ah, but we are part of the movie.'

'Jack is; are you?'

'I try not to get sucked in.'

'Turn off the recorder.'

'I already did.'

He stared fixedly at the road ahead.

'Is this going to work?' he said, meaning *The Making Of*, the relationship.

Make it glib, she thought.

'We have a postmodern relationship. Intimacy through a tape recorder, everything on the record.'

The big-name female stars dropped out for one reason or another: one was pregnant, another booked solid, a third had decided to go back to the theatre and had signed up for a season at the RSC, a fourth would not do the nude scenes.

'They're always bitching that there are no leading roles for women,' Daniel complained to Jack, 'and when one comes along, where are they?'

They were deeply disheartened.

'If we postponed it till next year, we might get Kiera or Cate or Gwyneth,' said Jack.

'I thought the idea was to get this on before *Shadow* comes out and bombs,' said Daniel bitterly.

They fell silent. The phone intruded on their grief. It was May, the casting agent.

'What about Amanda Compton?'

'The model?'

'Daniel, she's done three films.'

'None of them rang bells.'

'Wait, I've just seen a rough cut of her new film. She plays a homeless woman. She's done a Charlize Theron, made herself look like shit. I've got a tape. I'm biking it over to you. She could be the one. And guess what? She's run a marathon.'

Daniel watched her performance; it was a little ragged, but emotionally raw and daring. She was unafraid, reckless, but brittle enough to snap in two at any moment. He showed it to Jack the next day.

'She's untutored, but there is a raw energy,' said Daniel, as the end credits crawled.

'Do you think you could get a subtle performance out of her,' said Jack sceptically.

'I don't know, I need to meet her.'

Jack scratched his head, lit his pipe, sucked and puffed, and finally spoke.

'Seems we've gone from a Hollywood male star to an unknown English girl. As you said yourself, the object of this exercise is to do a mainstream thriller and get it financed before *Shadow* is released, because you and I share the same fear as all filmmakers, the fear that if we make another turkey, they will never let us make a movie again.'

'She's going to be a sensation when this picture opens. It's Charlize all over again,' said Daniel.

'Good as she is, the picture is crap, it won't get seen, it won't have legs. And it throws our financing plans for a loop. With an unknown, the estimates will drop through the floor. I made a killer deal with Jean Paul. If we go with this kid, he's either going to drop his bid or bail out. I can hear the dominos falling. We're hitting bottom here,' Jack said, mixing metaphors.

'We can cut the budget back. She won't cost us. We'll go 16-mm. We can make it for a price. Let me meet her, at least. We've been through all the big names, and we've nowhere else to go.'

Daniel spoke with her agent and suggested dinner at the Ivy. This was rejected. She wanted to meet at a restaurant in the East End, somewhere off the Commercial Road. He had difficulty finding it, and drove past it twice. To his consternation, it turned out to be a workman's café. The menu was scrawled on the window: egg and chips £1.50, portion of chips 50p, bacon sandwich 95p, and so on. The door was locked. He tapped tentatively. A man in jeans, wearing an apron, let him in and locked the door behind him. All six tables were occupied. Amanda sat alone at one of them. She wore no makeup. She was smoking, and invited him over with a raised, fluted, long-fingered hand. Her beauty in this drab setting made him catch his breath; her tawny hair waved and swirled about her head like the Red Sea, with a parting in the middle. Wide sloping green eyes took him in. He sat down across from her and gestured to the surroundings.

'Why here?'

'It's not what it seems.'

She offered him a cigarette. He raised an eyebrow.

'It's allowed. No rules in this place.'

He inadvertently recoiled as he realised it was a spliff. She laughed at him, a big raucous laugh revealing strong white teeth between bruised lips.

'Relax, take a hit.'

He was taken off balance. He took a big pull. It was strong. He felt his feet tingle and his head hum. He realised he was staring at her mouth, which was articulating . . .

'It's forty quid each and you get whatever they serve,' she said in her flat Estuary English.

A second man in an apron appeared, set out some cheap-looking cutlery and put a bottle of wine between them with a clattering of glass tumblers.

'They're artists, painters,' she explained. 'They have no licence or anything, but they cook to die for. They hop from place to place to keep the law at bay. They use these greasy spoons because they're only open during the day.'

'How did you find them?'

'You get on their list and they call you. The other one, the one who let you in . . . I'm fucking him at the minute.'

A fragrant miso soup appeared. She took the rolled-up script from her bag and swashbuckled the air with it.

'I don't get it,' she said. 'Why would a woman let herself be dominated by one man's dick?'

'Many women do. Have you ever been in love with a man who is not in love with you?'

'If you look like me, men come on to you all the time. I've had to fight them off since I was twelve, got date-raped a couple of times in my teens. Bad guys will never leave you alone, but the good guys are too intimidated by a beautiful woman to even try.'

'Didn't that put you off men, turn you off sex?'

'No, I liked sex, I just didn't like the people I was having sex with. No, I'd never let a man enslave me.'

Daniel was delighted with her, half in love already.

'We're not talking about you, we're talking about Heather.'

'Well, I'm not a proper actress; if I play her, she's got to be like me, or a version of me.'

Daniel hardly noticed what he was eating as each course was set before him, but in some separate sensual part of his brain he recorded the exquisite flavours and noted the roasted halibut on a bed of shredded vegetables that had been marinated in a ginger and garlic sauce, sweetened by a few drops of maple syrup.

Her directness disarmed Daniel. He found himself telling her how the script had evolved out of a need to make a hit to save his career. She was surprisingly shrewd about the script and put her finger unerringly on the weak spots. He, in turn, began to mentally improvise Amanda into the screenplay.

'You wouldn't have Heather's moral compass, would you?'

'I don't know what I'd do. It might be a turn-on having a lover who was capable of murder, who had murdered. That could be tasty for the audience. Is he going to kill her or fuck her?' Daniel watched her face as doubt, fear and desire played across it in turn, followed by a sly grin.

'I like when she takes the kid to bed and lets the old man feel her up. I know how to play those scenes.'

It got late. The other diners had gone home; the chef boyfriend was hovering. Daniel got up, apologised and got out his money. Amanda waved it away.

'It's on me.'

The boyfriend was a big blond-haired guy, relaxed, easy in his skin, nicely balanced, comfortable with her, Daniel thought, judging by the way they touched and moved together.

He drove home in a state of high excitement. He could not see clearly how Amanda would work out, but he knew in his bones that it would. The next day, he attacked the script, bending it to this new character. He called Brad and Jack and asked them to come to the house the next morning. He told them he had a new approach and wanted to discuss it with them.

'Bring Bella,' he said. 'This could be a crucial moment for her book.'

Despite Jack's entreaties, he refused to elaborate.

'Wait and see, Jack. It's good; it's a way forward.'

Daniel went back to the script and worked on it for the rest of the day. Brad was the first to arrive. Hope had coffee and croissants waiting in the kitchen. Brad appraised her approvingly as she leaned against the Aga.

'Are you cold?' he said, in a tone of voice that made it clear he was not merely referring to her warming herself on the stove.

'Why wouldn't I be, with you undressing me.'

He laughed.

'Want to come to church with me on Sunday?'

'Well, that's an original line, I'll give you that.'

'There's a Pentecostal preacher in Notting Hill who is sensational.'

Daniel burst into the kitchen as he always did, flinging the door open. He hugged Brad. 'Daniel, would you command Brad not to make passes at me in my own kitchen.'

'But Hope, he comes on to women all the time. You'd be insulted if he left you out.' Brad was already sublimating his lust to the hot buttery croissants, and was on his second one already.

'I was telling Hope about this amazing Pentecostal preacher; thought we might work him into the screenplay. And guess who I saw there: your lab guy. Nigel, is it?'

'Ah, that makes sense. His latest letter said that God demands that his film be made, and that if I don't see to it, I risk the eternal fire.'

Jack and Bella arrived, and as they all sat around the teak table, Daniel made his pitch. 'Now Jack, don't get alarmed, hear me out. I met with Amanda. She's sensational, but she's not Heather.'

Jack sighed with relief. 'Thank God.'

'She's better than Heather.'

Jack groaned.

'I want to cast her, and change the character to what Amanda is. It's a big switch but it works. Instead of her being sexually obsessed with the cop, it's going to be him who is obsessed with her, jealous, crazed and, in the end, unhinged. Amanda is a contemporary version of Wedekind's Lulu. We were heading that way at one point, and it's where we should be. She is generous, reckless, open, but tough and resilient. She's carelessly natural, exactly what these neurotic urban people who come to the hotel would like to be. They love her, envy her. She's untouchable, magnetic and therefore vulnerable. She's unaware of the effect she has on others, and just as with Lulu, all the damaged people unconsciously want to destroy her. Her love of life, her vitality, causes havoc in the hotel. Lionel becomes obsessed by her, and tries to rape her, which fuels the cop's jealousy.'

Jack stopped him.

'Hold it right there, Daniel, let me say something. I've just heard from the studio that they're going with *Shadow of a Smile* in the States on 2 September. They cancelled the two-thousand-print opening, and they're going to platform it in ten major cities. Just ten prints. Virtually no ad campaign.'

Daniel was stunned into silence, the breath knocked out of him, as Jack continued harshly, 'They're burying it, as we all feared, so let me remind you that our strategy was to get a commercial genre movie financed and everyone committed before *Shadow* opens and dies. A mainstream thriller with an American male lead was how we started out. I've been very patient, but now you want an unknown English girl to play the lead. You want to tear up the script and start over. I would be selling a different movie, and I don't know how to do it. The sex stuff is a problem, and it sounds like you're pushing the envelope even further with this approach. You're pissing against the wind. It's crazy, Daniel; this is going nowhere.'

Daniel was shaken by Jack's vehemence, as were the others.

'Jack,' Daniel pleaded weakly, 'if Brad comes on board we can turn it around fast, and I will go with you to the distributors and pitch it myself.'

'Kiera's picture has collapsed. Let's go to her and stay with what we've got,' said Jack, hard-faced.

'Please, let me test Amanda. I'll shoot two scenes with her; it will be sensational; it will sell the movie.'

Into the bleak silence, Hope ventured, 'She sounds like my kind of girl. I think we'd better have her to dinner so I can size her up.'

Bella's Notebook

Jack is angry because he believes that deep down Daniel never intended to do a straight genre picture and unconsciously has been taking it in a personal direction. Once he drew on Hope's infidelity, he was going to be in dangerous emotional territory. There's another issue, Jack says: D wants to control everything, yet is impelled to put it all at risk, to push the limits, to flirt with chaos. It is so difficult to make a movie, yet D seems compelled to invent fresh obstacles once the old ones have been overcome. Is this the nature of the process, or is D somehow deeply conflicted?

Hope has always provided balance. She is rooted, lets him fly, keeps things running, hauls him in if he gets too close to the sun, but her influence over him has waned. They are clearly still estranged. It is alarming that he has gone so completely overboard for this Amanda, though his idea of making Heather a modern Lulu is intriguing.

Bella arrived at five to help Hope prepare the dinner. She was wearing the dress Daniel gave her. She found Hope in full battle mode, banging saucepans, clattering cutlery. She was immersed in steam and flame, like a Valkyrie. She was cooking angrily, and even abusing her loyal Aga. Sophie was trying to feed the children, but Hope's mood had destabilised them and they were both howling.

Bella found an apron and quietly began to tidy up Hope's mess, filling the dishwasher, wiping the surfaces, putting things away. She had presents for the children, which mended their mood. She made a comforting pot of tea. Her presence always had a calming effect on Hope. They sat down at the table and Hope rolled a cigarette.

'As if it's not enough, I have to listen to him wanking on about Amanda. Now he tells me her boyfriend is a Cordon Bleu cook, and he has the nerve to suggest I'd better make it a special meal, and what am I proposing to cook?'

She took a furtive pull at the rollup and cupped it behind her hand, but the children looked up at her accusingly when they caught the whiff of smoke. Hope, not up for another fight, stubbed it out.

'Daniel's desperate for Jack to like Amanda,' said Bella.

'Yes, and he wants me to make a *Babette's Feast*. You know, the food's so delicious, all the nastiness melts away and we all love each other. Well, I'm making a volcanic meal, peppers and chilli, and everything spiced the fuck up.'

Hope placed Amanda's boyfriend, Rod, on her right. He praised her cooking and ate with relish, sweat breaking out on his forehead as a result of the hot food.

'You're so courageous to serve food like this, especially to people whose tastebuds have probably been made bland by Californian cuisine.'

'It's not courage,' she said, 'it's a hostile act.'

Rod threw his head back and laughed.

'It's Amanda, isn't it? She always makes wives crazy.'

Brad, on her left, was also sweating his way through the food.

'The sex war is fought on many fronts,' he grunted.

Hope was impressed by how at ease Rod was in this charged encounter with people he was meeting for the first time. She felt an impulse to unsettle him, put him on edge, like the rest of them. She nodded down the table to where Amanda had captured the fascinated attention of Jack and Daniel.

'What was that old adage?' she said provocatively. 'If you want to sleep easy, don't marry a beautiful woman.'

'Well, we're not married,' Rod said, laughing again, 'but it's not a problem for me. Beauty like hers intimidates men. They mostly take to their heels.'

'But not you?'

'I'm a painter. I paint nudes. So I possess her in a way others can't.'

'Are you gay?' Hope asked, causing Brad to choke on his beer – which Daniel had decided was the only drink he believed would work with this fiery food.

'Only when necessary,' Rod said, unruffled. 'Are you?'

'I've given it some thought lately, men being such shits,' she said.

Rod was delighted with Hope, and reluctant to leave.

'But I have to go and help my partner cook,' he said, waving and blowing kisses to the women.

Bella, sitting next to Brad, was managing to listen to this conversation with her right ear while taking in what was going on with her left. Daniel was next to her, then Amanda, and lastly Jack.

'Why Almodóvar is so good with women,' said Amanda, 'is because he's not distracted by wanting to fuck them, he being gay and all.'

Jack nodded, and smiled his approval. He glanced across at Daniel and his nod said, 'She's smart, I'll give you that.' Daniel gave him a 'What did I tell you' look. The truth was that her beauty doubled the value of everything she said. Jack's mind floated back to their shared epiphany at the Hotel du Cap, and the girl who had silenced them both. Then came the shock of recognition. *It had been Amanda.* Daniel watched the revelation dawn on Jack's face.

'Yes,' said Daniel, 'the girl on the rocks.'

'Did you see Bertolucci's *The Dreamers*?' Amanda asked. 'The way his camera was creeping all over that girl's body – it was so fucking prurient. It was like his tongue was glued to the lens.'

Daniel sprung to the defence of his fellow director.

'Oh, come on. The girl was completely at ease – which she would not have been if Bertolucci had been lascivious. No, as Marshall McLuhan once said when he was confronted by topless waitresses in Haight Ashbury: "They're not naked, they're wearing us."'

Laughter. Hope picked up on it and called to the table at large, 'A quote for every occasion. That's our Daniel. Imagine them all lining up in his head, waiting for their moment.'

'I agree with you,' said Jack to Amanda, 'there's always a sexual tension between the camera and the women in Bertolucci's films. The camera is his surrogate. He once said that, for him, camera movements were like the positions in the Kama Sutra, but I see it as something positive. It's what makes his films so erotic.'

Amanda turned her Charlotte Rampling eyes at full intensity onto Daniel, piercing him.

'How do you handle sex scenes with your leading ladies?' she asked.

'I fall in love.'

He said it softly but it coincided with one of those inexplicable moments of silence that fall upon a dinner party: an angel passing, perhaps. Everyone heard, and Daniel was obliged to include them all in his qualification.

'Not with the actress, but with her image in the movie, with her character. And if she knows she's loved, it becomes easier for her to give herself to the camera.'

'And they never kind of blend into each other?' said Amanda, giggling.

Strawberries in rosewater soothed their scalded palates. Daniel served a very cold dessert wine.

After dinner the three women drifted together into the kitchen. Hope was determined to give Amanda a grilling.

'I've been around a lot of actresses,' she said, 'and most of them are eaten up with ambition. You can smell it on them. But there's not a sniff of it on you. So what do you want?'

'I want life – as much of it as I can get. When acting gets boring, I'll move on.'

'And leave the wreckage behind?'

'Yes. There's always collateral damage.'

Bella watched the two women closely.

'Does what you want include children?' she asked.

'My body wants them, but I'm withholding permission at present.'

Hope felt a sudden surge of affection for this girl, and gave her a hug.

'I think you're great. He's going to cast you. I'm sure of that. And look, if you want to fuck my husband, you have my blessing.'

The three women erupted in raucous laughter, coven-like, alarming Daniel. A quote offered itself – 'The monstrous regiments of women' – but he suppressed it.

Jack, Daniel and Brad were huddled together in the sitting room drinking malt whiskey and talking about Amanda in low voices.

'Jack, she's a movie star if ever there was one,' said Daniel.

'She's beautiful, she's charming – but can she carry a picture? And can we finance it with her?'

'I'll test her. Next week. Brad, we'll polish those two scenes on Monday. Philippe will shoot it for me as a favour. He's in town preparing another Tim Burton movie.'

Brad was drunk. He turned his head back and forth between Jack and Daniel, a tennis match. He put his arms around them both and whispered confidentially, 'She can't have orgasms.'

'What?' said Daniel.

'See how wound up she is.'

'You base it on that?'

'On a lifetime of experience. That and her fag boyfriend.'

'Oh, fuck off, Brad,' said Daniel.

'I've been studying them all my life and I'm never wrong.'

'Go home, Brad, you're pissed.'

'She comes close but she never gets there,' he said sagely as he headed unsteadily to the kitchen, where he gave thanks to Hope and reminded her of the church service in Notting Hill.

TWELVE

Brad spilled out onto the Kings Road, where restaurants and cinemas were disgorging people into the mellow night, and clutching couples disappeared into taxis or walked home thigh to thigh. He had to remind himself sternly of the many advantages of living alone. The Kings Road has always had an air of tacky eroticism, and he kept an eye out for some abandoned woman, hoping to catch one on the rebound from a busted relationship, but everyone was taken, and he was partly relieved not to have to make the effort. He went to bed feeling old.

The next morning, Sunday, he slept till 10.30 and woke up with a moderate hangover, a bearable headache, a dry mouth and trembling hands. As he searched for a clean cup amidst the clutter of greasy plates and dog-ends, a wave of nausea engulfed him. As it receded, his beleaguered brain was trying to tell him something but could not put more than three words together – then one was enough – church! Then another: 11 o'clock!

The service had just started when he arrived: he was obliged to stand at the back. The Reverent Winston Omoto roared and sung the gospels, spoke in tongues, called the sinners to Christ, healed the sick, and comforted the bereaved. Omoto poured compassion upon the people and they were undone by it, helpless and forgiven, made pure. Brad looked for Hope, who was easy to locate as one of the very few whites. He could tell from her heaving shoulders that she was weeping with the rest. He wanted to surrender to it himself, and he opened his heart, but nothing would fill his emptiness. All these heated passions chilled him to the marrow.

Hope could hardly stand as she left the church, and Brad put an arm around her for support. He walked her around the corner to his flat, so she could clean up and compose herself.

She wept for all the hurt that she had given and received and for the pain her children would suffer during their lives. She saw the world in the soaring phrases of the Reverend Winston Omoto, a veil of tears, a river of blood. Brad held her in his arms to comfort her, and kissed her, but could not stem her tears, and she was unresisting when he fucked her. He fucked her with that hard hard-on that is the gift of a hangover. He made her come twice and finally she lay inert, spent. He thought she looked as broken as Meryl Streep in *The French Lieutenant's Woman* after her brief carnal experience. The expected satisfaction in having avenged himself on Daniel for having taken most of the credit for their joint work failed to fill his emptiness.

He rinsed a cup and made her tea. When he brought it to her, she had gone. He drank the tea himself and set about cleaning up his place, which was his wont on a Sunday, to avert the deadness of that day and to distract himself from self-disgust. Although his preferred method was to laugh them into bed, nevertheless, he had found that weeping them into bed was also efficacious.

For time and cost reasons, they decided to shoot only one scene: the rape of Heather and the death of her lover. Amanda held nothing back: she showed fear and anguish so effectively that Daniel found it acutely painful to watch. Even Philippe, operating as well as lighting, found it hard to stay detached.

That night, Daniel had his recurring dream of being a child actor in a movie, reaching for that terrifying door, being driven on by his adult self. He turned the doorknob, cried out and woke up gasping with a terror that was somehow related to the rape scene of the day before.

Phyllis gathered a carefully selected group of distributors at the Fox viewing theatre in Soho Square. It was expensive, but Jack had insisted on having the larger of the two rooms, hoping that the bigger screen would lend magnitude to their now-diminishing project. The buyers were all sympathetic to Daniel's work, and Phyllis had been obliged to include Jean Paul, since they had a deal with him in place, but she was worried that the changes in the script and casting would encourage him to seek revenge for the deal he had been manoeuvred into. He would certainly not put up $1.2 million for a picture with an unknown, and it worried her that his bile might spill out and poison the atmosphere. The whole strategy worried her.

Her company was in trouble. Her last three films had failed to reach her estimates. The survival of her business depended on the banks having confidence in her sales predictions and lending money accordingly. Typically, when she made a deal with a distributor, he would put up 10 percent on signing and pay the balance on delivery of the film – eighteen months or two years down the road. The production needed that money to make the movie, so the bank would lend against the contract and get it back with interest when the distributor paid out. France, Italy, Spain, Germany and the UK were represented, but they had excluded the United States.

Daniel stood up to address them. 'Thank you for coming. I appreciate it. We now call the movie *Crime of Passion*.'

He looked across the expectant faces and finally found Bella, who was at the back making notes. He hesitated, the story turning to ashes in his mouth. His dream had left him with an aftertaste of anxiety. Bella looked up and, feeling his discomfort, offered an encouraging smile.

'I believe you've all read an early draft of the script. Well, since then it has gone through many changes, many drafts, and has evolved into something . . . else.'

What had it evolved into? He had to swallow to hold down a rising panic.

'Into something quite different and very exciting, and, I believe . . . original.'

Shit, I let the 'O' word slip out, he thought. He caught the sneer on Jean Paul's face.

'We've found a stunningly beautiful and brilliant actress to play the lead, someone destined to become, I believe, a great movie star. After I've sketched out the changes for you, I'm going to screen a scene from the script, which we shot last week, a test, so you will be able to judge her for yourselves.'

He paused, suppressing the catch in his voice.

'Heather is working at an eco-hotel where people go to get in touch with nature. Lionel, a man hated by his staff, owns it. He takes pleasure in abusing them. He finds out their secrets, manipulates them to his own ends. Heather has to fend off his advances. Everyone is in love with Heather. She is a free spirit. No one can catch her or own her. The local police detective sergeant, Jake, becomes her lover. He is besotted with her, but his overbearing attentions are becoming oppressive. She is planning to move on, as she always does when her life gets complicated. We took a lot of Heather from Wedekind's Lulu: she's vibrant, connected, in touch with the earth, and unaware of the havoc her careless beauty causes. She has a great lust for life. She's a force of nature.'

He could hear his voice getting away from him, becoming emotionally unreliable. He truncated the story.

'So there you have it. Lionel the destroyer, cynical, predatory; and Heather, creative, generous, reckless. The setting is the mysterious Salisbury Plain, and there's a subplot about Lionel's involvement with a satanic sect that meets at Stonehenge.'

Daniel faltered, a catch in his voice. He surveyed the puzzled faces of the distributors and forced more passion into his words.

'So, Heather's running in the woods at night. It's hot and humid. She strips off her shorts and T-shirt and plunges into a dark forest pool. She hears voices and conceals herself. The dead body of Lionel is lowered into the water.'

Daniel could feel the distributors being drawn into the story. Violence always does it: one of the primary colours of the movies.

'She recognises one of the two men as her lover Jake, the police inspector. He searches the water with his flashlight and as it sweeps across her, she submerges. He finds her clothes and takes them with him.

'Naked, she finds a cottage in the woods, where an old woman gives her clothes. Heather explains her dilemma. She can't go to the police, obviously, so should she do nothing? Her lover, Jake, suspects that she knows. She confides her problem to an old man, whom she has befriended, who works in the hotel. It transpires that he was the second man at the murder of Lionel. So now Jake knows that she knows. He asks her to marry him, so that she would not be able to testify against him. She stalls him, still unable to decide what to do. Meanwhile, he hints that she would be a prime suspect in the murder: he has implicated her by planting evidence. As the tension escalates, she finally decides she must confess what she knows – but to whom? For his part, Jake decides that his only option is to kill her. He follows her out into the woods and tracks her down.

'He loves her, but must kill her. He is in tears. He makes love to her with a gun to her head under the trees close to the cottage. As he reaches orgasm, the old woman shoots him and he dies, lying across Heather.'

Daniel cued the projectionist and the final scene, he had just described, appeared on the screen. It was horrifying and intensely erotic. Over her lover's shoulder, Heather sees the old woman from the cottage approaching with her shotgun. Jake is crying and angrily proclaiming his love as he fucks her, alternately berating her for not giving herself to him – saying 'No one else will ever possess you' – and pushing the gun into her temple. As he approaches orgasm, the old woman shoots him.

The lights came up, to a stunned silence. Daniel had left the theatre during the film, unable to watch it.

Jack got up and spoke. 'Well, there you have it. First time I've seen it. I find I'm moved and deeply disturbed. Although I read it on the page, I had no idea it would have that kind of impact. I realise now that it's a Manichaean story: how the abundance of life, of great goodness – I might even say innocence – somehow attracts evil, and how evil will always attempt to destroy goodness. Thank you for coming.'

He left, and Phyllis huddled with the distributors.

She reported to Jack the next day. The distributors were favourably impressed and were willing to take the picture, but the eroticism meant that it could only be shown on TV late at night. This consequently reduced the fees the TV stations would pay. The lack of star names also worked against it. Phyllis had argued that surely the eroticism would boost the DVD sales and make up for the lower TV sales. It might, they agreed, if the picture did well, but TV revenues protected their downside, and for the most part their upfront offers corresponded to what they could guarantee from TV. Right on cue, Jean Paul slipped Phyllis a note saying, '$800,000 only, or I'm out.'

So Phyllis reported that her sales estimates would tumble down.

Kevan and Kieran, 'the K Club', as they were known, were crunching the new numbers. Shooting in England instead of the States, and the absence of star salaries and ancillary costs, clipped out a big chunk of money. The Movie Magic Programme automatically reduced the insurance (2 percent of the budget), the completion bond (3 percent) and the contingency (10 percent). They were soon down to $10 million: a tax shelter of 20 percent, bank loan of 20 percent and presales based on Phyllis's estimates, totalled $8.3 million. They were still $1.7 million short.

The two 'K's went to Daniel's house to report the situation and seek solutions.

'Fifty days,' said Kevan. 'Four weeks in the studio, where the unions will only allow you to shoot five-day weeks. But what if you did six-day weeks on location?' As Daniel leaned over the computer, Kevan replaced '6 weeks at 5 days equals 30' with '5 weeks at 6 days equals 30'. 'That way you lose a week,' he said.

'What's the saving?' Jack asked.

The computer calculated the reduced hotel nights, per diems, equipment hire and crew salaries, and gave an answer: $307,334.

Daniel sighed, turned away and paced the room.

'It's such a false economy,' he said. 'The crew gets tired, slows down, and you end up not making the days and going over schedule. And I lose the preparation time at the weekend.'

'Deferments?' asked Kevan, daring to mouth the dirty word. Jack and Daniel exchanged signals of defeat.

'I'll talk to Phyllis, make a gross deal so we get our fees back from first receipts once the bank has been repaid, but before she takes her sales fees,' Jack said.

Daniel signalled his acceptance. Kevan watched them carefully.

'So am I right: we take out Daniel's $1 million fee and Jack's half a million?'

He hit the buttons. The computer supplied the answer. Apart from the $1.5 million savings, it clipped $150,000 from the contingency, plus $75,000 from insurance and completion, making a total of $1,725,000 – almost exactly what was required to get down to the magic $8.3 million figure. It was a depressingly neat solution. Jack wanted to offer some solace to Daniel. 'If you decide to go for six-day weeks on location, you can keep the $300,000 savings.'

Daniel shook his head.

They had offered Amanda's agent $100,000 with back-end escalators, so that if the picture was successful she would eventually make $400,000. The agent was pressing for more up front, his rationale being that other agents would be trying to poach her, and that they would tell her that $100,000 was derisory for a lead role in a Daniel Shaw picture. She had got the same fee for her last picture, which had only half the budget of this one. Jack told the agent that he and Daniel were deferring in order to get the picture made, and there was just no more money. The agent called back the next day in a fit of breast-beating to say that Amanda was insisting that her fee also be deferred. She felt it was unfair for her to be paid and Daniel not to be.

Before the bank loan could be put in place, there had to be a completion bond. The several investors needed to know that whatever problems occurred, and however much the film exceeded its budget, they would not be called upon for more money, and the film would be completed. The bond company needed all the actors' contracts and the crew agreements to be signed, all the design work had to be completed, and all the locations chosen and secured, before they would sign off. They insisted on money being added to certain categories – that Daniel would need more film stock, for instance – and they would not guarantee completion until their representative had attended the final technical recce, which took place a week before shooting started. All this pre-production work would take twelve weeks and cost $1 million, mainly in crew fees, travel, legal work, the hire of studio facilities and other costs.

Here was the dilemma facing all independent pictures. You needed to spend all this money before you could get a completion bond. If the picture collapsed, for whatever reason, that money would be lost. So a gap in the market had been filled by a number of risk-takers. Jack went to a company called Film Risk Management. They came in and pored over the documentation, finally agreeing to put up the finance for the twelve weeks of pre-production, their investment to be repaid on the first day of principal photography, plus interest of $100,000 – which Kevan quickly calculated represented 40 percent interest per annum.

Jack railed against FRM, called them usurers, but there was no other way. The picture could fail for all kinds of reasons, so the risk was real. In this way, Amanda's deferred fee was swallowed up.

So, finally, it was done. Jack and Daniel signed up to do the picture on these terms.

THIRTEEN

Daniel, having fought to get the picture made, now fell into a humour of regret and inertia. It was always so. He had signed away a year of his life – probably closer to two. He would be chained to the movie for every waking hour. It was gruelling work, and much of it tedious and boring. At this stage he always felt an impulse to run away. They watched the ink drying on their signatures and Jack put his Mont Blanc pen back in his pocket. Daniel clasped him by the shoulder.

'Let's take our kids to the beach tomorrow. Get away before it all gets on top of us.'

As a gesture of escape, it was feeble enough, but it was something. Between my work and my family, how much freedom do I have? Daniel mused. Economists spoke of disposable income. What about disposable time? He mentally ticked off his committed hours: sleeping, eating, showering, dressing, domestic chores, kids' homework, and other activities he convinced himself were vital: reading the newspapers, taking exercise, keeping up with the arts – film, theatre, exhibitions. He felt obliged to do some teaching at film schools – which always led to an obligation to read students' scripts – and finally his own work, which filled all the gaps in between. And how would he use disposable time if he had some? He used to paint when he was younger and unmarried, when there seemed to be large stretches of time available. Didn't he walk for hours in the Lake District? Where had that time come from? And back further, to childhood, when days drifted into infinite space, when time was so profligate, it could be wasted at will, and he had allowed himself to wallow in boredom. As you get older, time closes in on you, he mused. It accelerates year by year and forces you to do everything faster and faster, just to keep up. Christmas seemed to come around every six months. Leaves appeared in May and were falling a month or two later, it seemed.

'Bournemouth,' said Jack. 'Let it be Bournemouth.'

They set out at seven, four adults and three children pressed into Daniel's ten-year-old diesel Mercedes with Hope's picnic basket, lavishly provisioned from the Harrods food hall, tucked in the boot.

Bournemouth enshrined and preserved some of the characteristics that Jack thought of as essentially English: the solemn taking of tea and scones at 4 PM in gloomy hotels; genteel ladies taking the air on the promenade; old men sunk in deckchairs, sleeping with the *Telegraph* over their faces. It charmed him. Bournemouth was a holy relic in his almost religious Anglophilia. Daniel despised the stuffiness of this Tory citadel, but tolerated it for another reason: it had the finest sand. He was a skilful sand-castle architect, and Bournemouth's sand was the best there was for this purpose. While Jack and the women lay in the sun, he set to work. He had brought his steel spade to stiffen up the plastic buckets and implements brandished by the kids. They gathered around him, sucked in by his fervent intent. Doing his bidding, they dug moats, fetched water, found sticks and driftwood to decorate the towers and turrets, the keep, the castellated walls.

Emma, her efforts scorned by the older kids, in an act of infant terrorism kicked over one of the walls. She was chased into her mother's arms, where she wept bitterly. Daniel lured her back with a promise that he would bury her in sand just as soon as the castle was finished, and would she look for ice-cream wrappers from which they could make flags and pennants. Orson had brought his collection of medieval knights and soldiers and began setting them out in the battlements.

Jack took a walk on the beach and felt, not for the first time, like Eliot's Alfred J. Prufrock: an ineffectual Englishman concealed inside a solid American. 'I shall walk upon the beach, I shall wear the bottom of my trousers rolled.' Right on cue, there was a man with rolled-up pants allowing the sea to water his big, flat, white feet. As the sand squeezed pleasurably between Jack's toes, he wondered if the mermaids would sing to him, but he knew they would not, for he was not an artist. He had measured out his life in styrofoam cups, the detritus of location crews throughout the world. Producing movies brought him close, and Bella could take him there, but even in his worshipful lovemaking, he was but an attendant lord, glad to be of use. Yet he was content, and took his pleasures from the marvellously mundane and fading banalities of English life.

The two women, lying side by side, kept looking up from their magazines at Daniel's progress, their ease ruffled by his industry.

'He's like some manic fucking ant,' said Hope.

She was grateful that he had committed to another film: it would keep him away from her and give her time to deal with her messy emotions. In a certain sense, putting another man between Paul and Daniel had somehow severed her sexual obsession with Paul, and she sensed that it might facilitate her way back to Daniel. Their lovemaking on Midsummer's Night had not been repeated. Daniel had made tentative advances, which she had rejected. She felt so ashamed of fucking Brad that the shame was turning into affection for her husband, but she was emotionally confused and not yet resolved enough to approach him and make amends.

They opened the wine, ate the fois gras on melba toast and the smoked-salmon sandwiches which Hope had garnished with shredded basil and fennel. Jack studied his wife's long thighs, her bold shoulders and strong back, which fluted to a delicate waist. He discreetly feasted on her body, for their lovemaking was in near-darkness and he seldom saw her naked in the light. Even now, she wore a severe one-piece bathing suit that exposed only her arms and legs. It made him think of the dress Daniel had bought her, which covered her neck and arms and revealed nothing but calves. It said something about Daniel's sensibility that he unerringly knew what she needed.

Daniel too was watching the women peripherally. Hope still had the poise of a dancer, but she was looser, more fluid than she had once been. She was sensual, whereas Bella wore her beauty like armour. Hope's body was open, inviting, its secrets gladly surrendered; Bella's guarded, implacable. Jack lowered himself down between them, and Daniel felt a wave of love that included all three.

The children splashed in the gentle waves. It was an English sea, unthreatening. Daniel waded in. He felt an urge to swim far out, to keep going. If I drowned, I wouldn't have to make the film, he thought. It seemed an attractive option. The water washed him clean of all thoughts of the film. He was purified, and the further he swam, the better he felt.

He came to himself with a jolt. He looked back. His children were hardly more than grains of sand on the beach. He was alarmed, and as he struggled to persuade his body to turn back, some logical corner of his brain informed him that he was in the grip of a death-wish. With a wrench, he turned back. The tide was ebbing and he swam against it, making paltry progress. Panic crept up from his gut. He swam harder, and soon his energy was draining away. He hyperventilated. His feet were cold, and the cold was creeping up his legs. A surge of new energy arrived from somewhere deep within him. The instinct to survive overwhelming the death-wish. Survival had a purpose, immediate and absolute, whereas the death-wish is complex and tentative, and quickly swamped by adrenalin. It took him half an hour to get back to shore, and he staggered up the beach, feeling a touch heroic, and disappointed that no one had missed him. He fell to his knees and hugged his kids, and they screamed, because he was as cold as a corpse.

Bella's Notebook

The pre-production will take eight weeks. They have hired offices at Shepperton Studios rather than Pinewood. Jack and Daniel are there at 8 AM in the morning and never finish before 9 PM, often later. Jack works with Kieran on the ever-evolving budget, making contracts for actors and crew, securing permissions for locations. Daniel spends most of his mornings with Tony Pratt, the designer. They are working on a very narrow colour spectrum – browns and greys, with an occasional flash of red to denote danger, blood. Tony makes cardboard models of the sets, which Daniel explores with a viewfinder. He works out the shots he will need, then picks up a pair of scissors and cuts away the parts of the set he will not see. I found it sad that Tony's lovely sets were chopped up like that. Tony was philosophical. 'It saves a lot of money.'

Daniel is constantly interrupted by the costume designer and the prop master and the set decorator and others, who offer him an endless array of choices: this lampshade or that, a book of wallpaper samples from which he must choose. Which of these sunglasses should Heather wear? Is this rucksack OK? Would he select a notebook, a name for the hotel. Two of the nastier characters have names that are identical to those of local people, and must be changed. What would he like to rename them? The afternoons he spends casting. There are forty speaking parts. The assistant director, Tommy Gormley, has been recruiting extras in Wiltshire and he showed Daniel polaroids from which he must choose. Daniel made a big selection. Later he will meet and audition them himself, when he and the heads of departments recce the locations in Wiltshire. Philippe Rousselot, the French cameraman, will come over for that and will spend two days with Daniel breaking down the scenes – where he needs tracks, a camera crane, a Steadicam, and so on, as well as analysing the lighting.

As the first day of shooting approaches, Daniel seems to be dragging himself through the process: he looks worn, he lacks the passionate intensity I witnessed in the writing process. Some of the crew, who have worked with him before, have commented on his short temper. Everything is urgent; no one has enough time. All the crew members are worried that their preparations won't be completed in time. They are like an army preparing for battle, and fear rules them. Jack, on the other hand, relishes crisis. He loves to solve problems. It brings out the best in him. He lights his pipe and becomes so reassuringly calm that the problems usually evaporate in his presence. I love to watch him working, it makes me love him so. I try to spend an hour or so each day observing Daniel. He lights up when he sees me, and my presence somehow comforts him. But I'm worried about him. I'll see if I can get him to have dinner one night this week.

Bella persuaded Daniel to eat at Thierry's on the way home, and asked him boldly what was wrong.

'It feels such a dead thing. Instead of it growing and burgeoning, all I do is give it artificial respiration.'

His wine-glass emptied very quickly, she noted.

'Once I start rehearsals and get Amanda and the actors in . . . '

The sentence petered out. The waiter filled his glass. He felt Bella's eyes on him, wanting a fuller explanation. Part of her technique as an interviewer was to wait silently, create a gap that the interviewee felt obliged to fill.

'How's the book coming along?' he asked, as a deflection.

'I have my doubts too, sometimes. Am I just a promotional tool? I mean, how critical can I be of you and Jack, people I'm so close to? I'm interested in the process and in the passion that carries it all along, but since the passion has dried up, I, too, have come to a stop.'

The food arrived, and he moved it around the plate without eating. He'd had a hasty sandwich for lunch, yet lacked appetite.

'Something is troubling you, Daniel.'

He dropped his eyes from hers and stared at his *loup de mer*, which looked back at him through a glazed eye.

'I have a dread of the rape scene. I threw up before we shot the test. I had a flash of Hope in Amanda's place, and it keeps coming back. At night, I see Hope being raped, and yet she is unresisting, and then she has an orgasm and I wake up.'

'It's about sex, this movie. You're dealing with dangerous stuff.'

'When I get home at night, Hope is either asleep or out. She leaves me food in the Aga but I never see her. I thought things were getting better but now she's so remote. Would you talk to her?'

'What would you want me to say?'

'I don't know. Forget it. Bad idea.'

'Have you ever considered that your emotional involvement in your films is a kind of infidelity,' she remarked.

'No, I have not.'

Bella let the gap of silence widen. He resisted, then fell into it.

'Truth is, I'm relieved when she's not there and we don't have to talk.'

'Maybe she understands you don't have the energy to deal with emotional issues right now.'

A surge of anger escaped his control.

'That's the kind of emollient you use to soothe your subjects. That's what I am: one of your subjects.'

She felt as though he had slapped her face.

'You know what?' he went on. 'I know nothing about you. You are so clever at getting people to open up, but you are even cleverer at concealing yourself.'

'What do you want to know?'

'OK, let's see. Where were you raised?'

'Minnesota. Father Italian, mother Swedish.'

'Siblings?'

'None.'

'Why did you marry Jack?'

'He was kind . . . is.'

'You had other lovers who were not?'

Another slap. She recoiled, then answered.

'Yes.'

He looked away, regretting his hostile tone, and caught an elderly couple at another table watching them. He gestured discreetly towards them.

'What do they think we are this time?'

'Oh, a married couple,' said Bella disarmingly. 'They think I've just found out you're having an affair – which is why you are so aggressive.'

He walked home feeling he had confessed too much, but a little more at ease. It was past midnight. He was startled to find Hope at the kitchen table with a vodka bottle and his prepared supper.

'How's prep coming along? Hardly seen you in a week.'

'Just fine.'

'You look whacked out.'

'Well, yes, you know how it is. We're shooting in three weeks.'

'The old sex drive goes wonky, I recall, once you start shooting. Or gets sublime . . . sorry, sublimated.'

She had trouble with the word. She was drunk, he realised. She had a malt whiskey in the thick tumbler waiting for him. He sat down beside her.

'Jack called, looking for Bella. She was with you, I suppose. You two having it off?'

'Of course not. Stuff for her book.'

'I wouldn't blame you. I haven't been very forthcoming. Sorry about that.'

Her eyes were wet. Tears always turned him on. He felt himself swelling. He held her. He tasted the tears on her face. She ran her hand down his chest and brushed across his crotch, felt his hardening penis. She slid down him onto her knees and looked up, her hands prayerful.

'I mean, really really sorry. Forgive me, I have sinned.'

She unzipped him. He ran his hand through her hair.

'Not now, Hope. Let's go to bed.'

'No, I want to give you a gift on this anniversary of our wonderful fucked-up marriage.' She took him in her mouth. How long since she had done this? Not for years and years. At least to him. She kissed the tip, then with each stroke she went deeper. She was able to push it into her throat without gagging, a technique Paul had taught her the first time round. An image of Bella at the beach sprang unbidden to Daniel. He banished it.

When Hope had finished her penance, she slumped to the floor. He sank down next to her and cradled her.

'You forgot,' she said.

'I was thinking about getting you one of those new diesel Minis.'

'But it was chased out of your mind by the dazzling Amanda.'

He handed her a bunch of keys.

'It's outside.'

She got unsteadily to her feet and stared at him.

'You did remember.'

'I've got an assistant now whose job it is to remind me of these things.'

'What colour?'

'British racing green.'

'Good.'

'Not a drop-head?'

'Absolutely.'

'Perfect.'

'An Aga and a Mini. My cup overfloweth.'

'I noticed,' he said, with a nod to her vodka glass.

She ran outside. He finished his whiskey. He felt pleasantly tired. He knew he would sleep, a deep dreamless sleep, a sleep as deep and welcome as death. He heard her cries of joy filter through the front door, and reflected that they were very similar to those of her orgasms. Sex defines it all, he mused.

FOURTEEN

Daniel surveyed the faces at the table: Amanda and the principal actors; Brad with his notepad; Philippe, the cameraman; Paddy, the script supervisor. Finally, his eyes came to rest on Bella, who smiled warmly.

They began the read-through, Daniel speaking the directions and the actors doing their lines. He had instructed them not to act, to deliver the lines flat. Try as they might to be non-committal, something always showed through, and it was that something that he wanted to identify and subsequently nurture, for it would be the very essence of the way the actor connected to the role, the point at which the actor and the role intersected.

Whenever a line seemed dubious or awkward or out of character, he would nod to Brad, who would note it for massaging later. Although Daniel and Brad had tried to make it witty and humorous, as a relief from the tension of the story, but the only things the actors laughed at were the typos. There was a palpable sense of relief when they got to the end. They laughed and chatted and made jokes about the sex scenes, which had been embarrassing to read. Daniel's stomach had churned at the rape scene, and as his voice had faltered he saw Bella's eyes urging him on, and he got through it.

He had made a rehearsal schedule for the two weeks: Heather-and-Jake scenes; Heather-and-Lionel scenes; Heather with the boy and the old man. It was all Heather. She was in almost every scene. Vanessa Redgrave had agreed to play the small role of the woman in the cottage. It was just three days' work. The other actors were in awe of her. Daniel had to remind Vanessa twice to speak the lines flat. Her sonorous vowels were so freighted with emotional nuance that it was almost impossible for her to express nothing. She was already inhabiting that woman.

The next day was devoted to Heather and Jake, the heart of the movie.

'We are going to study the scenes, not act them out,' Daniel warned. 'The style of the film is that we plunge into the middle of scenes, so what we will mostly do now is explore what the characters were doing and feeling before we meet them, so that you enter each scene with a history, and with vitality.'

Ned Nugent, playing the detective, was fretting.

'I need to know stuff about my character. Like, was he married before? Is he from Wiltshire or somewhere else? I mean, his accent will depend on that. And what is the hold Lionel has over him? I've got a million questions. The script is very sparse.'

May had described Ned as old-fashioned beefcake. He was close to being a star. He had played Robin Hood in a TV drama. He had a brooding, angry quality, which sprang from his resentment that he could not always follow the quicker minds around him. Daniel was hoping that Ned's vanity and insecurity would serve the character.

'Let's see what we need to know about him for each scene,' Daniel counselled.

'Well, I'd like him to have a complete history,' argued Ned.

'Invent one yourself. Don't tell me what it is, and I'll see if it works as we go along.' Ned was anxious. He wanted to shore up his character with facts. Daniel wanted to keep him on edge.

'How did they get together?' Ned wanted to know.

Brad spoke up.

'We figured he was a frequent visitor to the hotel and had dealings with Lionel.'

'What dealings?' said Ned.

'We don't need to know that right now,' cautioned Daniel, silently wishing that Daniel Craig had been available.

'He watches her training the guests,' Brad went on, 'and he's crazy about her. He volunteers for her survival course. Three days and nights in the wild. He's very fit. Lifts weights.'

'Jesus,' said Ned, 'I'd better get into training.'

'They get way ahead of the others, and make love under the trees. It is casual for her, but he's hooked,' said Daniel.

'That's a great scene. Can't we have it in the movie?' Ned asked.

'No, we start as she is tiring of the affair, feeling oppressed by it, because he is obsessed by her. You bring all that with you into the scene.'

Amanda had said very little. She was watchful, careful, holding her fire. When they rehearsed the scenes, she closed her script and approximated the dialogue, keeping very close to the original but testing it out, making it her own.

They were in the rehearsal room each day, locking out the world. Coffee and food were sent in. Daniel pressed hard, knowing he only had two weeks.

On his way to dinner that night, he realised that he had not seen or read the news for weeks. He had always felt that the world could not get along without him worrying about it, being aware of every catastrophe, act of God, or folly of man. But it seemed to be doing just as well – and badly – without him.

Dinner was with Philippe, to discuss the style and tone of the picture.

'Do you want it to be Heather's point of view?' Philippe asked.

'I was thinking that way early on – that the camera should see the world and the other characters as she sees them – but I've moved away from that.'

They were back at Thierry's. Philippe, though French, was indifferent to food, but in all other matters his tastes were exquisite. His contract required the production to provide him with a piano, and he played every night. He chose only the most difficult pieces, which he never mastered. He had accepted the idea of shooting on 16mm with a digital grade, and a blow-up to 35mm for the release prints. He was doing a series of tests on the chosen colour palate and determining how the various colours responded to desaturation. He reported all this to Daniel. They talked through the implications and finally got back to the style issue.

'How do you see it?' said Philippe.

'The camera should have the neutrality of nature – beautiful and indifferent – and this lovely creature is caught in the mesh of these nasty, petty passions. So I want an unyielding camera, unmoving, no creeping tracks or silky Steadicam follow-shots. Hard and still.'

Philippe could see it immediately.

'Then let's go back to shooting on 35mm. For this style, you need quality. Everything must be beautiful and hard and clear. Thirty-five millimetre, please.'

Daniel conceded, but worried about the extra cost, calculating in the back of his mind what he could save in some other area to compensate.

'And we should transfer the wide shots at 4k, not 2k, when we go to digital.'

More expense.

'Why not shoot on a digital camera, Philippe? If we are transferring to digital for the grade, and most cinemas are now projecting digitally, why not go the whole hog?'

Philippe winced. 'Because film is magic, and even when it goes through the digital transfers, some of the magic sticks.'

Daniel was warming to the argument. It was safe and technical. It relieved him from the highly charged emotional issues that pressed in on him from every quarter.

'Film was a nineteenth-century invention,' he said. 'Digital is twenty-first century. It gives us complete control over colour and density. We can paint the image in post. We should be embracing it. I've heard you complaining about film being over-saturated and unresponsive.'

Philippe was amused by Daniel's passion.

'Dan, I feel loyalty to film, love even. We have struggled together all these years, and I cannot bring myself to discard it.'

'But it was a lost cause years ago. Film was at its best, its purest, when it was black and white and silver nitrate. Those velvety blacks and subtle whites. But it was dangerously flammable, so they made Safety film, and the magic was lost right there. Downhill ever since.'

'You are right,' said Philippe, conceding gracefully. 'So let's do one last movie on film.'

'OK, Philippe, but the next time we go digital.'

Daniel had a dinner every night during rehearsals: after Philippe, the lead actors, one by one; then Tony Pratt, reporting on design progress; and on the following night, six days before shooting was to start, with Jack, who was at his most rabbinical and funereal.

'Something's eating you, Jack. What is it?'

'We had all our ducks in a row,' he finally said to Daniel, 'and now Jean Paul's company has gone belly up and the whole goddamn structure has fallen apart.'

'Oh, no. Oh shit. Oh fuck.'

'Until we can replace it,' Jack went on gloomily, 'no money's coming from the BFI or the tax shelter, and of course, no bank loan. The guy from the pre-production fund has been sitting on my back and has immediately cut us off dead.'

Daniel felt a moment of euphoric relief that he would not have to make the film, then he crumpled.

'I've been told to give protective notices to the crew, and that Tony should stop construction,' said Jack quietly.

'Have you done it?'

Jack paused, and stared gloomily at the Kings Road traffic.

'No.'

'Why not?'

'Because even if we get it going again, people will lose faith. Crew people will drift away and we'll get behind.'

'But if we go under, you'll be liable for what, $100,000?'

'In that ballpark.'

It was a soft, warm night, and they were eating outside to allow Jack to smoke his pipe. He was calm and relaxed – which made Daniel even more anxious for him.

'Don't take this on, Jack.'

'We'll get through it.'

'You love a crisis, Jack. I think that's why you do this thankless work.'

'Phyllis and I will go to Paris tomorrow and show Amanda's test to the other French distributors. Problem is, there are six other films out there which are affected, and they're all competing with us for a new home.'

The next day was Sunday, so the actors need not be told, but from late morning Daniel's home phone was hot from agents calling. Everyone had heard that the picture had collapsed. Daniel offered flat denials.

Since their exchange of presents on their anniversary, Hope had become more solicitous, but there was no passion between them, and no time to mend sexual fences. Now she came into his office.

'Let's go for a picnic on the river. Get you away from all this crap. Sophie can look after the kids.'

She knew his love of the Thames, and its power to soothe and renew him. They rented a punt at Henley and he poled them upstream towards a hidden backwater they knew well. He had competed in this archaic river sport when he was young and never felt more harmonious than when the varnished pole was slipping between his fingers: throw the pole forward, listen to the clunk of the metal claw as it touched gravel, hands high, push down, turn of the body, a final thrust facing the stern, then retract the pole hand over hand, one, two, three, then throw it forward again, away from the punt, to steer it to the right, closer or under the boat to move it left, but subtle, measured in inches. Hope lay back on the cushions and watched him from under her straw hat. He had wooed her thus, looming over her with his phallic pole. Unlike the awkward three-men-in-a-boat skiff, with its painful ribs, a flat-bottomed punt was comfortably suited for lovemaking, and so they had conjoined.

They ate their picnic lunch under a weeping willow.

'If Jack can't revive the corpse, you're not going to go nuts, are you?'

'I think I'll fall into a black hole. This project is tearing me apart and holding me together at the same time.'

'You'd be better off without it. You're having nightmares. You wake up screaming. Nearly every night.'

He considered whether he should tell her about his dream. He decided on an edited version.

'It's often the same dream. A woman is being raped, she struggles and then has an orgasm and I'm watching, but my feet are in concrete and I can't help.'

'Do you see who she is, or who's doing the raping?' she asked anxiously.

'I know them both, but I don't recognise them.'

She was relieved. She had not seen or spoken to Brad since the incident, although he had called her every day. When she heard his voice, she hung up.

On Monday, all the actors turned up for rehearsal except Ned. Jack had mollified the agents, told them it was just a blip. Ned called to say that his agent said he should not work unless his full fee was in escrow.

'Come right over here, or you're fired,' said Daniel.

He arrived thirty minutes later. Daniel was even more driving and intense, as though to banish the air of unreality, that they were preparing for something that might not happen. They were all aware of how frequently independent films collapsed. Daniel had all the phones switched off, so bad news could not penetrate. The actors had been inventing histories for their characters – the challenge Daniel had set them. They tended to be histrionic and overdramatic, and Daniel gently pegged them back; but it gave them a sense of ownership and commitment.

At the end of the session, Daniel called Jack in Paris, but nothing had been resolved. Distributors had received them coolly, still smarting that Jean Paul had been given preference. They had seen the test and Jack was awaiting responses. Daniel reported the news to Bella and left with Brad. He took him home. Hope was out at her pilates class. There was a steak and kidney pie in the oven, which they ate with a bottle of red wine. They went over the doubtful lines and revised them. They talked in a desultory way about the actors. Finally, Daniel raised the issue that was on his mind.

'When Lionel tries to rape her, it works fine because it's a fight. I'll stage it like that. It needs to be choreographed properly.'

'Will you get Hope to choreograph?'

The idea threw Daniel off balance.

'I don't know. Perhaps.'

'She would be great for it. I'll suggest it to her if you like.'

The notion unsettled Daniel. He let it slip by.

'I can visualise that scene, but I don't know how to shoot the rape at the end.'

'You've already made that scene for the test.'

'Just a test. It wasn't right. It was unspecific.'

'What worries you?'

'We've seen her fight off Lionel, so it can't be like that.'

'But he has a gun. That's different enough.'

'So how does she react? Is she cold? Rigid? Angry? What?'

'Want to know how I see it?' said Brad. 'She's limp. She doesn't resist. You see tears escaping her closed eyes. She opens them when she comes, and that's when she sees the old woman over her shoulder.'

Daniel listened carefully, visualising it.

'I'll put it to Amanda tomorrow.'

Hope came in, startled to see Brad, who got up and kissed her reluctant cheek and squeezed her rigid shoulders.

'We've been working on the rape scene,' he said.

'And I'm sure you're enjoying it.'

Brad watched her, smiling, teasing.

'Who was it who said that since sex and violence are the primary colours of the cinema, it follows that rape must be its apotheosis. Was it Tarantino? No. He wouldn't have used a word like "apotheosis".'

Hope took a glass of water and left the room. Daniel saw that she was distressed, and followed her out.

'What is it, Hope?'

'Nothing. I can't stand that shit. Why you work with him, beats me.'

The next day of rehearsal covered the Ned and Amanda scenes, and by the end of the afternoon they had edged towards the final rape scene. Ned had plenty to say.

'It's going to be tough for me to get to that place, emotionally. I mean, he loves her but he's going to kill her and rape her. How do I get there?'

'We take it step by step,' said Daniel. 'We'll get you there.'

Daniel told Amanda the new idea, and she watched Brad carefully.

'Sounds like a date rape. You been there, Brad?' she asked.

'Imagination. Comes from my feminine side.'

'It's plausible,' she said. Then added, 'Here's another thought. Supposing the reason none of them can possess her is that she can't come when she fucks men.'

'Has to finish herself off in the bathroom?' said Brad.

Amanda trod on his line. 'And this is the first time she gets an orgasm, with a guy about to kill her?'

What did I tell you, said Brad's triumphant look, and to her, to rub it in: 'Daniel told us you can only play yourself.'

'Ah, but there are many of me. We are legion.'

She gave Brad a blistering stare.

Daniel called Jack again. He had found a distributor, Pathé, but was still negotiating the terms. He had to get the price up to a level the bank and bonder could live with. Kevan Barker had been waiting outside the rehearsal room. In the absence of Jack, he needed guidance on pressing matters.

'Let's go round the corner for a pint. Too many little ears flapping in here.'

Bella tagged along, making notes, her journalistic instincts alert to the drama. Between great draughts of best bitter, Kevan gave his litany of woe. The film stock they had ordered was arriving and had to be paid for. Studio rental for five months was due, or they would be turfed out. Another picture wanted their space. The camera assistant was testing the camera equipment, and Panavision, though very understanding, would also like to be paid. The rumour that the picture had collapsed had spread far and wide, and smaller creditors were dunning Kevan. Jack had transferred funds to the production to cover the construction crew's pay, and told Kevan to fend off all the others.

Kevan, though thoroughly professional, saw life as a sacred joke. He believed in a god with a cruel sense of humour, intent on torturing his creations. This god's one act of mercy was the gift of alcohol – a gift for which Kevan gave daily thanks.

'I'm beating them off with a baseball bat. Can't do more than that. But if I may remind you, tomorrow is Wednesday. We start shooting on Monday, for which we will need certain toys that we don't have: a camera, some film, some actors, to name but a few.' 'Should we delay the start-date for a week?' said Daniel.

'Sadly, that would push the budget up and cost us money we don't have. However, I do have enough money to buy another round, thanks to Jack's munificence. I'll put it down to pain relief.'

There were further rounds, and the pain duly diminished.

Kevan left to have dinner with the head of Panavision. 'He's paying,' he said, draining his glass. Bella was still scribbling in her notebook. She glanced up guiltily at Daniel, feeling like a vulture feeding on carrion.

'It'll be a better book if we go under,' he said bitterly. 'Most disasters have secondary benefits.'

'Daniel, I couldn't bear that,' she said softly. 'If the film isn't made, I'll abandon the book.'

'Why would you do that?'

'Because I care about you more than I care about the book.'

Daniel felt a little woozy from the beer and exhaustion. He looked around and discovered that the crowded, noisy pub was now almost empty. He realised it must be late. Of course, they had not finished rehearsals until 8 PM.

He saw Bella in wide shot from the pub door, her long legs crossed on her barstool, then he snapped back into a close shot of her face, and dollied in to her mouth. He did it all the time, but especially when drunk – broke life down into camera set-ups.

'It all depends where you put the camera,' he said. 'Little girl skipping across a field of buttercups: sweet, charming. Extreme close-up of her foot crushing a flower: a violent image.'

'What are you talking about?'

'You. Me. The movie. I'm making it for you. I mean, you're my audience, which is why I'm always seeking your approval and trying not to let it show. But more than that. The story is about you, in some sense that I haven't yet fathomed.'

'We're in this together, for better or worse,' she said, 'all the way.'

'All the way.'

They had entered a pact which neither quite understood.

They unwound themselves from the barstools and went out into the wet night. A taxi disgorged a fare and they piled in. He dropped her off at her house and gave her a hug, kissed her. She offered her mouth and in his deepest, darkest place, inert matter erupted inside him. She broke away, and hurried into her house through the rain without looking back.

Entering his silent house, emotional turbulence banishing fatigue, his problems crowded in on him, filling the empty rooms like malevolent ghosts. On impulse he called Fred Schneider in Los Angeles – 11.30 PM here, 3.30 PM over there – and told him of their problems.

'That's tough, Dan. The fucking business is becoming a carnal house. I just fired two hundred people. There's blood all over my floor.'

'Fred, I want you to do me a favour. Give me a distribution deal. You don't have to put up any money, but if we can tell the bank we have a US deal with a major, they might make the leap.'

'Can't do it. The tenacious bastard is still hanging on. Got some better results from the other divisions, and I'm in pre-production with *Other Lives*. I'm slowing it up all I can, but it's crowding in on me.'

'Who's directing it?'

'That kid from Cannes. Sydney Abel. The one with the no-budget horror flick.'

'Remember when making movies was fun, Fred?'

'No, I don't.'

Daniel put down the phone and trudged up to his cold conjugal bed.

Wednesday.

The actor playing Mike, the fifteen-year-old son of Lionel, arrived for rehearsal, putting on an air of insouciance.

'Welcome, Luke.'

Daniel introduced him all round, then dismissed everyone except Amanda.

'OK, let's go over the scene. Your father has beaten you, you're humiliated. Heather finds you crying. Now, you worship Heather, so you hate for her to see you like this. She says, "Come on, you're going to sleep in my room tonight." We cut to them in her bed. You're turned away from her so she can't see your face, and she's whispering to you.'

Daniel gave a sign to Amanda, and she spoke the line: 'There are going to be a lot of good things in your life, Luke, and I'm going to show you some of them.'

Daniel took it up, 'Then she kisses him, we fade out, and fade up the next morning as he sits up in bed and says . . . ?'

Luke managed to croak out the line, 'Can we do it again?'

Daniel had chosen Luke very carefully. He was sixteen but looked younger. He was smart and not a virgin, and was sleeping with his girlfriend.

Amanda addressed the issue coolly and carefully.

'I'm afraid that's going to strike the audience as a cop-out. And it could get a bad laugh. Or did you mean it to be a joke?'

'Well, yes, we kind of skirted it, made it funny.'

'I think we have to play it out, not evade it. Let me improvise something with Luke.' 'Go ahead.'

'So we're in bed and he's turned away, like you said. I say, "Right now you hate your father." And Luke says, "I want to kill him", and I say, "I want to kill him too", and Luke says, "I hate what he tried to do to you", and I say something like "There's another way to take revenge: you can have what he wanted. He'd like to be in your place in my bed." Then I start to kiss him and stroke him.'

Luke was mesmerised by her.

'I think that's great,' he said.

'Then I guess he should come before they get anywhere,' she said.

Luke laughed, embarrassed.

'He might. I wouldn't.'

'And then what?' said Daniel, alert.

'I'd cuddle him and say, "We'll just talk for a while, and in an hour or so you'll get hard again and we'll keep going." And that's where you can fade out and up again and find them fucking. He's pumping fast, like he's masturbating, and his eyes are squeezed shut, and she's smiling at him, and when he comes, his eyes pop open, and he stops dead.'

Luke and Daniel fell into a fit of schoolboy giggles.

'Amanda, that's wonderful,' said Daniel, embracing her.

Bella came in unannounced, brandishing a mobile phone, and was startled to see Daniel in Amanda's arms.

'Sorry. It's Jack. You have to take it.'

He put it to his ear.

'It's done,' said Jack. 'We're back in business.'

On Friday Daniel brought the whole cast back in and gave them the revised dialogue, including the new scene with Luke and Heather, which he and Brad had worked on overnight. At 5 o'clock the crew joined them for champagne. After the tension of rehearsals and the near-collapse of the picture, there was an air of euphoria and a sense of closeness and affection. Jack clinked a glass and made a little speech.

'I want to thank you all for hanging in there. We had a nasty little blip, but we're all set and ready to go. This is going to be one hell of a movie, and I for one am proud to be part of it. I wish you all lots of luck, and broken legs and all of that.'

They cheered him, and the beefy Ned lifted Jack in the air and ran around the room with him, and they cheered again. They called on Daniel to speak. He stood up and held up a paperback book, Christopher Isherwood's *Prater Violet*.

'This is the best book ever written about making a movie – until Bella's comes out.' Laughter. 'I want to read you a short passage from it. "A film is an infernal machine; once it is ignited and set in motion, it cannot pause. It cannot apologise. It cannot explain itself. It simply ripens to its inevitable explosion."

'We've done all we can, prepared ourselves, and now it's time to set *Crime of Passion* in motion. Let's hang on to it and hope it takes us to great places.'

Cheers and foot-stamping. Ned, exuberant and drunk, having put Jack down, was now in a spontaneous scrum with two grips and an electrician. He extracted himself and called out, 'Hey, Dan, am I the only guy in the room who doesn't have a fucking clue what this picture is about?'

The grips who hadn't read it egged him on.

'What is it about, this picture?' said Daniel. 'Well, you know the story, but at the heart of it is the two extremes of sex. On the one hand, making love, which can be tender and transcendent, one of the highest gifts life has to offer.' Ironic cheers from the crew. 'And its opposite, rape, which is about hatred and war and destruction.'

The exuberant party fell into an awkward silence.

'Oh God,' said Hope, 'he is so fucking naive sometimes. They don't want to hear that stuff now.'

Daniel attempted to rouse them.

'So have a great time tonight, because on Monday we go into battle.'

On his way out, Daniel thanked Jack for making it work.

'Well, we made it,' said Jack, 'just the way we wanted. We'll be shooting when *Shadow of a Smile* opens next week. We're home free.'

Daniel worked all weekend with his designer and cameraman, and spent Sunday evening on his shot-list for the coming week. This was the most intense, creative part of his process. He visualised the scenes he was to shoot, projecting them on to the wall of his study. He shuffled the actors and the camera until the scene flowed the way he wished. This required an act of sustained imagination. He then wrote down a description of the shots, with thumbnail sketches alongside. Several hours later he had the shots for the week's work in his head. It was past midnight. He fell asleep immediately and woke an hour later from another familiar anxiety dream. He was on the set with the actors, but there was no crew. He raged and ranted and then tried to placate the actors, who were turning against him. Suddenly the crew were present and they started to shoot, but the camera was locked: it wouldn't follow the action. He tried to wrench it free, but to no avail. The camera operator shrugged and drank his tea. The actors were huddled with the financiers. They glanced at him from time to time. 'He doesn't know what he's doing,' said one. Then another, 'He's lost it.'

He lay awake, running over all that he had done and had to do, with the nagging feeling that he had forgotten something vitally important, but it would not come to mind.

Faintly and far away, the alarm rang calling him from a blessed oblivion. There seemed to be a choice. He could sink deeper still into a place from which there was no return, or crawl and drag himself back to life. He saw an establishing shot of his children and Hope and Jack and Bella at his graveside, then a close-up of each of them. Hope's hand was sprinkling earth on his coffin. A crane shot pulled up and away from the grave and a caption superimposed 'THE END',

221

and then a fade to the blackest of blacks. Panic helped to haul him back to the living. He felt ashamed to be dreaming in cinematic cliches.

Jack, exhausted from rescuing the picture, also fell into a deep sleep, the dreamless sleep of the righteous. At six, Bella woke him, her body pressed against him, clinging to him and whimpering from her confused dream, in which Jack was slipping away from her. He opened his eyes and kissed her, saw that she was half asleep but recognised the signs and sounds of her need.

'Are you ovulating?'

He ran his hand down to her vulva and found it wet. He climbed over her and gently allowed himself in.

'Don't ever leave me, Jack,' she murmured.

FIFTEEN

The first location was a stretch of the River Wey, a tributary of the Thames, standing in for Wiltshire in order to reduce the number of days they needed to be away on location, with all the attendant costs. It was ten minutes away from Shepperton Studios.

The extras, playing hotel guests, were being costumed. Heather and Lionel were in makeup; the crew were eating breakfast on trestle tables in the catering tent. Daniel greeted them all in turn, wished them luck, and smiled and kissed and shook hands, and gave a convincing impression of someone who was relaxed and confident.

In the larger world, there was imminent famine in the sub-Sahara: a deadly infectious disease was sweeping through Africa. Wars, genocide, pestilence. Vast acres of ice had broken away from the Arctic, and, ironically, as sea levels rose, drinking water was running out. We were overfed, undernourished, and each one of us a time bomb of toxic chemicals. And none were more concerned, none more responsive to the pleading letters from charities, than Daniel, Hope, Jack and Bella. But these concerns now felt shamefully remote when matched against the immediate artificial problems they had created for themselves. They were on compassionate leave, on holiday from guilt, and Daniel felt a surge of pure energy. The siren call of death was muted, and the cruel randomness of the universe replaced by the logic of film, the harmony of invented constructs, which, with a massive effort, he could have under his almost complete control.

They had hoped for sun, but in its absence Philippe had 'brutes' mounted on cranes punching light through the trees, dappling the light on the actors. Daniel and Philippe agreed on a lens, worked on moves with the actors' stand-ins, instructed the camera assistants to put down tape-marks for the actors' positions: red for Heather, blue for Lionel. It was the scene where Lionel lustfully watches Heather at work in the woods close to the pool where she will eventually watch his dead body being submerged. Tommy Gormley, the assistant director, brought on the extras. He had been working with them while Daniel was in rehearsal, and quickly had them in place. Daniel made some adjustments and then called for the actors.

Harry Fowler, playing Lionel, bridled when he found his moves had already been defined by Daniel, but was secretly relieved that he didn't have to make choices and could concentrate on subduing his fears. He had just thrown up his breakfast. Amanda was glad to be doing something physical. She followed her marks without complaint and was a dazzling sight. After several abortive takes due to a camera fault, a sound problem and extras missing their cues, they finally got a good one.

'Print,' said Daniel. 'Now we'll do one more. Let's try something different.'

He threw new lines at them and changed their moves. They loosened up. The new take had a spontaneity, a semblance of life.

Jack and Bella arrived at lunchtime, Jack anxious not to crowd Daniel on the first day. While Daniel was eating, Jack reviewed the morning's work on the video-assist, which recorded the scenes direct from the camera. He caught Daniel in a bear-hug.

'Brilliant, Daniel, staggering. She is magnificent.'

He more or less meant it, with some reservations, but would have said it even if he had been disappointed, it being the first day, and encouragement being required. It has often been said that the first week's work should always be re-shot once the nerves and neuroses have settled down. The director has to push hard in these early days, imposing tone and style. If a film is going to work, the actors and crew need to understand where the director is going. They start to hear the tune; soon they are whistling it, and finally can sing it themselves with the right words. They become a collective force that drives the process, and finally the director finds himself no longer pushing it up hill, but drawn along in the wake of the infernal machine, the runaway train.

As they approached the end of the first week in fairly good shape, Daniel's main concern was Ned's performance, as the police detective. His physical vanity worked for the role but it was perhaps beyond his powers to be obsessed with Heather – with anyone other than himself. He liked women all right, and loved their admiration. His agent was a woman, as was his assistant. His second, pretty but vapid, wife was tired of flattering him and consequently he was becoming bored with her. His saving grace was that he could make fun of himself and his vanity.

'I don't understand actors who won't sign autographs. I love signing my name. If there's a line of fans, after ten minutes I go into a trance. It's better than getting high.'

He was wary of Amanda. He appreciated her at a distance and would josh with the crew about her and make lewd jokes and threaten to 'give you one for real' in the sex scenes, but when he was acting with her he was withdrawn, avoiding her eye. He liked soft, submissive women. Amanda was threatening, and he found that unattractive.

Daniel posed the problem with Amanda.

'He doesn't like women; he only likes girls,' she said.

'Then be a girl for him,' said Daniel.

'Am I playing too tough?'

'No, but I think we need to see her weakness early on. Maybe we need a new scene. You are doing wonderful stuff.'

'I'm scared shitless,' she said, utterly surprising Daniel. 'You think I can handle it, so you spend all your time with the others. Well, I can't. I need help, especially now. I'm getting my period, and I don't trust my emotions.'

Daniel felt contrite and awkward for taking her for granted.

'You've been so dead-on, I felt I didn't need to work on you that much.'

'You should. I can do better than this. I've got a co-star who doesn't fancy me and a director who ignores me.'

He gave her a hug, and she clung to him and shed a tear.

Friday marked not only the end of their first week of shooting but the opening of *Shadow of a Smile* in America. As expected, it got mixed reviews but opened strongly on its meagre ten prints. Alison's performance was praised and the plastic tear was not mentioned. Jack flew out to LA to drum up interest and try to persuade the studio to spend more on ads and widen the release. Daniel gave several phone interviews but was relieved not to have to do the usual tour of American cities with a picture that was meeting resistance – something which always made the interviews hard work.

Daniel reviewed the week's rushes in the cutting-room with his editor, Ron Davis. They cut the Ned and Amanda scenes together and put them up in the screening room.

'Can you believe he's obsessed with her, Ron? He won't look at her.'

'That can work for us. She dazzles him. He has to look away.'

Daniel was not persuaded. His doubts about Ned began to haunt him. He wanted to talk to Jack, but what could be done about it short of recasting, paying Ned off and reshooting the first week with money they did not have? He could not ask Jack to jump through yet another hoop. He called May, the casting agent, at home.

'May, I don't think I can get a performance out of Ned. Not the one I need.'

'Danny, it's first-week nerves. You can beat it out of him.'

'Would you call around discreetly to see if any of the actors on our wish-list have come free?'

'They all know I'm casting for you. They'll cop on.'

'Tell them a Hollywood picture is enquiring.'

Hope invited Bella and Orson for Sunday lunch and afterwards, when Daniel went up to work on his shot-list, the two women strolled down the Kings Road together while Sophie took care of the three kids. As they passed the Chelsea Cinema they saw that they were just in time for the early performance of *Eternal Sunshine of the Spotless Mind*. They dashed in and joined the sparse audience. This most beautiful of cinemas was seldom full.

They drank coffee at Starbucks afterwards. Bella took a decaf low-fat cappuccino, Hope a double espresso with a dollop of cream on top. Starbucks appealed to Bella's residual patriotism: she felt it made up for McDonalds.

'I wish I could do what they did,' said Hope. 'Erase all the bad stuff that's piled up, and fall in love with Daniel again. What a great idea: a machine that can wipe out a relationship so you can start over. Sad, isn't it, that we can only fall in love with people we don't know.'

'Is it an immutable law?' Bella asked.

'Yes. We need a bit of mystery to get it on.'

'It's probably an evolutionary thing to prevent in-breeding, widen the gene pool.'

'I miss falling in love,' said Hope.

227

'Weren't you in love with Paul?'

'I was the first time round. The second innings was lust.'

'Love and lust. Can you always tell them apart?'

'It's so great at the beginning of a love affair,' Hope mused. 'All trust and truth, then a few white lies creep in. You say nothing when you should speak out, and a gap opens up. Passion only lasts two years. You fall into a routine. The oneness becomes a two-ness, then parallel lives, which leads to misunderstandings, then you bicker. He starts to irritate you. You don't talk any more. You can read him like a book, but it's not a book you want to read. You start to have a secret life, you dream of other lovers, or, like me, you hark back to an old lover, and because you have kids, the only way you can get it is by lying and cheating, and in real life there is no machine to wipe your sins clean.'

'That is so sad.'

'You telling me you don't recognise any of that?'

'It was different with Jack. We didn't fall madly in love. We were both so surprised that we got on so well and that we wanted each other. We knew it was fragile and we have always been very careful to protect it. We both thought it couldn't last and we are so grateful that it has.'

'I've seen how men come on to you. You must have had offers. Were you never tempted?'

'No,' she said, a little too emphatically.

'Have you ever thought about Daniel like that? You're with him all the time,' said Hope, whose jealousy was territorial rather than sexual.

'It's so abstract, our relationship. The closer I get to him, to his work and his mind, the further away I feel – I mean, physically. It's curious,' she lied, because ever since that kiss in the taxi, her heart jumped whenever she saw him, and she felt an ache for him when he was absent. She was sure it must be evident to others. Hope examined her closely, but apparently she passed the test, because Hope smiled and relaxed.

'Yeah, I know what you mean. His drive goes into his work. He's a good lover, not a great lover. He can't let go, always watching. I always felt he was fucking me through a viewfinder.' Two grown women in a fit of giggles over their coffee cups.

Daniel was alone with his shot-list in his top-floor office. He stared despondently at the pile of scripts on his desk. They were from his students and members of his crew, pressed upon him even when he warned them he would not read them for months. It was some time before he could compose himself to achieve the necessary concentration to make the shot-list. Suppressed doubts seeped out of the walls and rose from the floorboards, filling the empty room. He went to the window and envied the people strolling carelessly down the Kings Road. An urge gripped him to leave the house and walk west to World's End and beyond, and never return – to disappear from the earth. He shuddered as the feeling passed, and he sat down at his desk and began his mental projections.

He had almost finished his shot-list when the door opened an inch, and he saw Emma's teary eye peering in. Because this was the one process that required absolute solitude, the children were enjoined not to disturb him except in a dire emergency.

'What does that mean?' Andrew had asked.

'If the house is on fire,' Hope had answered.

'Dad, it's an emergency,' said Emma.

She was sobbing. Daniel jumped up, alarmed, aware that Hope was out of the house.

'What is it?'

She was desolate.

'I can't find my teddy.'

He picked her up and held her tight. His irritation dissolved in her tears. It *was* an emergency for her. After all, he reflected, didn't he get upset about *his* make-believe world.

'We'll search the whole house,' he said. 'You know how the woolly animals come alive at night and run all over the place having fun? Maybe you woke up early, and he didn't get back in time.'

'It's a she, not a he,' she rebuked him.

Downstairs he recognised the smirk on Andrew's face, and a half-nelson and a bout of third-degree tickling elicited a confession as to where the teddy was hidden.

Jack called from LA. Saturday's business had held up well and the studio had agreed to a further fifty prints next week, but so far were resisting spending any more money on ads.

Daniel viewed the scene on his laptop between Ned and Amanda, which was to establish that she was tiring of the detective's obsession with her. This was early on, before the murder.

'I need to reshoot it,' he told Jack on the phone. 'I'm worried about Ned. He's not intense enough, and consequently she just looks bored.'

'You should consider rewriting it, Daniel. It's under-dramatised,' said Jack.

Daniel pondered this.

'You may be right, Jack. Instead of a post-coital bed scene, maybe after they have made love he goes through her things while she's in the bathroom. He reads her diary, touches her underwear, and she catches him at it.'

'Good, and that's something a detective would do,' said Jack.

Daniel still lacked the courage to mention recasting to Jack. There was no point in worrying him unless a candidate emerged.

On Monday evening, May called. Since he was still shooting, she spoke in code.

'Been through the shopping list, Dan. No oranges, no mangos, none of the fruit you like. You'll have to make do with that banana.'

Next morning, when Ned arrived on the set, he stood very close to Daniel and glared. He was shaking with rage.

'Are you trying to recast me, you shit?'

There were no secrets in this business. Rumour was rife. Malicious gossip was the currency. Daniel did his best to simulate indignation.

'Where did that ridiculous notion come from?'

'Everyone's talking about it.'

Daniel was floundering. Denying it made him seem weak.

'Well, Ned, you've given me an idea. If you can't show you're obsessed with Heather, maybe that's what I should do. Recast you.'

Ned's fist clenched and Daniel flinched, waited for the punch. A girl from craft services put an espresso in Ned's hand and a kiss on his cheek. He turned on his heel and strode to the makeup trailer.

Daniel hesitated, then followed him in and told the makeup people to leave. He stood behind Ned, who was in the chair confronting his mirror image.

'I have to be brutal, Ned, for the sake of the picture. You have to find a way to look at Amanda that shows sexual obsession. You have to feast on her, and when she catches you looking at her like that, you look away, hide the lust in that look, convert it into a smile. I have seen you looking at yourself in that mirror there with an expression of self-love that would do just fine.'

Ned leapt up and, with a roar, threw the punch that had been lying in wait for Daniel. Daniel swayed back, and the fist only grazed his jaw. He grabbed Ned and pinned his arms down. There was a knock on the door and Hazel, the makeup artist, consumed with curiosity, could no longer resist entering. Daniel converted his grip into a hug and patted Ned's back.

'Smile, Ned. I love you.'

Hazel looked perplexed at the two men clutched in an awkward embrace. Daniel led the bemused actor out of the trailer, and they crossed the floor of the stage with Daniel laughing and hugging Ned.

'You love me, Daniel? You really love me?'

'I really really love you, Ned.'

Bella's Notebook

*We have been shooting nights all week. The weather has been kind, soft and warm, but with a chill coming in with the dew just before dawn. The drivers doze in their trucks or hang about the craft services, where a constant flow of coffee, soup and sandwiches comfort us **for** being up all night. There is a muted air of intimacy. As the world sleeps, we huddle together. Secrets are exchanged. I see hints of location romances. There is a feeling that whatever happens here doesn't count in the outer world. We are charmed, immune. We live inside an artificial construct in a magical place. The woes of the world do not intrude. Our lives are on hold. Love and affection abound and fill the spaces between us. Philippe's electricians are carrying the weightless lights inside helium balloons, great globes that float and drift above the trees and further seduce us into enchantment.*

Ned has undergone some kind of transformation. He seems much more fixated on Amanda. Is he falling for her? When Daniel offers him directions, there is no sign of the old arrogance; in fact, he is almost docile. He often consults a hand mirror before shots where he is required to express his obsession with Heather. The actor's process is mysterious.

Bella and Daniel were sitting side by side looking at the last scene on the video-assist. Daniel had set up the next shot and Philippe needed half an hour to light it. It was three o'clock in the morning.

'I feel I'm in Philip Pullman's *Dark Materials* – a parallel world just like ours but subtly different,' he said, looking up at the helium globes. 'Look, we have four moons in this universe.'

They watched in silence as the soft light fell upon them.

'In this other world, the unsaid can be spoken, but only once, then it's forgotten.' He paused, and she found she was holding her breath as though time had stopped.

'It can never be,' he said softly, 'but perhaps in a parallel world, in another life, it could have been . . . .'

They fell silent again.

'I would never hurt Jack,' she said.

'Nor would I.'

Philippe came up to say they were ready and, ever sensitive, knew he was breaking a spell.

They had shot the scene in the dark pool. Amanda had bravely spent hours up to her neck as the body was lowered past her, and Harry Fowler, playing Lionel, was braver still, being lowered into the pool, holding his breath, and keeping his eyes open. The detective and his accomplice take her clothes, and she finds herself naked in the woods. Her pale figure running away from camera through the trees was extraordinary. It expressed her vitality and fragility. She was somehow reborn, released from both Lionel and the detective. She finds the cottage in the woods. Daniel had planned that she would cover herself with twigs and leaves, but once he had given her the notion of rebirth, she wanted to remain naked. Philippe placed his helium lights high over the trees to get the effect of soft, dappled moonlight. She jogs through the patterns of light and shadow so that she is never wholly revealed. She stops and the old woman sees her in the faint light like a wood nymph emerging from the forest. The woman beckons her in. Heather explains that her clothes were taken, but does not tell of the murder. She confides that her lover has committed a terrible crime and asks whether she should tell the police. The old woman says, 'It depends on how much you love him.'

Jack and Brad both believed that the scene that followed would be too slow in the context of a thriller, but Daniel claimed that the audience would be so concerned about Heather's vulnerability that they would allow it. Vanessa held the crew in thrall as she spoke her monologue.

'You're not the first spirit to come out of those woods . . . . One summer afternoon he knocked, asking for water . . . . He was an artist, silent but aware, gentle . . . . He came each afternoon for a week and we made love and he took me on a journey on wings to such fearful heights that I wanted to die in his arms, but I was reborn instead, as you are now . . . . He left and I never saw him again, but I think of him every day and he visits me in my dreams . . . . And my dear, good husband . . . I never told him . . . but when he was dying, he said, "I knew. I made room for him, and I didn't lose you." He made room for him in his heart . . . it was such a beautiful thing to say.'

'Cut. Print. Wonderful. Vanessa, you've got some hairy-arsed grips in tears.'

'Story of my life, darling,' she purred back.

Yet in some technical part of his brain, he worked out how the monologue could be cut if it needed to be, the imperatives of narrative being what they are, eating away at anything that does not advance the plot. Bella touched Daniel's hand. She was deeply moved, and marvelled at the prophetic reach of the imagination. Daniel had written the scene as a romanticised version of his mother's confession, yet it spoke to their relationship, and she wondered if room could be made in Jack's big, generous heart for them. She smothered the thought, banished it.

Daniel told his dream to Amanda. He was a child, acting in a film. The camera was behind him, tracking with him as he moved forward towards a closed door. He reached out his hand to open it, but was seized with fear, and stopped. The director urged him to do it, but he could not. The child turned and looked back at the crew and camera. The adult Daniel was the director. He was angry. The boy tried again. This time he turned the doorknob and, with a terrible anguish, he cried out.

'Then I wake up.'

'What was in the room?' Amanda asked.

'I don't know.'

He had confided the dream to her because she was having disturbing dreams herself.

'This film is pulling me apart,' she said. 'I'm so exposed. I feel defenceless. You're using me up.'

He tried to appraise her condition.

'It's what you want: dangerous places, going as far as you can.'

They were walking to the set together from her trailer. She needed his undivided attention. She was as attention-seeking as a cruise missile, he realised. She claimed that her father had ignored her so she had seduced him, but Daniel hardly believed her. He was distracted at the time and he suspected it was her way of regaining his interest. Her beauty and personality ensured that she was showered with adoration, but it was a drug she could never get enough of. Beyond her openness and honesty there was a level of fantasy, he realised.

'This scene's bothering me.'

'About exposing your breasts?'

'Not that. What am I doing while he's looking at them? I have no role in this scene. I'm going to be upstaged by my own tits.'

'She's thinking of him, not herself. It is a gift, an act of compassion. Look at what his face is saying. Do nothing. Be still. Don't move. Don't blink. Don't think.'

She was nervous, unconvinced.

In keeping with the style of the film, this scene started with the old man looking at her exposed breasts.

'The audience will assume that he has asked her to see them, or she has offered out of compassion or pity,' Daniel explained.

They were sitting opposite each other, a coffee table between them.

'How should I sit?' asked the old man. 'If I lean forward it will seem too eager, but when I lean back it feels as though I'm not interested.'

'Change the chair,' said Daniel. 'Give him an upright one.'

One was quickly brought. The old man tested it, fidgeted. Daniel understood that actors project their anxieties on to props, furniture, anything they can blame.

'Sit to attention, sit upright,' said Daniel.

They rehearsed the scene as scripted. He tells her that he has been celibate for ten years, since his wife died, and that celibacy eventually became impotence. She responds, saying, 'I used to model for an artist and he said that one breast is always higher than the other.'

Words on a page are an inexact guide to moviemaking. When he saw it played out, Daniel knew instantly what was needed. He stopped the rehearsal.

'Cut the dialogue. All of it. You look at her breasts. She looks at you. Silence. Then you just say, "Thank you". And she covers them up.'

'I need those lines,' said Amanda rebelliously.

'No you don't,' said Daniel firmly. 'The two faces do it. The compassion, the beautiful curve of the breasts, the unsucked pink areole, the hint of a lattice of blue milk veins. His teardrop. Her serenity. His gratitude. And finally, her pity for his age.'

When it was done, Amanda left without a word, but threw Daniel a withering look. Paddy, the script supervisor, whose honed skills of observation extended to the emotional temperature, urged him to go after her. He decided to let her stew. The next day, he had a strategy for repairing the rift.

Daniel was against actors watching rushes. It made them self-conscious about the way they looked. But the next morning he edited the scene together quickly and took Amanda into the theatre and showed it to her. He explained how Philippe's lighting made the breast into a sculptural object, and how the old man's emotions spilled into her face. 'I get it,' she said simply.

'You see, you didn't have to do it all by yourself. The lighting is taking care of you. That lens I used is my own. It has a beautiful quality, soft and caressing. I only use it for your close-ups. The camera is on your side. It loves you; we all do. Sometimes you have to let us do it for you.'

They sat side by side, alone in the dark theatre.

'I don't care how I look. You must know that from my last picture. And I don't need your flattery, I need you.'

He took her by the shoulders and looked into her face.

'You need me to be objective. That's what you need from me.'

She looked at him with contempt.

'You know what's in that dream room that scares the shit out of you? Me. Women. That's why you like directing them. That way you finally control them. You can hide behind the camera.'

It hit him with the terrible force of truth. He had a flash, a waking vision of that terrifying door and that child, the father of the man, opening it, and what he saw inside the room wasn't Amanda or Hope, it was his mother. His father was vigorously fucking her, and she was crying out with what seemed to the boy to be pain, but which the adult Daniel recognised as pleasure.

His knees buckled and he fell back in his chair, the blood draining from his face. He was ashen. He felt he was going to vomit. It came back to him in a rush. He was five. He woke in the night, from a bad dream, wanted his mother, opened her door. Even though he had suppressed the memory, from that moment he had hated and feared his father, and saw his own role as the protector of his mother. He had fallen for women who had been treated badly by men but often found that they did not want his gentle consolations, but rather another man more forceful and masterful than the last. He had met Hope when she was a wreck from her New York lover, but she was too earthy and resilient to allow him to treat her like a sexual invalid, and bounced him into honest, exuberant fucking, which liberated him from his inhibitions – except for his pathological horror of rape and its simulation in the cinema.

Amanda knelt and took his hand.

'I'm so sorry, Daniel. It's not true. I was just being spiteful. Forgive me.'

The nausea passed and he felt the rush of euphoria that often comes after a fainting episode.

'Daniel, are you better? Please be better.'

He smiled at her. Took her hand.

'I don't think I've ever felt better in my life.'

They moved to the Wiltshire location. They took over the country-house hotel, filling all the rooms and reserving the exteriors and the lobby for shooting. The picture had settled down; the crew and the cast were close and harmonious. They were a tribe. They huddled and cuddled and shared their beds. In the bar, Ned told the story of an actor taking his wedding vows. When he was called upon to forsake all others, he said, 'Except on location'. As with primal tribes, the ultimate, unendurable sanction was banishment. A special-effects man, paranoid on cocaine, had been fired, and a stand-in, who was twice late, was sent on his way. They were both devastated. The rest were focused on a common purpose. The song was a good one, and they were hitting all the notes.

Daniel drew sustenance and inspiration from the landscape. It was an older, deeper England, unscarred by the Industrial Revolution, scarcely touched by Christianity; Avebury and Stonehenge pronounced a pagan knowledge long since lost, but recoverable, Daniel believed, by an act of imagination. His malaise had lifted and he was a furnace of energy. It was in this enviable condition that he got back to the hotel at the end of the week's shooting. Jack was driving Hope down for the weekend. They were all to have dinner together. Daniel went upstairs and, driven by an impulse, knocked on a door. Bella opened it. She had been in the shower and was wearing a robe. Her riotous curls were tamed and straightened by water, her face no longer hidden by them, but naked. He kissed her mouth, the robe fell open, and he held her against him. The power generated by the film, and pent-up passion, drove him into her. She came almost immediately with a guttural moan that welled up from a place she had never been, and he burst with his own cry, the cry of a falling man.

They lay wordless, still as death. He was half-hard. He moved slowly inside her and got harder. As long as they banished words, they were shameless and weightless, and drifted out into the night and over the Salisbury Plain, and Avebury's stunted stones rose up to what they once were, with lintel bars crowning them and sacrificial blood staining them, and their ancestors reached up to them, all the generations, struggling, suffering, their pain and scant pleasures, all reaching forward towards this point of epiphany between this man and this woman, as though it was the only purpose of their brief lives.

Joined. Moving. Prolonging. The second coming suffused and lodged into their bones, every cell proclaiming fulfilment. And at last it was over, and words came back, punitive words, words of shame, regret, confusion, but they pushed them aside, for other words were required and demanded, and they exchanged them. I love you. I love you.

They lay still, stealing a few more moments in that other parallel universe, where they were unencumbered.

'I will tell Jack,' she said finally. 'I must.'

He said nothing. She considered. Must something so beautiful be paid for in the coin of shame?

'We promised we would never lie, and we never have.'

He said nothing.

'I'll tell him it was an impulse. It happened once and never again, which it must not. Perhaps he'll forgive me.'

'Will he forgive me?'

'I don't know.'

'Then at least wait until the end of the shoot.'

She knew that if she lived with the lie for four weeks, telling Jack would be so much harder.

'Yes,' she heard herself saying.

She took a long hot shower, and dried herself, but his smell lingered, and her own odour kept rising up, surely, she feared, announcing it to the world. She looked in the mirror and was shocked by the drawn and radiant face that shot back at her, hardly recognisable. She looked at the bed's freeze-frame turmoil. How could she sleep in it with Jack? She called reception and asked to change rooms.

To Bella's relief, Amanda joined them for dinner, disrupting the ley-lines that connected the two couples that would have allowed them to divine the unspoken. Amanda was tired and brittle. Hope smelt something but could not pin it down. Jack was oblivious, delighted to be back in the magic circle. Bella did not trust herself to speak. Daniel was boisterous, regaling Jack with the week's blunders and trivialities, very self-mocking and funny. He was determined to prevent anyone else from speaking, in case they led the conversation to a place that would unravel him. He bludgeoned his way through the dinner.

'Well, you certainly found a second wind,' said Hope, as they lay in bed together. Now they were isolated from other influences, she was certain she could detect an erotic haze around him, and she found it arousing. If he was screwing Amanda, as she suspected, she preferred not to know about it. There were no territorial issues, since it was happening here, and if she challenged him, it would raise the old issues of her infidelities, and the Brad thing was hanging over her. Nevertheless she wanted Daniel to know that she knew.

'That Amanda, she's so gorgeous. What man could resist her?'

'Me . . . . I,' he corrected himself, in a tone that convinced her that it must be Bella, the only other candidate. Well, I never.

'You've moved rooms,' said Jack.

She had prepared excuses – the plumbing was noisy, the TV in the next room was always playing too loud – but little lies seemed worse than the big one, because of their meanness, and she could not make herself say them.

'Yes.'

Jack was content with that. She wanted to blurt it all out and tell him that this wonderful thing had happened to her, how she had been on a great journey with Daniel and that he had broken her open, and she had found out who she truly was, and would Jack please be happy for her, not threatened, because she would now know how to love him more than ever. She held him tenderly in the new, fresh bed, and he made the familiar tentative advances. She wanted to respond but she could not, not yet, but she was filled with love for him and told him so, and lay awake long after he had gone to sleep and rewound the episode and played it back in slow motion, and as she relived each moment, the euphoria returned and washed through her. Her armour had been penetrated, shattered. She felt remade, another person, set free, yet afraid of who she now was, where it would lead. She had lost herself, lost control; it was terrifying and exhilarating. She was helpless to resist wheresoever it would take her. She felt a wave of nostalgia for that distant, peaceful place with Jack, of gentle, loving ease. Her life till now was like a movie she had watched and mildly enjoyed, but now it was fading and receding and she could hardly remember the plot.

She slipped out of bed and sat with her notebook and tried to find the words that would capture the experience, but those that offered themselves diminished or distorted it. She was in an unknown land where language and experience would not serve her. She allowed her naked skin to get cold, to take the heat out of her flesh. It was like being pregnant: her body had taken her over and she could not subdue it. She shivered as her skin goose-pimpled but the fire within burnt on and warmed the . . . the what? A cliché offered itself and made her smile: the cockles of her heart. Her cockles were roasting. She crept back into bed and coiled herself around Jack's large and comfortable middle.

Jack had to go back to London on the Monday to attend to a play he had in rehearsal. Bella decided to go with him. She was longing for Orson, who was staying in Hope's house under the care of Sophie.

Daniel made several attempts to speak with her but she evaded him. She drove back with Jack in a comfortable silence. She felt safer as the distance between her and Daniel widened. Finally, she felt secure enough to ask Jack about the play.

'It's a revival of Tom Stoppard's *The Real Thing*,' he said.

She put her hand on his and held on tight.

'I've been so ridiculously immersed in this movie that I haven't even asked you about it,' she said with a sigh of apology.

'And I haven't talked about it for the same reason. Your complete immersion.'

'I loved the play,' she said. 'Stoppard finally came out from behind his mask of philosophical wit and wrote about the pain of love.'

'There's not much love in this production,' Jack chuckled. 'The leading couple are mad at each other and the director wants to quit.'

'How awful for you. Why are you laughing?'

'Because a big problem like this takes my mind off the many niggling little problems of the movie. It's therapy.'

'Darling Jack, is it healthy that you are only truly happy in a crisis?'

'I am only truly happy when I have you back from Daniel,' he said.

She started to tremble. He knew. She had an overpowering urge to blurt it out. The words churned in her stomach and she wanted to vomit them out. At the last moment she managed to sublimate it.

'I remember the woman has that great speech where she admits to an adultery, how this man got under the radar, was it, or under her defences.'

'It was Felicity Kendal in the original production. Wonderful,' said Jack, smiling.

Hope had sent the first part of her manuscript, already a fat sixty-five thousand words, to Betty Latimer, who invited her to lunch at the Ivy. Bella got there first and waited at the table. Betty swept in and swamped the room with her aura of glamour. Men rose to greet her and waiters were sucked into her orbit, so that she arrived with an escort ready to die for her. She was Zulika Dobson.

'Stunning,' she said of the manuscript.

In Betty's excessive lexicon this was simply a polite greeting, but from the tone Bella sensed reservations.

'So what's wrong with it?'

'Nothing. It's beautifully written, and the central theme – sex in the cinema – is fascinating, but I was dying to know more about the sex lives of your characters. I mean, what's going on between Daniel and Amanda? And that wife. Hope, is it? And the writer, Brad. What a womaniser. I love the Hollywood stuff – what monstrous people. I think you should do a piece, maybe up front, about sex in the cinema, put it into context how directors have shown it or found metaphors for it, that kind of thing.'

Two glasses of champagne arrived. The waiter indicated a nearby table, where one of Betty's admirers raised his glass up to his wishful, smiling face.

They ordered gravadlax and green salads – a staple of ladies who lunch at the Ivy.

'So how will it end?' asked Betty.

'Depends what happens.'

Betty engaged Bella's eyes and watched her closely as she delivered her core comment.

'Well, it's lovely to watch your scepticism gradually give way to admiration and then to see you, little by little, falling in love.'

Was it that obvious? Bella shuddered.

'Well, you have to fall in love with your subject, don't you?' said Bella, attempting to laugh it off, and finding herself using Daniel's words.

'Good for the book; dangerous for you,' Betty counselled.

Bella hurried back to her computer and scrolled through the manuscript, sharpening her comments about Daniel, covering her tracks; but conjuring him up made her long for him. When Jack got home, she ran into his arms – the only place she was safe.

In the days that followed, Daniel buried himself ever deeper in his work but could not drive Bella from his thoughts. He had scheduled the final rape and the killing of Jake for the very end of the shoot because he feared it so much, but the day inevitably arrived. Bella was no longer able to delay her return, and Jack drove her down to witness the last day of the shoot and celebrate at the wrap party.

On the eve of the scene, Daniel took Ned and Amanda to dinner. He told each of them one thing. To Ned: 'Although he loves her, in order to kill her, he must make himself hate her. We need to see that, see both.' To Amanda: 'You remember I wanted her to go limp when she's raped and only cry out when she experiences her orgasm. Would you try something different? Would you see if you can make cries of pain and anguish and fear that finally transform into the orgasm?'
He wanted the double effect of his dream, the terrifying confusion of pain and pleasure. They both had doubts about how to achieve it.
'Let's try it,' said Daniel, and took them up to his room and rehearsed on the carpet. They struggled with the technicalities of how to remove her shorts. They finally decided he should hold her face down with his hand pressing her neck into the earth and using his other hand to get the clothes off, hers and his own. 'If he fucks her from behind, he would only have to get her shorts down to her knees,' said Ned helpfully.
'But we need to see her face: she has to discover the old woman

approaching with the shotgun,' said Amanda.

'We can solve it with the camera,' said Daniel. 'Just pull the shorts out of the frame and turn her over. I'll cut to a close-up as her head turns.'

They experimented with positions and Daniel made sketches of them. They were all struck by the awkwardness of the sexual act and how physically difficult it was to rape someone, and they finally collapsed in hysterical laughter.

Daniel slept deeply and dreamlessly. He awoke thinking of something Germaine Greer had said about her own experience of rape: 'That it was better than a broken nose.' Sadly, women often got both. Daniel had searched the woods exhaustively for the perfect site for the rape. He believed that if he could find the ideal location, he would know how to shoot it. He settled on a stand of beeches, partly because the beech had a trunk suggestive of flesh, smooth and sensual. The day he found the spot was sunny and a dappled light lit the base of the trees. Tommy Gormley, his first assistant, took off his shirt and lay face down in a bed of leaves and beechnuts so that Daniel could see the effect of the light. A breeze was agitating the leaves and making the dappled light flicker. Daniel and Philippe examined the effect on Tommy's naked back, a kind of agitation. It was the visual metaphor Daniel needed, externalising the inner turmoil of the rape.

'What if there is no sun on the day?' Philippe asked.

'What can you do?'

Philippe gave his most Gallic shrug.

'What can I do? Put a brute on a cherry-picker as high as possible to punch the light through the leaves, but it won't be the same. I will pray for the sun.'

The forecast was for sun in the morning, clouding over later. Daniel called the actors early. If he could get the wide shots in sunlight, the closer shots could be achieved with artificial light. Philippe decided he needed two cranes, and his gaffer set about mounting lights on them. Daniel set up the camera for the establishing shot – the towering trees and the two small figures at the bottom of the frame lying in the milk chocolate brown bed of beech leaves.

'You enter camera left, pursuing her,' he instructed Ned, 'then pull her to the ground exactly on that spot and go through the whole action.'

The clouds were gathering and Philippe watched the sky anxiously. He fell to his knees and bowed to the east, to the sun, the god of light. The make-up girls were dabbing at the two actors' bodies. Daniel ran over and chased them off.

'Go away. No time. Save it for the closer shots.' Ned bridled at being rushed into the shot. 'Wait a moment, we haven't rehearsed it properly. This is a tough scene.'

'This shot is ant-acting,' said Daniel. 'We're losing the sun. We have to go for it.'

'Ant-acting' was a reference to the well-known story told by Lee Marvin. He was making *Delta Force*, directed by Menacham Golan. It was all kick, bollock and scramble, and the director was rushing them through a wide shot of several members of the cast getting on a plane. One of the actors complained of a lack of instruction. 'What are we doing? Are we in a hurry? Scared? Having fun? How do you want us to act?'

'Act like ants,' said Menacham, 'because that's what you look like from here - fucking ants!'

Philippe had his dark glass to his eye as the clouds approached the sun.

'Let's shoot. We have to go now!' he cried.

The camera turned. Bella and Jack watched, holding their breath. Daniel called 'action'. Regardless of what the actors fretted over, the imperative of 35mm film running through the gate at twenty-four frames per second catapulted them into the scene. At this distance, dialogue was not important, so Daniel hollered instructions to them throughout the shot, and they did his bidding. The anxieties, the nuances were swept away in the urgency of action. They managed one good take before clouds blocked out the sun. There was palpable relief; they were committed. Daniel sent the actors to makeup and put in the stand-ins. He called for the close-up lens and set up a shot of Amanda over Ned's shoulder.

'Dingle!' Philippe called. 'Bring me dingle.'

The grips quickly cut several branches of different sizes, which were mounted on C- stands, and Philippe set about adjusting their height and matching it to the elevation of the brute on the cherry-picker, so that the leaf shadows made hard shapes on the bodies. The stand-ins complained of the cold, and Philippe said he was sorry but that they would have to endure it. He brought the leaves closer, and lowered the brute, and soon its heat was happily warming them. An electric fan was set to agitate the leaves. Philippe had two of his sparks handholding Chinese lanterns on poles to add fill-light. The actors were sent for. Amanda laughed out loud when she saw the paraphernalia that surrounded the bed of leaves.

'All this just to get me raped.'

'You know what they say about moviemaking,' said Daniel. 'Ninety-five percent technique, 5 percent emotion.'

'Well, here comes my 5 percent,' she said as she lay down. A prop man put fresh leaves around her head to cover the ones that had got crushed and trampled. The makeup people moved in to freshen the scratches and spritz water vapour to simulate sweat. On the previous day they had shot the pursuit that led up to this point. Daniel had told Ned to think of a man stalking a stag. He admires its grace and beauty and feels a surge of love and pity for it because he knows he will kill it, but as he follows it and it continues to elude him, he begins to get angry, and as the day wears on, he finally comes to hate it and, when he kills it, he is consumed with bloodlust.

Amanda was panting and lacquered with sweat and slashed with dirt and scratches from the chase when he threw her to the ground and ground her face into the earth.

'Do we have to go through the whole rape? Can't you pan up to the trees or something?' said Ned, his nerve failing.

'We've been through all this, Ned. It has to be played out in real time, otherwise it's just titillation. Think of the power of the rape scene in *Irreversible*.'

'Look, come on, I'm ready,' said Amanda. 'Let's do it.'

'You made that great roar when you threw her down in the long shot. Start with that. To get you going. Action!'

Jake roared, she fought and struggled, and then the pistol was at her head and she froze. He entered her and she cried out and there were tears of anger and pain and she spat at him and her face twisted into a mesh of hatred and words came, searing abuse, and contempt. She was every woman who had ever been humiliated by a man. Then moans of despair, and over her shoulder she sees the old woman approaching and at that moment she makes an extraordinary transformation into an orgasmic state. Jake's face, watching her, changes too. He is filled with love and his face alters again as the old woman discharges her shotgun into his back.

There were eight other setups required to complete the scene, but the heart of it had been captured. Daniel and the actors were emotionally exhausted by the end of the day, but relieved that it was over, and happy that they had achieved something important. When the last shot of each day was done in any film, a cry would go up from the director, or more often from the first assistant director – 'That's a wrap' – thus the party to mark the end of the shoot was known as the wrap party. Daniel never let this go by without challenging the spelling. He claimed that it should be 'rap', the acronym for 'report and print' – which is what the early silent films were required to do at the end of each day – but 'wrap', 'wrap it up', was too convenient a metaphor, and easily overwhelmed its officious and prosaic origins.

Back at the hotel, Jack and Kevan Barker were preparing the party with the hotel manager, who proudly produced a cake in the shape of Stonehenge. Fred Schneider, who was doing business in London, picked up Brad and drove down to celebrate with them. Kieran Corrigan came over from Ireland. Hope took the train to Salisbury and was picked up by the transport captain. The crew and cast washed and scrubbed, the women reclaiming their femininity with heels and frocks, from anoraks and boots, the men shaven and shining. They gathered in bonds of affection to eat and drink and sentimentally reminisce. They had gone to war together and survived. Armistice was declared to rivalries and petty enmities. Jack and Daniel made speeches declaring this film to be the finest experience of their careers (as they said after every film, and so it honestly seemed at the time).

Bella had pulled her hair back with the bold air of a woman coming out of purdah. It revealed her long neck, and Daniel caught his breath at the distant sight of it. She wore the pale blue dress he had given her. Hope had got the hair and makeup people to do her up, putting herself in their hands and even abandoning her beloved lipstick for theirs. Her short, floral silk dress showed off her strong dancer's legs. She had the determined sexuality of a woman out to reclaim her man, or, failing that, to find another. Amanda made a dazzling late entrance, escorted by the long-absent painter boyfriend Rod. She looked so magnificent that the assembly broke into spontaneous applause. For the most part, she had played down her beauty, wearing no makeup and dressing in sloppy, casual clothes. Now she looked done up for the Oscars, and gave the party a zing of showbiz parody. She had become a woman who knew what to do and when to do it: a star. Daniel circulated amongst the crew, recalling contributions made by each of them, a vital suggestion or a moment of wit, and they all assured him that the picture would be a big hit. He found his way to Fred and hugged him close.

'What's happening?' said Daniel. 'I'm out of the loop, making this monster.'

Fred's eyes searched the far side of the room, where Stonehenge stood in all its icing-sugar glory. Daniel settled down to wait for the pause to wear off.

'They got him in the end.'

'Tannenbaum?'

Fred affirmed, with the slightest of nods, and then silence, a moment's respect for the dead. 'Problem is, he hung around long enough for me to be associated with his fuck-ups, including *Other Lives*.'

'That much I heard. Cancelled a week into shooting.'

'At least I did that. Take a bath now for the five you've spent, and save a hundred million down the line.'

'So now you're out of a job?'

'Hey, Daniel, you know Hollywood. You fail up, not down. I got a severance package of $30 million and a producer deal for five pictures. That kid who was directing *Other Lives*, you remember him from Cannes: Sydney Abel. They had to give him a break when they dumped his movie, so they passed him over to me. He scratched around at the agency for a script he could make, and he found that piece of crap by your lab guy.'

'Nigel?'

'Yeah. The kid's set it in New York instead of London and we start shooting next month. A horror flick. He's got Dracula and Frankenstein escaping from the film cans.'

They sighed at the endless waste and stupidity of their masters.

'At least it will get Nigel off my back,' said Daniel.

'Don't bet on it. He hates the rewrite, and blames you for taking his holy words to America and letting the barbarians loose on it.'

They hugged again and Daniel drifted over to Brad, who was weighing up the women. 'Picked one out yet?' Daniel asked.

'I learnt one thing in college in Italy,' Brad said. 'I used to get a train every day and I walked down the length of it looking for an attractive girl, and I would find one, but I would think, maybe there's a better-looking one further down, and more often than not I would find myself at the end of the train and I would have to jump on as it was moving and sit for the whole journey with a couple of grannies. Go for the first one that looks half-decent, is what I learnt from my university education.'

'You are remorseless, Brad.'

'Who's that squelchy blonde over there?'

'She's one of the caterers.'

'Half-pissed already, by the look of her.'

He walked over to her.

'Do you have a man?' he asked.

'Not here,' she answered coyly.

'You do now,' said Brad.

Kevan Barker had found a Brazilian band from somewhere and they struck up. Daniel asked Amanda to dance and they were the first couple to take the floor, accompanied by whistles and cheers.

'It was magnificent what you did today. Beyond acting. It was gut-wrenching, and in the end strangely beautiful. Thank you.'

'I feel used.'

'No you don't. You loved going the distance.'

'You took me further than I wanted to go.'

'I had to push you. You were holding back.'

'You raped me.'

'Paramount called asking about you. I sent them some of your scenes. It's for the lead in a big big movie.'

'You've changed.'

'How?'

'You were in love with me at the beginning.'

'Besotted. And not with you, with Heather. I still am.'

'No you're not. There's someone else.'

Before he could prevent it, his eyes flashed towards Bella, and Amanda caught it.

'You'd better go and dance with your wife before you get busted,' she said.

'You look wonderful,' Daniel said to Hope as they moved on to what had become a crowded dancefloor.

'I thought I should scrub up for the occasion, what with all the competition,' she said, getting in a dig.

'I'll take the kids to the Science Museum tomorrow when we get home.'

'That should bring you down to earth. With a bump.'

'I'm longing to do things with them.'

'Only with them?'

'With you too.'

'You seem very together, considering.'

'In what way?'

'Not at your wits' end, like you usually are.'

'Perhaps I'm growing up, finally.'

'Oh, I wouldn't go that far.'

Daniel wasn't much of a dancer, but Hope was. Her moves were both erotic and funny, and she surrounded him in a parody of a mating dance. Her intentions were clear – and not lost on Bella.

Daniel slumped onto a sofa next to Jack, who put an arm around him and squeezed.

'Well, you made it.'

'No. You did,' said Daniel. 'You busted a gut to get it released before *Shadow* came out, and you did it for me.'

Jack shrugged off Daniel's gratitude.

'As it turned out, we kinda got away with *Shadow*. I was concerned it might become a famous failure, like *Heaven's Gate* or *Cleopatra* – a career-breaker. But although the picture won't make any money, it kind of squeaked by. The critics didn't piss on us too much, and fortunately the studio had a big hit going and we got sucked along in its wake. They were able to strong-arm us into a lot of play-dates we wouldn't have got on merit. Upped our gross by 20 percent at least.'

'That was down to you again, Jack,' said Daniel. 'You went out and sat on their distribution people.'

Jack's face darkened, and his eyes dropped.

'I was driven by fear, Dan. The fear everyone in Hollywood shares but no one speaks of. It's strictly taboo: what if we make a movie and nobody comes? You see this nightmare in your mind: the picture playing to an empty house.'

They shuddered at the thought.

'When my first film opened in Paris,' Daniel reminisced, 'I thought I'd take a look at the audience on the first night. I walked up to the theatre on the Champs Élysées and there was no line, not a soul in sight. I crossed to the other side and sat in a café and watched. Still no one went in. I was devastated. I would never get to make another movie. Then suddenly people poured out of the theatre. I'd got the playing times wrong.'

Jack chuckled. Across the room, Bella was huddled with Hope.

'I sometimes wish I'd never told Daniel about Paul,' said Hope wistfully.

'Could you live with a lie like that?' said Bella, her words so emotionally freighted that Hope looked at her sharply. Where was her customary cool?

The men watched them and wondered.

'Do I get my wife back now?' said Jack with a smile that hit Daniel like a cattle-prod. At the same time, he took note of Jack's delivery: what an original way of playing an aggrieved husband confronting his wife's lover. He filed it away.

'Now she doesn't have to follow you around all the time,' Jack added.

Relief flooded through Daniel like morphine, but as the drug wore off he felt sorrow that the lie still lay between them.

'Go and dance with Bella,' said Jack. 'You know I don't.'

Daniel was detecting a subtext in everything Jack said. He was glad to get up, get away, and sought out Bella.

Daniel walked over to the two women.

'Jack asked me to dance with you.'

Bella glanced at Hope.

'He's all yours,' she said archly.

They danced silently together, fell into an easy rhythm, divining each other's moves, harmonious, careful not to touch, eyes not meeting.

'You've been avoiding me,' said Daniel.

'Of course.'

'I want to say something.'

'Don't.'

'I must.'

'Just keep dancing.'

The Brazilians had taken a break from the samba and, responding to the sentimental atmosphere, were attempting a waltz. Daniel held Bella a little closer and struggled to find the words he needed.

'What's happened to us is . . . . I don't know how to play this scene, I have no reference points.'

'You mean, you've never seen it in the movies.'

'Uncharted waters.'

'And I'm drowning in them, Daniel. Please save me; please let me go.'

'Are you going to tell Jack, now the film's over?'

'I don't know.'

'Please don't.'

Proximity rendered them helpless and she knew that her only hope was distance. She stopped dancing and eased him away from her.

'Here's your reference,' she said. 'We'll always have Paris.'

She walked over to Jack, her legs barely supporting her, and fell onto the sofa, alarming him.

'What is it?'

'Dizzy, for a moment.'

She put her head on his chest, and he held her.

Hope's face was turned away, eyes closed. She was abandoned, lost to herself, writhing and whimpering, far away. Daniel fucked her with detachment. Fucked her hard, like punishment. He was his father fucking his mother. This is how she is with Paul, he thought. He felt as lonely as death.

'God, you were such an animal. Where did that come from?' said Hope afterwards, dreamily.

Bella clung to Jack, a child to an old teddy bear. She was reassured to have him inside her but felt no passion, and finally faked an orgasm in order to end it – something she had never done before. The big deception made it possible to commit a smaller one. She lay awake, feeling Daniel like an occupying army inside her, and ashamed of her capitulation.

SIXTEEN

The following morning, crew and cast drifted back to their lives, abandoning temporary lovers for comfortable spouses, as Bella was doing, leaving the detritus of a film, used-up props and costumes, and sets devoid of virtue, taking with them a few anecdotes and the residual glow of amity. Jack took Bella and Orson to Paris for the weekend, where the child ate *moules frites* at every meal. Daniel took his kids not only to the Science Museum, where they played with hands-on exhibits illustrating gravity, centrifugal force and other wonders, but also to the London Aquarium, housed in the old GLC building, where they gingerly stroked the stingrays, and finally to Legoland, an alternative universe made of plastic bricks. On the following Monday, Daniel took the No. 19 bus, got off at Shaftsbury Avenue and walked to the cutting-room in Wardour Street. As he turned into the building, he caught a glimpse of Nigel. He hurried inside, hoping he had not been seen.

What they had captured on film had been digitally transferred to the Avid editing system, and the editor, Ron Davis, was awaiting him. During the shoot, as they watched the rushes each day, Daniel had chosen the takes he preferred, and told Ron approximately where the cuts should be made. On this information, Ron would cut the scenes together loosely, and so had an assembly of the film awaiting Daniel, who, unable to face the impact of watching the whole film, elected to look at it one scene at a time, easing himself into the process. The Avid was too fast: an edit could be made so quickly that there was no thinking time; only second thoughts were of value. Cutting with film was another process altogether. You held the film in your hands. Time became spatial. You took hold of a shot, measured it from your outstretched fingers to your chin and knew that that section represented three seconds. You marked it up on the Movieola or Steenbeck with a chinagraph pencil and then cut it and joined it with tape, wound it, rewound it, laced it up, ran it, assessed it, revised it. It was a satisfying physical process involving hands and arms, standing and sitting, in which you were constantly aware that film was a series of still photographs that could be converted into movement, like those little 'flicker' books you'd marvelled at as a child. It was a conjuring trick. You were looking at the image itself, whereas the Avid presented you with an inferior electronic approximation that often led you to misjudge its value. Such were Daniel's thoughts as he entered this reflective and solitary stage of moviemaking – and the most rewarding, because the film would begin to take shape and reveal itself.

Three weeks later, Daniel had produced a rough cut. It ran two and a half hours. Having edited it scene by scene, he had no idea of the overall effect. The assistant editor had been conforming the 35mm print to the Avid cut. Only then was it possible to screen the picture. Daniel invited Jack and their two wives to watch it with him. He booked the Fox screening room in Soho Square from five to eight, and a table at the Gay Huzzar afterwards.

When the lights went up, both women were in tears. Jack was pale and shaken. Daniel was alarmed at what he had unleashed, but in a world where we are confronted by the day and hour with tragic events and emotional shocks, they sat down to dinner somewhat recovered, and with the ravenous hunger that follows a funeral or a wedding. Daniel chose the wine he thought appropriate – Bulls'

Blood – but Hope wanted a vodka martini and, surprisingly, Bella asked for one too. They studied the menu, ordered, made a toast wishing the film well, and then Daniel posed the question.

'What is it about?'

'I can't answer that yet,' said Jack, 'the movie is still emerging, but I'll say this: it packs a killer punch. I was wiped out. And Amanda! What a performance! If we promote her right, this picture could go all the way. I'm talking blockbuster. I'm talking critics. I'm talking awards. We set out to make a commercial picture and we have, but it's much more than that. And Ned! I know you had to use a whip and a chair, but he came through for us.' Daniel smiled, always grateful for Jack's loyalty and optimism and professional hyperbole, even when it was false. Hope dispatched her drink during Jack's brief speech.

'I'll tell you how I saw it,' said Hope. 'It's about how everyone hates a free spirit. They all want to lock her up, or tame her, or kill her. She's given, she gives out, and it's a great idea that she can't get an orgasm, because she gives and gets nothing back. It's sad, and it's true.'

Daniel took her hand and squeezed it in acknowledgement of what he and time and kids had done to her spirit.

'And you put your mother in there, that was Jenny to a "T",' Hope added.

'I think a lot of women will feel what Hope felt,' said Bella, 'but more than that, for me Heather is on a quest. She wants to find out who she is, rather than other people's views of her. It's come out much closer to Wedekind's *Lulu* than I thought it would. Remember that Lulu is finally murdered by Jack the Ripper by him stabbing her in the vagina, and she welcomes it, sees it as an act of love, and yet it is the antithesis of love. Her sexuality has caused this havoc, and death is the only solution. It's very bleak, yet curiously exhilarating, because we're invited to believe the Ripper's knife does give her the orgasm she has lacked, and his blade is the surrogate of an impotent man.'

Bella stopped abruptly, having said more than she had intended to. 'I don't know. I'm not making sense. I was moved by the old woman's story of the man who came to her door and made love to her, and how they achieved this epiphany and it released her. It's what Heather wants.'

'Do you think the old woman should have told her husband?' said Hope. 'Did Jenny ever tell your Dad?' Daniel marvelled at the subterranean level at which women knew everything.

'There are some things that are felt and not said between couples,' said Jack in a soft voice. Bella looked at him sharply. What about their pact of truth?

Daniel caught Bella's anxious eyes fleetingly. Was Jack sending them a signal?

'Jack, Bulls' Blood is too heavy for me,' said Hope. 'Can we get some white? Do you know what they have here? Lacrima Christi. It's as close as I get to Jesus these days.'

'I've got doubts about linking the rape to the orgasm,' said Daniel. 'It's incendiary. I like Hope's interpretation, but I'm afraid people will see it in other ways.'

'Like what?' said Jack.

'Well, equating sexual fulfilment with violence. She only gets an orgasm when she is raped. We are back to *Letter from an Unknown Woman*. The idea is that her body is loyal to her first lover, who effectively raped her, and it's only through rape that she is finally released. Now if we stay with that, I think we need to reshoot the scene where she's in the bathroom and Jake is snooping through her things. He's frustrated that she cannot give herself to him and she tells him about this first lover – the rape. The alternative is to edit the final rape so that she does not orgasm. The old woman shoots him before the climax, but I find that deeply pessimistic.'

'When I was sixteen,' said Hope, swallowing the tears of Christ, 'I had this horny father confessor. He told me about the debate in the church to do with when nuns get raped. Is it a sin if she gets an orgasm, or, since she can't help it, it's not? He wanted to know my opinion.'

'What did you say?' asked Bella.

'I opened my eyes wide and said, "What's an orgasm?" Since I'd never confessed to having one, I wasn't going to let on to him.'

Hope always knew how to lighten things up. They laughed, and agreed that they should digest the food and the film, and see how they felt about it on the morrow.

Sophie was sitting in the kitchen with Emma, who had woken up and refused to go back to bed until her mother got home. Hope took her in her arms and unsteadily carried her upstairs. She put the child to bed and laid down next to her and instantly fell asleep. Emma tugged at her arm.

'Mummy, you're supposed to put *me* to sleep.'

Daniel went up to his study and wrote notes to himself. 'You only ever see the film for the first time once. So, initial impressions. What did I feel? Compassion for Heather, but beyond that, deeply unsettled, disturbed. The attempted rape by Lionel, and the rape by Jake, feel like the source of all human conflict, the rivalry of men, the humiliation of women. Men like war because it is a metaphor for rape. Making love with love can be the highest place we can reach, the closest we can get to another person, the nearest we can come to escaping the bonds of self; and yet the same act, when it is rape, is the lowest, the most violent act. Sex elevates or debases.'

The image of his father fucking his mother floated into his mind. Even with an adult's eye and understanding, it still felt violent. Perhaps because of that, he had only ever been able to make love with tenderness, yet with Bella he had been forceful for the first time and it had been transcendent, yet the same force with Hope came out of anger; consensual rape, he thought, conjuring up an oxymoron.

He decided to show the rough cut to Brad. He needed the balance of Brad's contempt for lofty ideas and his cynical attitude to sex.

Daniel arrived at the viewing theatre a little late, to find Brad sitting in the foyer. Having watched the film, he was reading *Vogue*, window-shopping for girls. One of his ploys when one appealed to him was to call the model agency and tell the girl he was a filmmaker looking for the most beautiful woman in the world and she was a contender. It sometimes worked.

Brad's advice was, trim it back hard, keep it moving, go for the suspense and don't push the sex angle so hard.

'You know,' he said, 'sex for most people is simple. They feel the urge, they do it, and then they forget about it. You might find that there are some bad laughs in there.'

The next day Daniel had notes from Jack and Brad, and discussed them with Ron.

'Shall we get started,' said Ron.

But Daniel was reluctant: he wanted to discuss it with Bella. The film was so entangled in their relationship that he felt unable to do more until they had spoken. He called her. She picked up the phone as Jack was getting ready to take Orson to the Test match at Lords. Jack was dressed in grey flannel trousers, a navy blue blazer and the tie of his Oxford college. His passion for all things English had its source in his spell as a Rhodes Scholar. Daniel often jested that Jack's admiration for him was not to do with his films, but with his prowess in poling a punt. Through discreet lobbying, Jack had acquired membership of the All England Tennis Club, the Garrick, and finally, and most gloriously, the MCC. Considered together, they almost conferred citizenship, except that Jack was not interested in becoming British but rather, more subtly, in assuming an honorary Englishness. When Jack was insomniac, he would imagine himself at the wicket, batting at Lords, and playing a repertoire of strokes – the cover drive, the square cut, the late cut, the leg glance, the hook, the sweep, the pull to midwicket, the on-drive – and if he was feeling immensely confident, he would dance down the wicket and hit a mighty six into the members' stand, before falling contentedly to sleep.

With due modesty, Jack liked to include himself amongst a distinguished coterie of cricketing outsiders: Sam Beckett, the Irishman; Harold Pinter, the Jew from the East End; Tom Stoppard, the Czech immigrant; the late Paul Getty, his fellow American. Cricket, he told Orson, was not just a game but a preparation for life.

'Does that mean life is always going to be boring?' his son replied.

Daniel and Bella met at four o'clock in the Groucho Club, a neutral venue. Although jammed from five o'clock onwards and busy at lunchtime, in the afternoon it was usually vacant and silent. He was waiting when she arrived. They sat down without touching. A bored barman served them tea. She slipped off her jacket, revealing a sleeveless dress. He became Bertolucci's camera, panning over her arms and shoulders, pausing at the long neck, then up to the mouth and the eyes, and tracking back to take in the tumultuous hair. They had no need to speak, presence alone filling their need. The longer the silence ran, the harder it was to begin. Daniel felt he should say something for the sake of the barman, who was watching them curiously.

'It's lapsang suchong – a masculine tea, I think,' he said at last.

'I can handle it.'

They fell back into the blessed silence, then, as the barman stared: 'Brad says I should go for the suspense and cut back on the sex.'

She considered that, her eyes on his. Unwavering.

'Well, I'd go for sexual suspense,' she said with an ironic smile.

She knew that there was no choice, no decision to be made.

'Don't they have rooms here?' she said.

He went out to reception and took one. As with the first time, they were lost in each other. Afterwards, they lay content and spent, side by side, as still as a knight and his lady on a crusader's tomb.

'I was fourteen,' she said softly, falling into her stream-of-consciousness mode. 'An uncle, a smiling uncle. I was fond of him. He had a hypnotic voice, sonorous. He did it. I still can't say the word.'

'Raped you?'

'Yes. I grew up afraid of men; there are a lot of men, I discovered, who are turned on when they sense fear in a woman, and enjoy making her more afraid. I had bad relationships. I grew a shell. I gave up on men. I thought perhaps I was a lesbian. Found I wasn't.'

'Heather's story.'

'Yes.'

'And how did Jack save you?'

'He was therapy, so patient, and gentle and loving. I found trust and safety and I enjoyed sex for the first time. It was like prayer, homage to an absent God. I never imagined I would ever lose myself in another.'

Silent tears fell from her eyes into the greater silence.

At last, she drew away from him, back into herself.

'However beautiful this is for us, Daniel, from the outside it's two people cheating on their spouses. We both love Jack. How can we do this to him? And Hope. How can I look her in the face again?'

'Remember I told you what Nietzsche said, "Whatever is done in the name of love, is beyond good and evil".'

'Darling Daniel, your quotations won't help you now, and you're not shooting this scene. We're living it. We're at the core of things. This is as deep as we'll ever go, or need to go. We found something so perfect and deep and alive – and it's also a betrayal.'

They became aware of the expanding noise, talk and laughter climbing the stairs from below as the club was filling up. It threatened them.

'When I hear laughter, I hear the roar of the wild beast,' said Daniel.

'Another quote?'

'Baudelaire.'

They showered and dressed. Bella suggested that they go down separately but Daniel insisted they went together. He refused to subject the relationship to the squalid coin of a clandestine affair.

'We will not skulk,' he said firmly. Part of him, as is often the case, wanted to be found out.

In the lobby there were people that they both knew, and Bella was convinced that everyone was aware of what they had done, but Daniel was affable and relaxed.

They stepped out into Dean Street, and there was Nigel Bateman. Daniel was startled.

'What are you doing here, Nigel?'

'Waiting for you, Daniel. Saw you go in. Thought I'd wait. Try and catch you.'

Bella's stomach turned at the words 'catch you'.

'You haven't answered my letters, Daniel.'

'I haven't even opened them, Nigel. Just finished shooting.'

Bella was stranded. People were going in and out of the Groucho, several greeting Daniel, including one or two she knew. It was unendurable.

'I must go,' she said, and walked towards Old Compton Street.

'They've stolen my script, Daniel.'

'For God's sake, Nigel, they bought it. You took their money.'

'Thirty pieces of silver,' said Nigel, choking on his shame.

Bella was getting into a cab on Shaftsbury Avenue. Daniel broke into a run, Nigel at his heels. The cab pulled away. Daniel made a despairing attempt to reach it. He stopped, chest heaving, realising how out of shape he was. Nigel came clattering up.

'You never should have taken it to America, Daniel. God will punish you. I want it back.'

Daniel turned on him.

'Fuck off, Nigel. Leave me alone.'

When Bella got home, Jack had bathed Orson and was making him an egg-in-the-hole, his favourite comfort food. Bella kissed them both.

'How was the cricket?'

'A little slow today,' said Jack, bent over the stove.

Making sure his father was turned away, Orson pulled a face at his mother and she responded with a gesture that said, I know, but we have to humour him.

With a start, she realised she was ovulating. Supposing she was pregnant! She had options. There was the morning-after pill. Yet how could she suppress the pregnancy she had so yearned for. She had an image of Daniel's sperm, motivated by their urgent love, forcing its way over whatever barriers her ovaries had constructed. Yet this was a journey only Jack's sperm deserved to take. If Daniel had opened her up, Jack deserved access.

Jack, tired and dreaming of the perfect cover drive, found his reticent wife moving over him, seducing him from the coils of sleep in which he imagined himself reincarnated as a big square blond Lancastrian, Andy Flintoff, the English cricketer. Flintoff was retired but in Jack's dream he was triumphantly recalled to save England from the marauding Australians. He knew so much about Flintoff that he could inhabit him, and so he responded, still half asleep, and muttered, 'Aren't you Jack Diamond's wife?'

'I am.'

'Would he mind me making love to you?'

'No,' she said. 'He won't mind in the least.'

His sperm oiled her tight vagina and she came. It was a kind of reserve orgasm, seldom called upon, like an echo, rich in memory, but lacking presence. So there they were, all that sperm from the two men she loved bombarding her ova, all the billions of permutations of genes, doubled, redoubled, double or quits.

Daniel walked the night streets knowing it was unsafe to go home until he had brought his emotions under control. Hope was sitting at the kitchen table when Daniel came in. She had been reading a script. She slid it across to him and took off her glasses. He looked at the title page. It read, '*Conquests* by Brad Tullio, an original screenplay'.

'Now that's a surprise,' said Daniel.

'It's his story,' said Hope. 'Screws all these women, they mean nothing to him, his life is empty, then he seduces this married woman, the wife of a friend, and to his dismay, falls in love with her. She won't have anything to do with him. He suffers. It doesn't ring true. He probably felt it made a better ending if he was punished.'

A fleeting anguish crossed her face, which Daniel misinterpreted as her insight into what he had done. He felt guilt, remorse, and a rush of compassion for her. He took her hand. She held on tight.

'I'm sorry,' he said.

'For what?'

'For everything.'

'Me too.'

Back in the cutting-room, Daniel approached his task with a clear head. The emotional connection between Bella's life and the film had been made. He marvelled at all the emotional undercurrents that had found their way into the story. Everything gets into the movie.

The script had been constructed to plunge the audience into the centre of scenes. He found himself shortening the scenes even further as Heather's predicament became more threatening and claustrophobic. He shaved shots to their bone. He gave space only to Heather's vitality and exuberance and athleticism. He reflected on how the language of film had developed. When Griffith introduced the new grammar of close-ups, and reverses and the inter-cutting of parallel action, older people were confused and disorientated but the young embraced it. Now TV commercials and music videos had developed an elliptical style of editing that brutally eliminated whatever was not essential and central. There were no beginnings and endings, only middles; no foreplay, no apologies, no explanations. This method had been applied to mainstream movies by young directors. Daniel had criticised it as a new primitivism, as they had thrown out all the rules, consigning the history of film to the cutting-room floor – or the Avid's virtual trash can. How tame it made the jump-cuts of the Nouvelle Vague look, but now he understood how audiences read these new movies, and he was adapting to it. When he had previewed *Shadow of a Smile* to young people, they found the film predictable. They were half a reel ahead of him, they could absorb information – visual and aural – much faster than his own generation. There was a new cine-literacy, which he had attempted to respond to with this picture. The more narrative could be achieved by gesture, looks, visual metaphors, rather than words, the more compression was possible. Another quote popped out: 'All art aspires to the condition of music.' He saw the story as a melody, and editing was about pace and rhythm and harmony and counterpoint.

Throughout the Paul period, Hope could not bear Daniel's touch, and he learned how distant two people who lived cheek by jowl could become. As in many marriages, as she gradually warmed towards him, he had grown further away from her. It was only when they were together with Bella and Jack that Hope and Daniel reconnected and felt affection for each other.

Hope invited Bella and Jack for dinner on the eve of their departure for New York, where they would preview the film. Jack and Bella were to remain in Manhattan, so it was also a farewell dinner. Despite, or perhaps because of, the deception that divided them, they were connected by a thread of love that filled each of them with a joyous sense of elected affinity.

'How goes the book?' Hope asked.

'I can't decide how to finish it,' Bella said as a signal to Daniel.

'Won't events decide for you,' he replied in code.

'I mean, whether to stop now or go on until the movie is released,' was her cryptic response.

'I think it must stop now,' said Jack, alarmingly, but then added innocently, 'The book should come out to coincide with the release of the film. You have to give a publisher time.'

Hope had gone berserk in the Harrods food hall for the occasion: truffles and lobster and a Chablis Premier Cru.

'I hate to see you go,' Hope said. 'I wish we could be in that Buñuel film where they're eating dinner and no one can leave, and we could go on like this forever.'

'That's more *Groundhog Day* than Buñuel,' said Jack jovially.

'But better than being in *The Discreet Charm of the Bourgeoisie*, where they couldn't get dinner at all,' said Bella.

'How would you shoot this dinner,' said Jack, 'to express all these feelings?'

Daniel found himself making a shot-list in his head.

'I'd fade out the dialogue, bring up the music, go into slight slow motion – say thirty-two frames per second, to give it a dreamy look – and then track from face to face.'

'What about a shot under the table to see if there's a hand or a thigh or toes touching?' said Hope.

'No,' said Daniel. 'To express our friendship, I would have us levitate and float about the room, dancing and hugging and making our goodbyes.'

'Don't forget the tears,' said Bella, supplying them herself – which made Hope cry too. Tears came to Jack's eyes.

'There is something else to celebrate,' said Bella. 'I'm pregnant. At least I'm pretty sure I am.'

Hope hugged her and the tears flowed freely. Daniel got up abruptly, ostensibly to fetch the Armagnac, but in truth to break eye-contact with Bella.

SEVENTEEN

Testers Inc. had set up an American preview at a suburban theatre in Westchester. They claimed it was an upmarket catchment area. They had students at the local mall giving out tickets to people with the right profile – the audience they believed would be attracted to the picture. In practice, people often gave these tickets away to anyone they came across, so it was always pot luck. The students were directed to describe the picture as an English erotic thriller. This proved attractive to some but abhorrent to others. Ron Davis had got there early, to rehearse the print. Since it was unfinished, it had to be run with a separate magnetic soundtrack.

Daniel watched them filing in with their buckets of popcorn and gallons of coke and glazed eyes. They were mostly young and overweight. Are these the people I made the film for? Daniel asked himself. The audience was riveted by the opening scene, the flash-forward of the murdered Lionel being submerged in the pool, and generally went along with the story until the sexual initiation of the boy. Of the 380 members of the audience, forty-two walked out at this point and a good many of the remainder laughed at it. There was more derision when Heather showed her breast to the old man, and eight more people left. As Heather's jeopardy became more intense, they were gripped and held to the end. During the final rape scene, three young women left in tears.

When it was over, the man from Movie Testers asked the audience to stay, and cards were given out. They were asked to give their comments and rate the picture: Excellent, Very Good, Good, Fair, Poor – and to say if they would recommend it to their friends. The marketing people estimated that, for a movie to be successful, the Excellent and Very Good categories combined should score over 80 percent. The Movie Testers made a rapid analysis of the cards and found that the approval score only reached 63 percent. There was some consolation in that 78 percent said they would recommend it to their friends. *Shadow of a Smile* had scored in the eighties, but the 'recommend' was only 58 percent.

Jack, Bella and Daniel were driven home in a limo with piles of cards on their laps and read the comments as they went along. They were shattered by the results, having convinced themselves they had made a hit movie. They climbed the stairs of Jack's brownstone in the Lower West Side and collapsed into armchairs and drank Jack Daniels without, for once, feeling companionably conjoined by their names in whiskey. Jack sorted through the cards mournfully.

'I guess we have to reckon those walkouts, 10 percent, would have voted in the bottom boxes, so realistically our score should be even lower.'

'They hated the sex scenes,' said Daniel. 'They were either embarrassed or they laughed at them.'

'Don't be so despondent,' Bella counselled. 'Over half the audience really got it. And they were mostly women. Listen to this: "I was very disturbed, but grateful that someone has treated rape seriously." And this one: "I was raped. I've never been able to acknowledge it until now. Thank you." Here's another: "I could hardly bear to watch it, but everyone should see it." Women are going to make this a success, and they loved Amanda.'

'But they hated the things she had to do,' said Daniel, shaking his head. 'It's hard to recover from these scores.'

'Daniel, you've always derided this way of testing a picture,' said Jack.

'Let me do a fast re-cut,' said Daniel. 'Maybe Brad was right. We should go for the suspense and cut back on the sex. I can do that in a couple of days, and then we can test it again.'

Daniel asked Ron to find a cutting-room where they could make cuts directly to the film. This proved difficult. Editing had become so universally digital in America that younger editors had never handled film or seen a sprocket-hole. Daniel called his friend Joel Coen. He and his brother owned a building downtown that claimed to be the narrowest house in Manhattan, not much wider than a door. They had only recently, and reluctantly, gone digital, and still had an old flatbed machine with joiners and a rewind bench.

Daniel sat with Ron and eliminated the boy's sexual initiation and the exposing of the breast to the old man. He shortened Lionel's attempted rape of Heather, and pared down the final rape. They also shaved down the sex scenes with Jake, the detective.

Jack had a separate apartment at the top of the house, where he insisted Daniel should stay. Bella found this impossible and took Orson upstate to Woodstock to visit her mother, who lived there and helped run the summer stock theatre. Bella took her laptop and worked on her manuscript. She had written a piece as Betty had suggested – 'Sex in the Cinema' – which had got so long it was almost a book in itself. Given the cuts Daniel was making, she wondered how relevant it would now be. She set out to write an account of the preview.

Four hundred vacant faces stared at the empty screen. They chomped on popcorn and guzzled Coke. There was no sense of excited anticipation. Expressions were blank or seemed to say, amuse me, amaze me, thrill me. I realised that every movie has to deal with this inertia, has to seduce the audience, charm it, scare it or make it laugh, as Mr Witt said. This film lacked the booming Dolby soundtrack, and those synthetic sound effects that are like waves crashing on rocks, which punctuate mainstream movies. Perhaps that is what these faces were saying: bludgeon me, arouse me with a cacophony. The film made them uneasy. It did not fit the patterns they were used to. They were insulted, assaulted, confounded by primal sexual impulses. They ran away. Jack Diamond was deeply depressed. 'How could I be so wrong?' he said. 'I don't know what they want any more. I should give it up. Stick to theatre.' Daniel has gone back into the cutting-room in a murderous mood, ready to kill his creation, or fatally wound it.

She told her mother about the preview, and how Daniel was devastated, and she started weeping. 'You've fallen in love, poppy,' said her prescient mother. 'I never thought you would.' She consoled her daughter and held her. 'Does Jack know?'

Bella shook her head.

'Well, don't tell him. Play it out.'

She fell into her mother's arms.

'And I'm pregnant.'

She saw the question on her mother's face.

'I don't know.'

Daniel completed his savage cuts on the second day. He left the cutting-room and took to the streets of Manhattan, walking hard and fast but without purpose. At each intersection he would take the green light, wherever it led. He found himself on the Upper East Side and came upon a theatre playing the latest *Spiderman*. The performance was about to start and he went in. It was a massive hit and the critics had lauded it as better and subtler than its predecessors.

Jack had cooked dinner and was waiting for him, anxious to hear how the editing had gone, but Daniel wanted to talk about *Spiderman*. 'Jack, it's mawkish, repetitive, predictable. It's nineteenth-century melodrama. As I watched those computer-generated images of apocalyptic destruction and this virtual cipher swinging through the canyons of Manhattan, I thought, the audience that lapped this up is not going to get much out of our picture.'

Jack served up the truffle risotto and laughed.

'Daniel, it's not the same audience, and even that audience you sat with have other moods and needs.'

Jack's native optimism, which always vied with his Jewish melancholy, had struggled back into a fragile ascendency.

Another mall: Brooklyn this time. Another audience, much like the first. Only half a dozen walkouts – and two of them came back with popcorn. Daniel's nervous system was connected to each person like Spiderman's strands of web, and every restless twitch was a dagger to the heart.

They waited nervously for the scores. They were up to 76 percent, from 63 percent, but perplexingly the 'recommend' was down from 78 percent to 66 percent.

Bella was waiting for them when they got home. They gave her an account of the screening. Jack was mystified and Daniel said, 'It's tough to make sense of it.'

'I thought about it a lot while I was upstate,' said Bella. 'The movie is upsetting, but people realise how important it is. That's why they recommend it highly. I think you should go back to the cut you had and stick with it, and let the film find its audience. It's too good not to work, and it's too good to make hasty changes.'

The next evening they sent out for Chinese food and talked into the night, for Daniel was leaving the following day. They finally resolved to follow Bella's advice. To leave it alone. There were minor changes Daniel wanted to make. Despite the pain of exposing a film to the public in an unfinished state, there are always lessons to be learned. There were several places where the laughter (of the good kind) swamped the lines of incoming scenes. He needed to open them up, and there were other places where he had cut too hard into a scene. The whole picture needed some breathing space.

'What about the boy?' asked Daniel. 'Maybe we should drop the sexual-initiation scene. It's a turn-off for a lot of people.'

'No, it shows her generosity of spirit,' said Bella. 'He's been deeply humiliated. What she does probably saves him five years of therapy.'

When Daniel came downstairs the next morning, Bella had already left to take Orson to school. He drank coffee and ate bagels with Jack, who was also about to leave for a meeting with the investors in a play he was putting on. He was immaculate in a black silk suit, white starched shirt and his MCC tie.

'We'll have a late lunch at the Russian Tea Room and I'll drive you to the airport.'

When Bella got back, she found herself vulnerably alone with Daniel. She wanted to touch him, but with an effort of will she turned away. She made coffee and Daniel came up behind her. The cups rattled in her hands as she sensed his nearness.

'Please don't touch me. Please don't.'

He slumped down at the kitchen table with his coffee. She sat opposite him and pushed her tape-recorder between them, a mechanical chaperone. She turned it on and announced, 'Daniel Shaw, Final Interview.'

It sounded like a death knell. She played it back to check if it was recording, then: 'So how do you feel about the preview, now that you've had a night to sleep on it?'

He gathered his wits and, avoiding her eyes, looked directly at the tape-recorder.

'Chastened. It's not the blockbuster Jack predicted, and I've had to accept that a lot of people won't like it, so we'll have to work hard to find an audience that does. That was your suggestion. One of several that has shaped the film.'

She ignored his reference to her views, and continued with her impersonal questions.

'What do you have to do to finish the picture?'

'Well, as you know, I go back today. I have to reshoot the bedroom scene, to have Heather confess to her lover that she was raped. More and more, that feels central to what the movie is about. You know that.'

Bella struggled to hold her nerve as the film collided with her life.

'I'll complete the editing: that will take a couple of weeks. Then I'll work with Alex Desplat on the music score, and supervise the sound effects. I'll do a week of ADR with the actors.'

He was relieved that it was just technical stuff that did not require input from his unruly emotions.

'ADR?'

'Automatic Dialogue Replacement. It used to be called "looping". For instance, in the rape scene, we're using wind machines, so the dialogue is not usable.'

'You mean she'll have to simulate those primal cries and screams?'

'Only in the wider shots.'

'For the close-ups we used a smaller, silent fan because it only had to cover a limited area.'

'How much of the dialogue has to be redone?'

'Maybe 10 percent is necessary, but I go through the entire picture with the actors, and it gives them and me a chance to review the performances. We replace it wherever we can improve it.'

'But surely you can never recapture the emotion of the moment, the original voice.'

'There is no original voice. It's not the actor's voice, it's a reproduction of it. Film is mechanical; an actor should use its possibilities: the chance to improve it. On the set you can do several takes, and choose the best in the cutting-room. In the ADR studio you can make it even better.'

'So that takes a week, and then what?'

'Another week with the crowd, twenty or so mixed voices – there are actors who specialise in this. When we shoot a crowd scene, we ask the extras to mime their conversations so that we can record the principal actors' dialogue clean. Now we add in crowd dialogue and we can mix it in at the level we want. It's all about control; it's about having all the elements – sound effects, dialogue, music – separate, so they can be balanced.'

She smiled at Daniel's need to control, to iron out life's ragged edges, to counter emotional entropy. Running counter to that was his reckless compulsion to push the boundaries, to risk destroying everything he had built.

'What are you looking for from the musical score?'

He lit up, some embers from the old fire beginning to glow.

'Well, I will tell Alex that I want long sustained notes on cellos and basses, and at other times, on high strings, to enhance the suspense. Also some synthetic sounds, deep hums and drones. I know that sounds a bit conventional, but I want to give the audience some help, something they can recognise. The only melodic element would be a theme for Heather. I imagine a female voice, which at first is barely heard – two or three notes – as though it's struggling to find a tune. Gradually, the melody emerges and finds full expression at the end. Alex will listen patiently to all this, then come up with something much better, I hope.'

'So how much would all these elements improve the preview scores?'

Daniel laughed and sipped his coffee.

'Surprisingly little, in my experience: maybe 5 to 10 percent.'

'Even so, that can get your recommend "up to 90 percent".'

'Let's hope so.'

'Then what?'

'Oh, the sound mix takes five weeks, then digital grading another ten days, and then getting the prints right in the lab.'

'So how much work in all?'

'Another five months.'

She turned off the tape-recorder.

'I'll be seven months pregnant.'

'When will I see you?'

'I shall stay here until the baby is born. Bring the movie over when you finish it.'

The question hung heavily in the air between them.

'Is it . . . ?'

'No. It's Jack's.'

'Have you told him about what happened? I keep getting the feeling that he knows.'

'I haven't, but maybe at some level . . . .'

Bella had her back to the window. The sun burst through clouds, streamed in and set fire to her hair. It took his breath away. She recoiled from his reaction and got up abruptly, then turned away to the window and looked down at the patch of garden, dominated by a fluttering, rust-coloured Japanese maple, last night's raindrops cupped in its leaves, delicate, ephemeral. She felt herself dissolving. With an effort of will, she turned to face him, and hardened her heart.

'It's illusion, Daniel, what happened to us. It was a chemical euphoria developed by evolution to get women pregnant. It's a fever, a temporary insanity. Can't you see how ludicrous and sneaky and silly this looks from the outside?'

She fought down her feelings, her voice betraying her.

'I'm not on the outside, I'm on the inside,' he said quietly.

She turned away to the window and her tears fell silently, and a breeze ruffled the raindrops on the maple leaves and it wept with her, and they heard the front door open and Jack toiling up the stairs, and Bella fled to the bedroom.

Jack puffed in, sweating from the heat outside and winded from the stairs. He unbuttoned himself – jacket, shirt, pants – and expanded into the kitchen.

'Oh, my profligate, impossible investors. They don't care if they lose their money, they think of me as a charity. I'm almost tax-deductible. But they are patrons and they are determined to patronise. I'm condemned to listen to them. They have purchased my attention and they have opinions. They think they're performing in *The Producers* and I am Zero Mostel – whom, sadly, I'm beginning to resemble.'

He swallowed a glass of water, noted the tape-recorder on the table.

'Another interview?'

'The very last.'

'She's closing the book?'

'Yes.'

Jack nodded and took another prodigious swig of water, while the first broke out on his face and neck.

'I'll change out of this suit of armour and we'll go to lunch,' he said, mopping his leaking skin.

Bella had to collect Orson, so could not go with them. She saw them to the door. She and Daniel kissed awkwardly, and she slammed the door.

'That sounded very final,' Jack chuckled. Once again Daniel had a sickly feeling that Jack knew, and was toying with him.

Everyone who came into the Russian Tea Room not only knew Jack, but had the need to hug him and slap his back and kiss him.

'I hear the picture's great,' they all lied.

In walked Fred Schneider, to another round of hugs and slaps.

'I hear the picture's terrific,' he said.

'Now who told you that?' said Daniel.

'That's the word on the street.'

'And how's your horror flick?' Jack asked.

'Studio's high on it, they're going out with two thousand prints and a $30 million ad buy.'

'That will upset Nigel,' Daniel said, laughing.

'Yeah, he's suing,' said Fred. 'The guy's a freak.'

'Tell me about it.'

'He wrote to me,' said Jack. 'Wanted me to take up his case against your studio, and if I agreed, he offered to follow my wife and take pictures of her. He claimed she was having an affair.'

'Who with?' said Fred.

Daniel urged the ground to open up and swallow him.

'He would only reveal this if I agreed to help him,' said Jack.

'There's one under every stone,' said Fred, and ambled off to meet the studio head he was lunching with. Any ex-studio head is like an ex-president of the United States. However badly he may have failed, whatever humiliations he has suffered, he is still a member of the anointed, and entitled to enduring status.

'I'll come over in a couple of weeks to see a final cut,' said Jack. 'And here are a few thoughts.'

He handed Daniel a sheaf of notes, which Daniel tucked into his pocket without reading.

'Bella's going to hang in here. As you know, she doesn't want to take risks. She's been yearning for this child for so long, and I'm so damn lucky to have hit it. I never told her just how low my sperm count was. Afraid she might take off if she knew.'

'She loves you, Jack. She never would.'

'And I love you, Dan. We both do. Whatever happens to our movies and our lives, nothing will ever change that.'

Despite Jack's protests, Daniel insisted on taking a cab to the airport.

'Go home and take care of Bella.'

It was a night flight. His habit was to take a sleeping pill and hope to wake up at the other end. Instead, he spent the night writing a letter to Bella – a letter he would never send.

I'm writing this on the plane. The lights are dimmed and everyone but me is asleep. The large man next to me is sprawled out with his mouth open. I nudge him every so often, which stops him snoring. When I press my face to the window, I see a deep chaos of stars, can't make out any constellations. Are we in the right galaxy? Am I in one of Philip Pullman's parallel worlds? Am I the only sentient being in this spaceship? Speak to me, Hal. My journey takes me eight miles further away from you every minute. From our conversation at lunch, I'm sure Jack knows, and suspects that the child is not his. He was so loving and gracious, I was humbled. He is such a good man: far better than me, miles better. You are lucky to have him, and so am I. Sorry I was so stilted in that last interview. The tape-recorder sat between us, frowning its disapproval. What I wanted to say was that we have cared for this movie, loved it and held it close for all these months, and now we have exposed it to a cruel world. We want everyone to love it as much as we do, but I know from experience that they never do. Now I'm going to make it stronger and more presentable, more able to face an indifferent public. If you are lucky, your film touches a nerve, a mood, and the world embraces it; if your timing is wrong, however good it is, it just won't connect. The real value of a film only becomes clear after several years. It is reassessed when it comes out on DVD, and again a year or two later, when it plays on TV. It gathers a reputation, or loses one. How often we see a film years later that we have loved, and find it disappointing. The film hasn't changed, nor have we, but the world has. The film has lost its connection to the zeitgeist. Seen at a cool distance, a film, whatever else it is, is a repository of its time and place. Everything gets into the movie: all the ideas, love, spite and energy, and bits of all the people who made it. I predict that in ten years' time our film will, amongst other things, reveal itself as telling the story of a great love between two people who, even now, exist together in blissful harmony in a parallel world. Let it be our testimony, and I will hold to this thought as I now help our movie on its way.

He looked out of the window. In the north-east, the sun was rising and flooding crimson light over the soft folds of the carpet of clouds below, which covered England. Up here in this other universe, in this billowing cloudscape, the sun always shone. The same clouds, seen from London below, were a flat, grey, dreary blanket.

It all depends on where you put the camera.